Gabriella
and
Dr. Duggan's
Secret Dimensional
Transport Machine
Book 1 of the NuGen series

James Cardona

Gabriella
and
Dr. Duggan's
Secret Dimensional Transport Machine
Book 1 of the NuGen series

2nd Printing April 2013
1st Printing February 2012
ISBN: 978-0-9850284-5-9

Printed in the United States of America

Any similarities to persons real or imaginary are purely coincidental. Most of the locations in the book, such as the Phillipines Islands, Ipanema Beach and Corcavado in Rio De Janiero, Brazil and Princeton University's Main and Forrestal Campuses have been visited by the author although some liberties have been taken in the descriptions.

Table of Contents

Men in Blue-Black Suits

It is clear they will kill him.

My hands trembling, carrying another box out to a half-Spanish half-Indian woman, mumbling the shoe size through shaking lips, my pulse pounding, my heart bursting, I stare through the store front window at my father, barking excitedly, pleadingly, fearfully, shaking his arms at the two militant looking young men wearing blue-black suits shimmering in the dark, dull, cold red of the fading sun, sinking low, extinguishing itself, falling into darkness and gloom, as if death draws it down deep.

Mom's eyes bulge. Ignoring the customers, her hands involuntarily shake as she folds and bags their purchases.

The two men, like stone cold prosecutors in an open and shut case, simply state their demands and that is that—no need to argue for something that's already decided. Quickly the two leave, blending into the crowd, and as my father returns, body trembling, exhaling a troubled groan as if everything has suddenly changed, mother runs to him, a storm of tears, nearly knocking over a rack of blue jeans, crying out, "Not again! Not again!" falling into father's arms.

I baby-step toward them, confused, pleading, "Papa, what is it? Who were those men?"

"Nothing, mi vida." Hugging my mother, his hand lovingly caresses my head then wipes a solitary tear from his cheek that she doesn't see. It is the first and last time I see my father cry.

*****

Pulling down the metal accordion cage over the front entrance to the store a few hours later, my father latches the heavy metal padlock and announces unexpectedly that we're going out for dinner at the Brazilian restaurant up the hill. My mother was born in Brazil and she loves that food, I guess it reminds her of a different time. We never eat at restaurants; my parents can never justify the expense when there's always plenty of food at home, even if it's sometimes just lentils, so I am very excited. The tension of the day's earlier events is fast fading, as if nothing happened, and I laugh hysterically at Dad's stories, holding his hand as we walk up the hill to a special part of town containing two small rows of restaurants. The cobblestone road is closed to traffic in the evenings and the restaurants fan tables out into the road space. String-lights holding red, yellow, green and blue incandescent bulbs run across the street from building to building and lamp post to lamp post casting funny colors onto customers' faces.

Chapter One

I love the colored lights and Dad laughs as I bounce up and down in my chair, letting the red and green light alternately strike my face, sticking my tongue out, pulling my cheeks, smiling, giggling, laughing.

Men in Blue-Black Suits

My father urges me to order anything I want and appears uncharacteristically happy to see me cautiously order Paella served in a half coconut shell, one of the most expensive dishes. Everyone is having a grand time, the second and third floor apartment dwellers above are eating out on their balconies and several mariachi belt out their interpretation of old favorites such as *Guantanamera* at the Mexican place whose tables blend into ours at the center of the closed-off road. Many of the customers sing the words they know or yell the typical Mexican, "Aaaaah-Haah" at just the right moment.

Just as it seems that the evening can't get any better mother suddenly turns pale white and kicks father under the table, pointing behind him slowly with her fork still holding a baby shrimp. He and I turn our heads at the same time, slowly and cautiously, just enough to see the back of a blue-black silk suit gleaming in the neon lights of cerveza signs out of the corner of our eyes, only a handful of tables separating us. It's one of the blue-black suit-men from earlier today and he seems totally engrossed in the Ultraball game on the wall screen behind the counter, laughing, eating, drinking and hoarsely bellowing out "Goal!" The green and yellow colored lights morbidly shimmer across his blue-black suit and his skin is a sickly pale of undead flesh. He appears creepy, fetid, rotten and zombie-like. The waiters stare at him, not sure what to say, as he is quite loud. Maybe they can't understand why. But we know.

Quietly we finish our meal, no one saying a word, and skulk back through the closed-off cobblestone road, down the hill on the zigzagging streets, no one saying a word, back toward our apartment on the second floor above our store as odd, dark shadows from flickering streetlamps play tricks on the closed gates of the family-owned stores: dry cleaners and coin laundries, bodegas and small mercados, Portuguese, Chinese and Korean groceries, and the tiny appliance store owned by Tony Motorola's dad. Just as we reach our street, our dread seeps into reality as we are somehow not surprised to spot the second blue-black suit-man leaning casually against a telephone pole, intentionally not looking our way. The single streetlamp streams down upon him like a spotlight in a Broadway musical and the way his shadow crawls away from his feet I can't help but wonder if he is standing under that light so that we would see him.

Mother steadies father's terribly shaking hand to help him put the key in the lock, then, just as we enter, the screen rings, my father answers, says a few words and heads for the door, face covered in cold sweat but now suddenly resolute.

Mom bursts into tears, screaming, "No!" diving in his path.

"I must. I have to," he says, his voice slow and calm but on the verge of cracking.

"No you don't! We can go to Tio Ernesto's! We hid once, we can hide again!"

"They'll just find us again, mi cielo," he pauses, "I'm tired of hiding."

I stand motionless, in a sort of shock. The minute particles of dust in the air stop cold, floating, stagnant. I blink. My eyes refocus, almost unnaturally, and my parents, just across the room, are suddenly so far away.

He tries to sidestep around her without meeting her gaze directly.

"No!" she squeals, violently grabbing his shoulders, water leaking down her cheeks.

He hugs her, holds her tight for a moment then says, "I love you. I will just give them what they want then I will be right back," and walks out.

The two of us are left standing there, micro-tremors crawling across mother's back and arms, me cold and clammy, lost in a daze, the door creak still echoing in our ears, me not knowing what is happening, desperately afraid of the unknown, mother's body racked with fear, a fear that seems to have been here before and knows what happens next, us both staring at the open doorway and dark hall beyond; empty. I can't move. Only stare. Frozen solid. I can't breathe. My heart feels like it has stopped beating. I'm only fourteen and I think I am losing my father.

For three unbearable hours Mom and I refuse to look at each other for more than a few moments at a time as if seeing the fear might unleash it. A silence full of dead stillness is broken by a short, stiff, hard knock and as the two police officers enter my mother bursts into a shower of tears, falling painfully to the floor before they can tell us that my father is dead, killed in a "tragic car accident." The wind is squeezed from my lungs and I cannot breathe. I feel like something is squeezing me and my chest is so tight; I cannot get enough air. I wonder why I feel dead inside as if there is a giant empty cavern in my chest, immense and unfillable. I wonder why I feel nothing, no emotion. My eyes are wide open and vacant and it is like I do not know what to look at because nothing makes any sense. The clock, the table, the plate, the fork; nothing makes any sense. I wonder why I feel empty and dead as if my insides are missing. In shock, I don't cry. *This is NOT happening! Something's wrong. Something's terribly wrong here. I can't believe this. This must be some kind of sick joke.*

I overhear one of them just outside our window as they leave; chuckling as he says that he knew who it was before he even reached the crushed car, wrapped sideways around a telephone pole near the cliff edge, as it was the only big black Buick in town that looked like one of those old FBI cars from the 1960's.

Just as they drive off, Mom barks at me, "Let's go!" shaking me from my stupor. She runs to my bedroom, rips open my drawers, throws them on my bed, stops, turns to me and hollers, "Move! We're going! Now!"

I hustle into the room, wide eyed. She throws me my back pack and says, "Fill this up! We're outta here in five minutes!" then runs to her room.

What's going on? What do I do? I don't understand! Why?!

"I, I... Mom?"

"Just do it!" I hear over the crashing and banging coming from her room.

I grab some things but I can't think. I don't know what to take, what to do, or what is happening.

I don't understand. And Dad. What about Dad? This can't be happening!

The five minutes pass too fast. Mom grabs my arm and yells, "Lets go! Now! There's no more time!"

Men in Blue-Black Suits

We run out of the apartment and down to the store. Mom opens our tiny safe, snatches what little cash Dad saved and we jog to the bus station. *I can't believe we are leaving my entire world behind! No, no, no! This can't be happening! Where is my father? We can't leave him!*

As the bus pulls out it all hits me loud and sudden like the day Mr. Ortiz let all school kids ring the school bell and Marco pulled the rope too hard and I was standing too close. I begin to cry and I feel terrible for it because I didn't cry just some minutes ago when they told me Dad died. Mom holds me and it seems like it is more so people won't see than it is to comfort me. She seems suddenly cold and hard; different, not the mother I know. I want to close my eyes and wake up like this is all a dream.

Why? Why? Why?

Mom tells me that we are headed for Brazil. We will hide in the favelas. She speaks so plainly as if nothing just happened, as if Dad didn't just die, as if we are not running for our lives. It's not so bad there, she says, just a few blocks from Ipanema, a very famous beach. She acts like we are going on vacation. *Who is she? Dad just died!!! How can she be so calm? How can she act like nothing just happened?*

We will change our name, she says, from Martínez to something common to Brazil, maybe Conceição, to help us blend in. A creeping, crawling, goose-bumpy feeling falls on me that this certainly hasn't been the first time we changed it and I suddenly have no idea who we are or who I am. All of my life, all that I can remember anyway, I was just the girl from the family that owned the neighborhood clothing store. But that was all a lie. Obviously. Some strange men just killed my father and for what?

What just happened? What we are hiding from? Who are we? Who am I, really? I don't understand!!!

Chapter 2

The Giant L

"**Y**ou should try out too, Gabriella," says Ms. Eiras, stirring a dinged-up pot full of hot water, a few tomatoes, sickly looking carrots and not much else.

"Yeah, I guess." I shrug my shoulders. Anything Mara does I am willing to try. She is Ms. Eiras' daughter and the only friend I've made in these four miserable months in Brazil. I met her only by chance as Ms. Eiras and my mother both rent their pathetic shanties from the same spiny-finger-twiddling landlord.

Looking at the corrugated sheet metal walls and ceiling screwed to a rusty, round-metal tubing framework perched on hard packed earth, I am still amazed that they can actually charge rent for this. Ms. Eiras' rent must be a little higher than ours as she has an orange extension cord running through the dirt, under the wall, into the single room space from who-knows-where to give her a little electricity, unreliable of course. We don't have an electric cord in our shanty. The shanties, technically illegal since they are built on government land, are piled on top of each other, strewn all over the side of the mountain, raw sewage running down between them in open trenches, and when it rains down on their steel roofs it sounds like the end of the world.

"It will be fun! And you're fast too. Mara told me you always beat her to the top of the mountain." Ms. Eiras looks just like you would expect a woman in her situation to look; strong, muscular arms; worn and beaten hands, like the hands of a hard-working man; hair cut short and economical, all one length, cut at the shoulders like maybe Mara did it for her; and clothing that doesn't seem to fit her quite right.

"Alright, I'll do it." I really like Mara and her Mom so I don't need much convincing. Ms. Eiras loans me Mara's old uniform so I can go to school and Mara lets me borrow her books. It's almost comical here, being poor. Attending school is free, but no one is allowed to enter the building without a uniform and the school doesn't provide books. Education is supposed to be the great equalizer but there are still walls to climb. Mara is the only one who helps me. The other kids would rather play their favorite sport, pick on the new kid.

The Giant L

I am trying to blend in here, in Brazil, in the favelas, and not say too much. I tell no one where I am from, what happened to me, or, God forbid, my real name. It seems like everyone has a past that they don't want to talk about so no one asks too many questions. Mara helps me so much, not as much with the physical things—although she does that too—but the mental; she helps me forget, to not think about what happened and not think about the questions, especially the big one—*Why?*

"Mara, tell me about this again," I say in Spanish, slowly, as we leave for the tryouts.

"<You know Ultraball don't ya?>" Mara says slowly in Portuguese. We can understand each other in our native tongues as long as we stick to the common words, speak slow enough and use lots of hand gestures.

"Yes of course. Who doesn't? It's the biggest sport in the world." Everyone knows Ultraball, a sort of football-soccer-rugby hybrid that uses two balls and is ultra-violent. It seems like every game-night the injuries are more gruesome than the last. It has only been around about five years but it is extremely popular.

"<Well, now they trying to change it.>"

"Who?"

"<Dunno—advertisers I guess, they control everything don't they. Heard something about an in-ter-na-tion-al com-pe-ti-tion, like the Olympics or something. All different countries will send teams, so they're making some changes. Now the schools are adding the new thing. Everyone's going goofy about it.>"

"I thought we were trying out for a running team. I definitely don't want to play Ultraball."

"<I know, I know. Me neither. They're adding something; I think it's called pre or something like that. Short for pre-lim-i-nar-y 'cause at first the running part, the new part they're adding, was gonna be before the main game, pre-lim-i-nar-y ya know, but they decided to run it at the same time but never changed the name. So it is a running thing.>"

"So, we run around the track while they are playing the game on the field?"

"<Yeah, like that. And the points won during the pre go right on the score board, so we girls running changes the score and we can win the game just as much as the field team. Cool right?>" Mara stops for a moment, hesitant to continue, "<Except for one thing though.>"

We are almost at the school track. "What?"

"<There's ob-sta-cles on the course.>" We round the corner and the field opens up in front of us. About fifty people are on the field, some adults, some high schoolers, waiting for the tryouts and another fifty or so are in the stands gawking. It is on the oval track surrounding our school's football-soccer field but there are all sorts of obstacles, things you must go over, others to go under, some impossibly tall, ropes hanging down in another area, and even a small kid's swimming pool about ten feet long. I can't understand how we are supposed to go over the big wall. It is about ten feet high and there isn't a rope or hand holds, nothing but another wall leading up to it forming a giant L. "How do you get over that?"

Staring, Mara says shallowly, "<I don't know.>"

After scanning the stands and seeing three of my most vicious tormentors eyeing us, Roberta, Gomez and Salvadora, both of us turn our heads away and move toward the sign up table, their gaze burning the side of my face. We are the last two to sign up for tryouts.

"Three times around the course, just make it around three times," the coach pleads loudly, unused stopwatch in hand hoping for someone, anyone, to at least finish the course. Apparently it is not going too well.

Finally one young woman figures out how to go over the L. Running toward it at full speed, she leaps and lands a foot on the side wall, pushes straight up, then lands the other foot and barely grabs the top of the wall, then over she goes. The stands erupt. She rounds two more times and completes the course. Later two more are able to imitate her.

Mara tries out but can't pass the wall and then it's only me, the last one left and everyone's watching.

Roberta calls out, "<This oughta be *good*! Watch her fall!>"

It has been all down hill with that group since the first day when I tried to include myself in one of their conversations about the coming holiday saying that my grandma visited last year flying in on a plane. Big mistake. An explosion of sneering insults boxed my ears.

"<A plane! Ha!>"

One explained how her grandmother rode the bus for twelve hours arriving nauseous and exhausted for the twisting turns through the narrow mountain roads.

Another lamented about how her grandmother rode on the back of a farmer's truck with the pigs, enduring eight hours of hitting pig butts with her pink umbrella to stop them from stepping and snorting on her.

"<You think you are rich! Grandma flying on a plane! You live on the side of the mountain!>"

It didn't matter if I was telling the truth or lying, they despised me either way.

Standing at the start line, unable to start running, I try desperately to block them out, desperately to focus.

Focus! Focus!

Everyone staring, me remembering racing through the crooked favelas pathways, racing through the winding streets, girls chasing after, they could never catch me, me always first to escape, bouncing off shanties and ranchos, dirt and rocks, as I cascaded down the bent paths, accelerating with each twist and turn, ducking under carts and tables made of old sawhorses, bounding over old women stooped on broken concrete stairs, dodging the slow moving, weaving around children playing in the crooked streets, I sped away, faster, faster, faster.

Standing there, at the start line, the coach pleading for me to start, everyone watching, my breathing slows on its own as if I am no longer in control and suddenly my mind is clear, suddenly I can see the path, the way, my way. The vision is so clear, I can somehow see where to place each foot, each hand, twist, turn and move as if someone is pushing, pulling, controlling me as if I can see the entire course already completed in my mind.

"Let's *go, girl! What's your name? Gabriella? Let's go!" The coach looks down at his screen, frustrated that the evening has been such a waste of his time with only three barely making it through the course.

Suddenly, I go, full speed down the course, arms pumping.
Gomez screams, "<This is going to be *great!>* " obviously excited at my upcoming demise.

I hurdle the first obstacle easily then speed toward the second, higher one. I know I can't hurdle this one so I dive-vault it, using my arms to increase forward momentum and land in a body-roll and bounce up to my feet, still at full speed. The crowd hushes, eyes suddenly on me. The ropes and water hazard are easy enough. Finally I head toward the giant L, my heart racing faster than my feet. *Can I do this?*

I try to imitate what the young girl did, running up the side of the L, trying my best to push up instead of away, and I find myself much higher on the wall than any of the other three. My hips are above the second wall and my arms reach down as if they already know what they are doing. My hands plant themselves on the top of the wall and I swing my legs between my arms like a monkey, catapulting my body and landing several feet in front of the wall, almost overshooting the landing pad. I don't understand what just happened but a feeling of fierce joy steals over me as I realize that this is something that I am good at, something I can do without being taught.

Running at full speed, blood pounding in my ears, I glance back to see many now standing and the coach involuntarily clutching his watch and baby stepping toward the track, in a trance, as if a hypnotist is drawing him in. I can't believe what I just did myself, but I can't stop.

I repeat the loop again and this time it comes more easily, naturally, as if my body is made of water. I am fluid. It feels *wonderful.*

On the third pass, I go for it; full speed. Electricity is in my veins and I can't understand it. Hurdle, hurdle, vault, swing, swing, swing, vault, and on to the L.

I see Roberta sneering. She wants me to fall; I want to shut her up.

Placing a foot on the sidewall I kick myself up, up with all my strength, arms pointed skyward, swinging my knees around and turn my body 180 degrees, tuck and over. I back flip the wall. The group in the stands stomp on the aluminum seats and scream so hard that the traffic stops outside and I think the stands might break. I sprint to the finish and the coach is bent over staring at his watch saying, "<No, no, no. I can't believe it>," then mutters something to me too fast. I can't understand his accent.

Mara runs over to me along with many of the others who give me highfives.

"What is he saying, Mara?"
"<He said, 'You broke some record.' >"

Now everything is surreal. *Broke some record, broke some record, he said I broke some record?* Like a dreamy dream, the voices are muffly and the clouds are fluffy. Little fluffy clouds, little fluffy clouds, white and blue and orange, who painted them? Exotic. The blue sky screams at me, "Look at me, look at me." Foreign. My skin is suddenly tingling, jingling, ingling as if the sweat on my shoulders is changing to needles, a liquid acupuncture, pin and prick, pin and prick. My hairs are on end and the voices are neon and blue and green, fading in and out, fading in and out, a satellite warble piercing the thick atmosphere of silence around me.

What? I can't believe it. I didn't hear right.

"What? Are you sure?"

"<It's what *he* said. I dunno but what you just did>, que magnífico, que puro," telling me 'how magnificent, how pure,' her voice is like butter when she tries to speak Spanish and it's hard to focus on it with so many around me hooting.

The coach is already on the screen with his finger in his other ear, bent over slightly, and glancing over to me every so often, then he hangs up and comes over saying, "<I just spoke to the director of the Bahía team, he is going to find out if we can train you and, who knows, you might make the national team.>"

Roberta and Gomez return with orange traffic cones they stole from the street and begin screaming through them as if they are megaphones, "<Go Gabby Go! Go Gabby Go!>" while a group of girls dance to samba rhythms that Salvadora bangs out using two broken broom sticks and a metal trash can.

We leave the field, Mara bouncing excitedly on the balls of her feet, me in a complete head-spinning daze, Mara chirping like a baby bird calling for food, proud of how great I did, me wondering how bad I just made my life, Mom's life, wondering if we will have to move again, hide again, leave everything behind again, Mara yelling out to every passing car or person on the street, bragging to them how her friend just broke the record, even though she has no idea what record it is, me wanting to disappear, hide my face from their eyes, and sink into the earth. Mara can't understand why I'm not excited. Today I wish I never woke up, never left home, never visited Mara, never listened to Mara's mom, and just ran away, far, far away as soon as I laid eyes on the course.

In the dusk we pass the shanty people gathered around piles of burning wood, singing songs and talking about nothing. After climbing the steep earth steps up the side of the mountain, I leave Mara at her shanty, smiling and beaming up at me, and head for home. Dread blankets me like a wet wool sweater shrinking as it dries, pulling in tighter and tighter the closer I come to my shanty, the closer I come to having to break the news to Mom. I sweep the shanty's hard-packed dirt floor with a broken broom, unroll my bed mat, lie down and squeeze my eyes down tight in the black darkness.

"Gabriella, what's wrong? Why are you so quiet?"

I stay silent for a while, listening to the wind blow through the large openings in the sheet metal then, bursting into tears, I release it all in one breath, "Mom! I screwed up bad this time!"

"Mija, Mija, what happened?"

She quickly lies next to me clutching me close as I squeal, "I'm sorry! I'm sorry, Mom! I ran a race and I was so fast. Too fast! I'm sorry! Everyone knows. They made screen calls. Important people want to see me! I'm so sorry! It was the girls! I just wanted to shut them up! To show them! Now they will find us! We just got here now we are going to have to hide again! And where will we go?"

"Mija," she says lovingly, calmly petting me. "I don't know; I don't know—Let me think."

The sun is gone and in the pitch black she holds me. We are both silent for a long time and my stomach is twisting. It hurts.

"Maybe it will be okay? Yes, it will be okay."

What?! What is she talking about? What about Dad? He died!! And we had to hide!! What about that? Now she says, "It will be okay"! It's the last thing I thought she would say. "What? What do you mean? We're not leaving?"

"I don't know... Let's see what happens."

"Let's see what happens? Let's see what happens! They killed Dad! What do you mean, 'Let's see what happens!' "

"We don't know that. Mija, please, stop. He was in a car accident. The police. You were there. You heard what they said."   She is lying next to me but her voice sounds distant.

No! No! No!

"No way—Those two guys in the suits—And why were you so afraid?"

"What are you talking about?"

"Mama! Your hands were shaking! I saw you!"

"Oh... I don't remember that. Listen Mija, we had some debts, that's all. It was nothing. We left the store. We changed our name. You're older now. They wanted your father, not you."

The sheet metal creaks and the voices of the folks outside by the fire are dwindling.

"Something just doesn't sound right, Mama. Are you telling me the truth?"

"Yes, my love. How could I lie to you?"

Coach Murray

The next day at school the whole place is buzzing and alive. Like Moses at the Red Sea, the mob of students in the open courtyard parts when I come through and everyone has a good look at me. I feel embarrassed by their stares. After a few classes, the principal brings the coach from yesterday and he introduces himself. His name is John Murray and he is working for the government trying to form the national team.

"John Murray is a funny name for a Brazilian," I say.
His skin is light, almost translucent, veins showing through; hair sandy brown; eyes a shade of almond with hints of green; and so thin that he looks much taller than he is, the classic runner's build. He laughs and tells me he is from North America then asks if he can train me and I agree. We go to the library and set up my account. He will send me workouts and I can send him my progress. He says he will try to pass through this area at least once a month. He tells me that the national tryouts are in less than six months then he leaves and I feel lost and alone.

After a few days of running the practices on the high school field my world seems to be completely different; it is almost as big a change as when we moved from Venezuela. It is really weird the way people treat me different now and everyone seems to know who I am all of a sudden and it strikes me odd seeing as I really don't know who I am myself—I am living a lie. A few are jealous of my success, I think, but most want me to do well and everyone wants to know all about me. I am no one to them but now it is like they own me and if I do well then they somehow own a piece of that success. Some ask a few questions and start conversations with me and I don't know what to say. I don't want to lie but I can't tell the truth either. All I can talk about is what is happening right now, the tremendously difficult workouts that John Murray wants me to do.

The workouts are crazy unrealistic and I can barely do half of each day's assignments. I feel like I am sending him questions all the time just to try to understand what I'm even supposed to do.

'Twelve interval repeats of 1200 meters at tempo pace'—*what does that mean?*

'Lactate threshold, tempo pace, race pace, fartlek.' *Huh? He can't be serious. They actually call it that?*

"Fart. Lek." I roll it over on my tongue then laugh.

*****

Several weeks pass and not only am I finishing the workouts but I'm becoming faster. Most of the kids who were trying to practice with me have abandoned the effort and Mara only comes to watch, encourage and keep my time a few times a week now. We don't talk much anymore. I think we are growing apart already. Maybe she thinks I will be leaving soon and never coming back. If she brought it up I would agree with her but for an entirely different reason and I know I can't tell her.

I bury myself in the workouts as it helps me to not think about what happened in Venezuela, what happened to Dad and why Mom acted so peculiar that night. I train and train and train and in some odd way I enjoy the workouts more if they are more punishing. The suffering helps to stop me from thinking about the past and what happened and the questions. And the future too. That is something I don't want to think about either. I have none, not here in the shanty village, on the side of a mountain, hiding. It is also kind of cool that the brutally punishing workouts are actually giving me results and I am making progress. But that is not really why I kill myself doing them. At all.

Today Coach Murray tells me, "Remember this always Gabby, any endurance sport is almost completely mental. If we can make your brain, your mind, believe in yourself, to have faith in yourself, to believe that you *can* not only win, but that you *will* win, that your winning is a done deal, that it is already decided, then we really have already won." He is the most positive person I have ever met and I love when he stops out unexpectedly. He stares deep into my eyes, like he is searching, looking for something, *almost as if he is looking down into me.*

"Here is what I want you to do everyday and at every practice, okay?"

I return his gaze, eyes watering, trying not to look away, to not melt. "What do you want me to do?"

"You are going to pick a different phrase everyday, make it personal, make it real, not real to me, but real to you, something that means something to you at a deep personal level and you are going to repeat it all day to yourself."

"That's screwy," I say doubtfully, giving myself a chance to look away. "Give me an example."

"Now these are personal, you have to make up your own, but I will give some of mine. For example, I might repeat in my mind 'I am fast, I am quick,' or another one, 'No one can beat me, I am the fastest.' " He says the next one more slowly, "or another, 'I am a leaf on the wind, I float on the air,' like that see?"

I don't reveal it in my voice but the last one touches me somehow, it sounds like something I came up with, something I can relate to. "I'll try it."

A few weeks go by and Coach Murray adds new, more difficult workouts, "Gabby it is not only speed and strength, but balance that is going to win this. That is the missing element. If you can develop all three, you will have a real shot at this." He gives me pictures of all these weird looking yoga poses and tells me to make the pose and hold it for at least thirty seconds then, without stopping, smoothly transition to the next pose. It is the hardest thing I have ever done. Standing there on one foot with the other pointed straight forward, both arms and head pointing directly up is nearly impossible. As the last of the impossibly long thirty seconds finally comes, sweat drips from every pore and my body is suffering an earthquake of spasms. Pulling the elevated leg back and pushing it behind me without touching the ground and laying my body out front vertical, like a board, provides me just a few moments a rest. Just being able to move feels great, then the hold, the excruciatingly painful hold, comes and it is almost unbearable all over again.

Another thing he wants me to do is run barefoot every other day. We rely on our shoes to support our feet, he told me, but what we are doing is not allowing our feet and ankles to develop themselves properly. At first I run barefoot at Ipanema and my feet kill me, but after about two weeks my feet wake up and I start to notice each of the individual muscles in my feet, gaining discrete control over them.

This is such a new experience for me, training, having a coach, and actually playing a sport. In Venezuela my life was the clothing store. Sure, I snuck outside to play with my school friends once in a while but I was never on a team, never played a real sport. Now that I think about it, I did love to run back then. I ran to and from school and with the other kids in the mountains, usually playing tag. I was always the fastest. But it was nothing like this.

Even here in Brazil, Mara and I ran the mountains together, just to break away from the stench and the feel of the shanty village. My favorite was Corcovado, that famous mountain with the huge statue of Jesus perched on top, arms wide open as if he is hugging the city. A paved path leads up it and the tourists who ride the buses always stared at us in disbelief when they saw us passing them. But I never realized that I might be good at a sport, it was all just being outside and having fun for me. But now nothing is fun. I am alone and I run and run and run until it burns or until I break just to block it all out. I don't want to think about the past. I don't want to think about the future. I don't want to think.

*****

Crossing the days off on the calendar I shudder as I realize that less than two months remain. At school today Coach Murray's message provides another set of completely different workouts. No longer just running, strength and balance exercises, he adds dynamic agility exercises and he finally sends a lengthy explanation of the true nature of the competition. Apparently there are minimum and maximum numbers of each of the obstacle types allowed but there's much room left for variation on the tracks. We really will not know what we are up against until the morning of each event. Reading between the lines it seems suddenly like he is unsure how to train me now. He said he was a running coach and that the Pre is completely different than anything anyone has ever trained for. He gives me dodging exercises, running back and forth from side to side on the track; hurdling exercises, the hurdles being at different distances and different heights, always changing; and climbing and leaping exercises, running up the sides of walls and back tucking over, I love these the best.

Finally the day comes and Mom, Ms. Eiras, and Mara wake up before dawn to walk me to the bus stop and wish me luck. I cry. It is my first time away alone. The buses are chartered just for the tryouts and mine is already half full with athletes of all ages. I sit in the back next to three girls wearing matching red spandex outfits that say NuGen down the leg. They ignore me so I try to go to sleep.

Several hours later we arrive at a huge football-soccer stadium with a sign on it that says Arena Itaquera and someone says it is used by the professional teams of São Paulo. Inside it's the exact opposite of the stomping and banging stands and traffic-cone megaphones; everything is quiet and deadly serious. People in suits with screens are everywhere and appear to be in charge of something but I am not sure what. I smile when I see Coach Murray and run up to him as he speaks to a team of about twenty people, several wearing those same red outfits I saw on the girls on the bus. A few of the others from my bus are right behind me.

"Hola, Gabriella, Velocity, Carilla and T'mekah, come over hear and join the rest of the group," he turns back to the others and introduces us, "Girls, here are Gabriella Conceição, Velocity Jones, Carilla Fang and T'mekah Turkah, all from Bahía state. Everyone, this is it. As you can see there are thousands of athletes and hopefuls here today so competition is going to be tough. There will only be about two hundred of you who advance out of this round and after tomorrow's round only twenty-five left and then finally only seven who eventually make it to the national team so I want to be realistic with all of you up front. Now of course I discovered and have been coaching all of you so how well you do is going to be a direct reflection on me as a coach. If some of you do well enough to advance, it will bode well for me making the national team coaching staff, so I absolutely want you all to do your best." He went on to tell us who some of the audience were; other coaches, some from other countries or states hoping to pick up athletes who just miss the cut; medical and drug company representatives looking at new athletes to sponsor; and advertisers and Ultraball representatives overseeing the whole operation, trying to have a better feel for how well their investment is going.

There are five tracks set up in the stadium and only eight runners per heat so I am waiting nervously for what feels like forever. They call out the names and some of them are really odd like Speed, Mercury, Axle, or Hammer and I wonder if they made them up themselves to intimidate the other runners. I overhear one girl say that her parents had her test-tubed. They could only afford one enhancement so they picked speed and then named her 'Flash.'

The course here is much longer than I am used to, six miles total, each slightly different and everyone has only one shot which seems so unfair. One trip, one slip and it is back on the bus for a long ride back to the shanty, back to nowhere. I look at my assigned course and it is an 800 meter loop with one of the big L shaped obstacles so I will have to run twelve times around and twelve times over the L which gives me twelve opportunities to miss it, lose and head back to the shanty village to sleep on the dirt floor.

About ninety minutes before my turn, my only shot at this, I go for a long, slow, eight-mile run to loosen up followed by some light stretching, balancing and then very short, powerful sprints to wake up my legs. Pulsating waves of blood ripple through my body and in my mind I am transitioning, becoming water, becoming fluid, becoming beautiful liquid motion.

They call my name and my mind is suddenly hyper-aware as I line up. The gun fires and I am off too fast. Oh so fast, I am at full bore and I know it. *It's six miles, girl! Slow down!* At two-hundred meters I am out in front of all of them. Hurdle, hurdle, vault, rope, rope, rope, run, run, vault, and I slow a bit for the L. I can't mess this up. Over the L like we are old friends and I finally take control and slow myself down. By the end of the second loop I am dogging the heels of the slowest runner. I hold my pace for the next few laps and take the L cautiously but right in the front of my mind I know that the other runners in my heat don't matter; I am really competing against thousands. I have to run fast no matter what the others do.

I am water, I am water, I am water, I flow, I go. I am water, I am water, I am water, I flow, I go.

I let myself become water, beautiful water, moving in my way, my beautiful liquid way. My focus intensifies and I do not think about the exact movements, my body moves where it is supposed to be as if the course is directing my body to be where the obstacles are not. I speed up, faster, faster, faster, and my energy feels limitless. I am out in front by a long way and with two laps to go I have passed all the girls at least once, all the girls except one, Velocity Jones, who is right there with me, looking completely fresh, one of the girls from the bus who was wearing a red NuGen track suit, muscular, tall Velocity Jones, an Amazonian Adonis, beautiful, fierce, enchanting and savage all at once. I am running so hard I feel like I am going to black out. Unconsciously, uncontrollably, I try to rest somehow, even for just the smallest moment, slowing down ever so slightly. My head tilting back and slightly to the left on its own, I half-close my eyes on the back half of the loop where there are no obstacles, trying to collect energy for what is coming. The front half has all the obstacles, the audience and the suits with screens watching us close. I accelerate on that half and smile at them trying to show that I am full of energy. They watch us as if we are thoroughbred horses and they are placing bets, looking at the quality of the bristle of muscle, the quantity of sweat, and the choice of foot placements, steps and gait. Finally, fearfully, I cross the finish line and collapse, just so glad it's over. Coach Murray spends a microsecond with me saying, "Good job," and walks away toward others in his group.

Waiting for the evening results I notice something I didn't see before, some of the suits are up in the stands, somewhat far away and they are using binoculars. It strikes me odd. Then I see them, two men in those same blue-black suits, and I am suddenly ill, suddenly back there, back almost a year ago and it is playing in my head over and over again as I duck away, hiding from their eyes.

Did they see me? Do they know? What am I going to do? Are they looking for me? Where can I hide?

One of them looks like one of the men from that day, the day my father died, but it is so hard to tell from such a distance. The bile is collecting in my mouth but I refuse to spit. I swallow hard and feel disgusted.

My name has been changed; my hair is different; I am older; they can't find me, can they?

An intense pain in my head, stronger than any headache I have ever experienced strikes lightening fast like a cobra. The overhead lights are unbearable and I am almost too dizzy to stand.

They don't want me anyway. Mom said so, right?

I can't stop shaking and I want to go to the bus and hide.

No! No! No! This can't be happening! Not again! Where can I hide? It is safer here; I can't go to the bus. They wouldn't try anything with all these people around, would they?

I move toward the safety of groups and distractedly try to talk to a few girls until all the tryouts are over. I can't think of anything but getting away.

Run to mom! Escape! Get out of here and hide like we did before! But where will we go?

I mill around with the girls, trying to not be too obvious and trying to not look up at them too much. The staff hands out brown bags of food which is cold and not very good then some guy in an oversized suit announces the top 250 names. Only the top 200 advance; I am 201 and just ready to go home and get out of there. Four of Coach Murray's prospects were called and he gathers us while the rest of the people start moving towards the buses to leave. Some are angry at the system but there is no one to listen to their complaints. It's Carilla, Velocity, T'mekah and myself and I definitely don't look the part. The others have brightly colored track-suits with names on them and I still don't understand why, but of the 250 almost all do.

Coach Murray says, "Okay, girls. All of you did great. I am very proud of you, all of you. Now tomorrow is the next level and if you want to advance you have to bring your all. The blue buses go to the hotels where there will be nurses to take your blood sample for testing then they will assign you rooms. Get some good sleep and I will see you in the morning."

I find myself glancing up at the stands and scanning them, looking for the blue-black-suit-men, but I can't find them anywhere so I begin to calm and focus in on what he is saying. As he speaks, I feel the relationship between us somehow different now. Before I felt like he was my own personal coach and now I am sharing him and I don't like it.

As we start to leave he calls me, "Gabriella, one second."

"Yes Coach?" I smile broadly.

"I have always encouraged you, right?"

"Of course Coach, but why?"

He holds his hand up. "I always speak positive, right?"

"Sure but—" He stops me again. We are mostly alone, out on the field.

"So now I need to do something different with you. I need to tell you the truth and I don't want it to take you down. Can I do that?"

"I think so... Yes. Yes, you can. Go ahead."

"Right now, you are eliminated. The only reason they are keeping the last fifty is in case some of the other girls fail the drug or genetic testing. You are 201 so you have a real good shot, but right now we don't know."

"I kind of figured that much." Genetic modification has been legal for a long time but Ultraball was the only sport that permitted it. Of course they only permitted athletes with human DNA so everyone had to be tested. There was such a shock a few years back when a few were caught with hybrid animal DNA. They test everyone now.

Coach Murray continues slowly, "So now for the hard part. Almost all the girls you will be facing tomorrow are modified, designed before birth, in test tubes, to be the greatest athletes that their own personal gene pool could provide. Most of these are children of good athletes, some even great athletes, who contracted with one of the genetics companies to boost up what was already there. So they are going to be almost impossibly tough to beat. Additionally, the companies who hold those contracts have been training these girls and investing in them, so they don't want to see you win either." The weight of truth hammers me and with the two men in blue-black suits in the back of my mind, going home feels like a good thing.

"So I am going to say one thing here and I don't want you to answer. I just want you to think about it. I want you to go to the hotel thinking about it. I want you to think about it all night tonight. When you wake up in the morning, think about it. While you are eating breakfast, think about it. And when you come back here, I want you to think about it."

He pauses for a long time and then looks hard at me. Finally I nod then he says, "Here it is. Plain and simple. Those girls are better than you. They are genetically modified to be better than you. They are faster than you and stronger than you. They have been training all their lives and have trained harder than you. They have the full support of the biggest and richest mega-genetics companies behind them with their staff, trainers, coaches, and doctors. So I only have one question for you—"

He pauses, staring deep into my eyes, then says,

"What—

Are—

You—

Going—

To—

18

Do—
About—
It?"

His face is stone. Those words, like heavy sledgehammers banging steel anvils, sharp, tight and abrupt, echo painfully in my ears, then I leave for the blue bus.

Top Twenty-five

All natural, all human, pure and original, just like nature intended, born from two people in love, no test tubes, no scientists, no experimenting doctors, no DNA cook books, I am just a clean and simple, fifteen year-old girl and I don't have a chance. Over twenty-five of the girls who were in the top 200 were eliminated, all for some form of banned substance, mostly performance enhancing, so now I will advance but everyone else is a modder, genetically modified, a super-athlete, everyone except me.

How can I compete with that?
Coach Murray's words are still ringing in my ears like the memory of a once fired gun. He kept saying, 'Think about it,' like I would have to concentrate; I have to concentrate to not think about it. Don't get me wrong, I would love to win, but I can't really see how that's possible. Some of these women are in their early twenties and have been training for longer than I have been alive.

The only strategy I can come up with goes against all of Coach Murray's training, to go all-out right from the beginning. He always told me to hold back until the second half of the race. He called it a negative split. He said that the second half of the race should always be faster than the first half. I am always supposed to run the first half as fast as I can without going past my lactate threshold, that point where my body is creating more lactic acid than it can get rid of, because lactate acid causes fatigue. It took me weeks of training, experimenting and feeling out my body, learning to understand my body and its subtle cues, to even figure out where that point was. The second half of the race I am supposed to gradually speed up and at the very end of the race shoot to maximum effort, the VO2 max. *Coach Murray is a great teacher; I sure am going to miss him if I don't make it.*

Well, all I can think to try is go all out right from the beginning and hope I don't fatigue as bad as the rest, run them into the ground and try to burn them out, a loser strategy really, but it's all I have.

There are only 200 of us and with three races each there will only be 75 heats. Across five tracks, it should go pretty quick which makes me even more nervous because I won't have much recovery time between races.

I go straight into my warm up and try to block out everything. This morning I haven't seen the two blue-black suit men so I am starting to relax more. I'm in one of the first races and as the gun sounds I am running full blast, just like yesterday, but this time it's intentional. Yesterday I was out in front and lapping girls, today they are all right there with me, dogging my heels. I can see long hair and flashing blue and green clothing just out of the corner of my eye.

These girls are quick!

By the end of the second lap I am starting to feel fatigued and all the other girls have pulled back, about twenty meters behind me, watching me, like turkey vultures hanging in tall branches waiting for the cars to go by so they can resume their road-kill feast. I push hard for two more laps and then, uncontrollably, lungs on fire, legs burning, full of lactate acid, I start to slow down. The others are holding their pace and creep up on me, slowly beginning to pass me. I feel it all slipping away. I dig deep, searching deep inside for something, anything, even the tiniest morsel of energy that I can give, to sacrifice it up, to give it up to the unforgiving tarmac of this track. Just then something weird happens, I feel something there, something deep inside, like a tiny hidden well of energy that I didn't know existed, I dig deep and find something. I burst forth, somehow recovered and reestablish my twenty-meter lead. I keep pushing, waiting for the moment it happens, the moment my muscles finally explode and I fall out of this race. Four more laps gone and the girls are still in vulture mode as I increase my lead to almost fifty meters, a quarter of the track. Each time that I slow for a handful of seconds I seem to recover really quickly. *I didn't know I could do that.*

We're halfway and now they start their push while I have been red-lining the whole time, the air burning hot in my lungs. As the last lap rounds the bend two of the girls catch me and we fall into maximum stride, maximum effort and maximum exhaustion, like a life or death struggle, all that matters is who's first to the finish line. As I cross the finish in third, I burst into tears knowing that it was all I had and it wasn't enough.

John Murray gathers me off the track like a wounded calf and hugs me briefly saying, "You did good, you did good, two more to go." But in his voice he knows I can't make it to the top twenty-five.

The next two races go pretty much like the first one except the girls know I am going to push the pace so they don't give me as much of a lead and I finish closer to the middle.

After lunch they call names of the top twenty-five to much celebration and high-fives while I wither, trying to hide my disappointment, ignoring the pangs of failure, thinking about what other options I have left to escape the favela. Well, at least there is marriage, I guess. Mom has been hinting already. Soon she will be sending out feelers to all the matchmakers in Venezuela, Peru, Spain and the Mideast, maybe even in UNA.

I pack up my gear, what little I have, into my tiny backpack, upset that I failed but somehow relieved that it is all over, and start toward the buses when I hear Coach Murray call my name. So wrapped up in my own feeling of failure, I almost forgot to say bye to him. Guiltily I step past a group of girls, toward his voice, and freeze, eyes bulging when I see him standing with two young men wearing those evil looking blue-black suits, all three looking my way.

"C'mon over here Gabriella, I have some people I want you to meet."

No! No! No! Now they are going to get me! It's happening all over again! I want to run, to hide, jump on the bus and steal away, but I feel cornered. Suddenly something twists in my stomach, a hard knot of flesh, grimy and black, swirling, curling, banging around against the walls of my gut as if it's a mental patient trying to escape a padded cell. My breath is choked as an ice-cold fist wraps its paw around my heart.

I walk toward them, in a trance, staring straight at Coach Murray, refusing to let my eyes veer away, as if they might somehow betray me, as if the men might be able to discern something in my eyes. *Okay, Gabby. Calm down, calm down, calm down. Just be ready to run and don't get too close.*

"Sorry Coach. I was so distracted that I forgot to say bye." My voice shaking, I give him a quick hug and begin to turn away, terrified that they will figure out who I am and grab me. *Can I just get out of here!*

"Gabriella, hold on." Coach grabs my wrist lightly and I want to tear it away and run, but I don't; I am too afraid. "I want to introduce you to these two men. They liked what they saw in you. Your spirit. They are interested in you for their farm team in UNA."

I exhale softly and contemplate what he just said for a moment. *What is happening here? Is this some kind of trick?*
I allow myself to look at them, quickly, glancing their way for a split second, then back, and I am surprised that they do not grab me, do not recognize me. I am confused. *Could this be true?*
My tongue is clammy in my mouth and I feel slightly nauseous. I want to leave this place but maybe, just maybe, this is real, maybe this might take Mom and me out of the shantytown. *I have to take a chance.*

"A farm team? In North America? How would it work? I am only fifteen. What about my mom?" My voice quivers. *Is this a dream? Maybe the suits are just a coincidence.*

The two men look at each other for a moment and one begins speaking calmly, as if he is explaining a used car warranty for the millionth time, almost bored, "As you might already know, United North America has five Ultraball teams; one out of Sacramento, another in Chicago, the others in Montreal, Mexico City and Philadelphia. Each has a minor league farm team. We are interested in you joining the Northeast farm team, out of Philadelphia. The team trains near Cherry Hill which is just over the bridge in New Jersey. We will pay for your move, and your mother's of course, and all members of the team take a salary, nothing outlandish, but it is decent money. We can talk about negotiating a contract after you speak with your mother if you like."

My mind is splitting open and I don't know what to think, I just need to be on that bus and think about this for a minute, away from these two. It is all I can do to keep myself calm and say a few words so I can escape, "Okay, I will contact you through Coach Murray after I speak with Mom."

I hug Coach one more time, turn quickly, and walk away, too fast I think but I can't help it.

It's a long bus ride back and the more I think about sleeping on hard-swept dirt floors, the choking stench of raw sewage, the children that play bare-foot in the trenches and the lack of opportunity or even possibility of escape, however slim, the more I convince myself that those men wearing the same blue-black suits that the men who followed us that day, long ago, in Venezuela, was just a coincidence, nothing to worry about.

Those suits were probably not the same. Not the same, not the same, no they're not the same. No, not even similar, now that I think about it.

Gabby, you worked in a clothing store for years. You know they were identical.

But I was just a kid, what do I really know about clothes looking the same? Oh, what to think, what to think, I don't know what to think!

Maybe I'm fool, worried over nothing, a coincidence. Yes, yes, coincidence, it is all just a coincidence. Maybe I can trust them? Trust them, trust them. Maybe? Maybe I can trust them. Yes, maybe I can trust them.

But what if they find out who I am?

The New Face of Ultraball

"**A**lright! Gather round and listen up!" The large framed woman bellows, entering the Philadelphia Freedom locker room, the Philadelphia Liberty's farm team, wearing a thick white sweater, khaki shorts, nearly knee-high tube socks accentuating her tremendous, muscular calves, holding a screen in her hand and wearing a whistle around her neck.

"My name is Michelle Donavan and I am not your friend!" She pauses as the seven of us girls move to surround her and sit on the wood benches. She is not exactly screaming but her voice is loud enough that it feels like it. "I am not your enemy either, although some of you will grow to think so. I am not your mother or your sister! I am not here for a relationship; I am here for results! The Philadelphia Liberty hired me because they think I can get those results out of you. And I will do what ever it takes, including working you until there is nothing left, grinding you to a pulp if I have to, until either I get those results or you fail and you're gone!"

She stops, scans the group of serious faces and pauses at three who are smiling at her like puppies looking for a treat.
Donavan looks down at her screen, exhales in disgust, then, looking up, says, "Okay! Let's get to know each other, as I call your name, stand up, tell me your background and something about yourself! Gabriella Con– Con-See– I'll just call you Gabriella."
I stand up and say, "Hello everyone. I'm Gabriella. I come from Brazil. I speak Spanish, not too much Portuguese—and English obviously. I just turned sixteen and am in high school. Ahh... I am looking forward to racing with you? That's it, I guess."

Donavan goes on calling off the names and listening to their stories.

Maxine Stone, a massive woman, easily six and a half feet tall and solid muscle, says she was chosen as an 'enforcer,' whatever that means.

Sidney Scott, a tallish, thin, medium-brown woman, probably of African descent but it's hard to tell, says she's a local, just out of college and has always been great at sports; soccer, field hockey and track, so when the Pre came out she jumped at the chance.

Cyndi Battle, a short waif of a girl, probably weighing in at eighty-five pounds is a NuGen girl. Her parents were sprinters, both Olympic medalists, who contracted with NuGen to test-tube her in the hopes of something great. At twenty-five, her career was ending until the Pre came along and gave her a second chance.

I zone out, wondering what I am doing here, as the last three, the three smiling puppies, Jena Abdel, Dart Milwaukee and Mercury Kwik tell their stories.

I am this little sixteen year-old high schooler from another continent against these twenty-something, super athletes. Can I possibly fit in? Can I keep up?

Donavan bellows, waking me from my daze, "Great! Now that that's over I don't have to hear anything personal from you all ever again! Remember all I care about is results! I am glad Maxine mentioned about being an enforcer. As you may already know, you girls run on the track at the same time as the field game. There will be two races, one during the first half and another during the second. We can run seven runners total across the two races. So, for example, we could have five runners the first race and two the second—or three the first and four the second—and that is part of the strategy we will work out each game. Since only the first three runners score, three points for first, two for second, and one for third, the fourth and fifth runners, if we have them, will be enforcers. It is their job to block the opposing team's runners or provide defense for our girls."

I raise my hand, saying, "Coach Donavan, I thought physical contact wasn't allowed?

"Correct! There are only a few penalties in the Pre; starting before the gun, physical contact or stepping out of bounds. In any of those cases that runner is disqualified and must immediately leave the track and will not score. But that doesn't stop enforcers from pushing opposing team runners off the track and taking them out, now does it?"

Looking at Maxine's tremendous girth, I shudder at the thought of being smashed off the course from ten feet up and then I remember and the fear rushes back in; this is Ultraball. *What was I thinking!* It's Ultraball, the most violent sport on the planet. No pads, no helmets and no breaks in the action although plenty of breaks of the players' bones. Mom and I always hated when Dad would put Ultraball on the screen. It seemed so vulgar, base and almost inhuman. Now I am in it and a slack-jawed shock rolls over me; I can't believe it. My body is on the dinner table.

After Donavan comes the team dietician, who tells us to basically to not eat anything good like hamburgers, then the therapist and on-call doctor, who don't say much except, "Try to not get hurt," and, "Stay clear of the men crashing off the field." My mind blanks to the next few staff members: planners, schedulers, media liaisons and others, as I can't stop thinking that I made a huge mistake coming here.

A few days later, Mom and I are unpacking when our new screen rings our first call. Answering it, I hear, "Is this Gabriella?"

"Speaking."

"Great! This is Norman Gellman. I work for *Sports Illustrated.* We are doing a piece on the Pre and would love to have you featured in it." He goes on to tell me all about the feature and how it would be great for my career.

Career? I never thought about this as a career.

I call the team media liaison and she agrees so a few days later Mom and I arrive at the studio and a swarm of people surround me, makeup people, hairdressers, another measuring for clothing and shoes, another doing my nails while the photographer speaks about all the different shots and how beautiful I am and how the camera loves me already and I am so overwhelmed. Jena and Cyndi are here too, and the lady in charge says that the issue will feature runners from many of the other teams, both farm and pro teams. Mom won't allow me to wear the ultra-tight Ultraball shirt they provided but whatever they put on me looks so great and I just can't believe that this is happening. I am in heaven. *What a great day this is!*

*****

I go to training right after school everyday, the days pile on, the training is impossibly hard and now I know that Donavan wasn't lying. She is trying to grind us to a pulp and it is not until our first game, against Chicago, that I understand why.

We meet at our practice facility and gather our gear then are bused to the stadium. The team is quiet and pensive. A thousand bees are buzzing in my chest and I would love to do something, anything, to get them to stop. We dress for the field quickly, Donavan tells us that Chicago is a speed team, like us, and we need to be faster. She says many other things but it is like I can't hear them and I can't focus even though it seems like she is yelling her instructions. All I can hear, all I can focus on, is the howling, hollering and cheering fans, a reverberating rumble that penetrates through the concrete walls.

We walk out of the locker room, down dark, sparsely-lit halls, the pulsing sound of the crowd getting louder, up a gently sloping ramp and out onto the field just as the announcer calls out, "And here comes our local girls! Our Pre runners! The Philadelphia Freedom!"

Spinning around, spinning around, they are everywhere. Fans, fans, fans, screaming fans wearing bright Philadelphia red, dancing, shaking and holding home-made cardboard signs.

The men have just started their game as we reach our bench. Donavan tells me that I will run first and I am in a daze. Two men smash into each other just in front of us, one careening off the course and crashing to the floor just in front of me, Donavan leaping out of the way, and his head comes to rest on my foot. *What am I doing here! Mom was right! I am going to get killed!*

Sidney, Cyndi and I line up and before I know it the gun fires and we are off and I am running but my body's not connected to my brain. *My head is just floating, floating way up here and there, all the way down there, is my body, and how could I possibly control it? It's just too far away!*

Run, run, run. *Okay! I'm running!* Run, swing, swing, swing, vault and up the warped wall. *Okay! I got this! Just catch those girls! You can't let them beat you, Gabby!* Run, run, dodge, duck, run. Two men crash off the field just in front of me—leap! I vault over them as the dread seeps into my joints. If they had been a microsecond later they would have smashed into me! I catch the back of the pack and try to pass but they know I am there, the Chicago girls, and they force me to stay back. Some of the obstacles have to be taken single file as there's not enough space or not enough ropes, bars, or swings. Just as we hit an opening on the curve I burst into full speed and pass the last girl. Two Chicago girls are in front of me and Sidney and Cyndi are in front of them. *We only have one lap left! I have to pass these two!*

I am dogging their heels but I just can't seem to get by. Just as we swing wide on the final curve, the blue ball flies off the field at what seems like one-hundred miles-per-hour and smashes the Chicago girl's head just in front of me. She tumbles off the course and is disqualified. *That could have been me!* I speed up but can't catch the Chicago girl in front of me. There's just not enough course left and she is too far in front. I finish in a disappointing fourth. Donavan is not happy.

A few weeks pass and next we race Sacramento, an enforcer team. They are big, brutal and aggressive and seem to thoroughly enjoy taking their opponents out of the game by slamming them off the course. I race in the second half with Max and Jena. Jena and I take off fast and quick and after the first lap we have almost a half-lap lead. Running next to Jena, I say, "What's going on?"

She says, "I think they are waiting for us over there."

Two of their enforcers are running really slowly, almost not running at all, near a small grouping of obstacles. About one-hundred yards before we reach them, Jena says, "Spread apart!" so I slow way down and give her some space.

As she reaches the tilting balance beam and mounts it, a Sacramento beast, easily three-hundred pounds of pure, pulsing muscle grabs the beam and slams it down hard, sending Jena in the air like a catapult, then rushes up and swats her airborne body off the course and laughs deeply.

I want to stop running. I want to stop. I want to walk off this field, right here, right now. I want to quit. But I can't. I can't be deported. I can't go back to Brazil, to the dirt floors of the shanty town. I can't go back to picking bugs out of my hair. I have to run. I have to move forward. The fans demand it.

Swing, swing, swing, run, leap. I run up the tilted side-wall and reach out for the rope, trying to dodge the enforcer, standing there, waiting for me, saliva glistening on her broadly smiling lips. Smiling? No, it's more like leering, like a playing card Joker. She dives for me and I try to lift my legs as I swing but it is not enough and she latches onto my hips. She is so heavy! I can't hold on! The friction of the rope burns my hands and I let go. We splash into the watery mud below and are both disqualified.

*****

In my first few races my two best showings are fourth and third and with the enforcers trying to knock at least one of us (if not more) off the course each race, sometimes just finishing is an accomplishment. So far our season is sizing up to be pretty average and Donavan is not happy. We are two wins to three losses, though most of our losses have been due to the field team, not us Pre runners, but since our scores are tabulated together it doesn't really matter. A loss is a loss.

Life in UNA is so foreign for me. It is as if I am a different person here and my life in Venezuela and Brazil was just a dream. Everything that happened before, working in the clothing store, the day that Dad died, Mom and me running for our lives, hiding in the favelas, running with Mara up the mountains, the shanties, the open sewers, all of it; it was as if it all happened to someone else, not me. Yet here in UNA I don't fit in either. No matter how rude or welcoming the people are I always feel like an outsider. No matter how close I come I always feel like there's still some barrier. It's like I am pressing my nose against the glass and looking at the sharks in a fish tank and I can't understand how to get past the invisible barrier of the glass. I still haven't figured out who the sharks are either. And I still haven't figured out who I am. Or who I want to be. That is a weird thing too. I can invent myself, be who I want to be, start all over if I want but I have no idea who that person is. All I know is that I can't tell anyone the truth. And the truth, what is it? I don't really know. I only know what I saw and experienced and that was an illusion. I was the girl from the family that owned the clothing store. A lie. What is the truth? Where am I really from? Why were my parents hiding? And what from? What did those men want from my father? And how did they find him? Will they find us? Too many questions and all I can do is try not to think about it and hope Mom and I are doing the right thing by being here. And hope I don't slip up and say our real last name or something else stupid like that.

A few more matches fly by and it's two weeks before our first big international match, against Brazil, when the *Sports Illustrated* issue hits the screens and seeing it, I am ready to vomit. Maxine throws it down on the bench in front of me, screaming, "What is *this*?"

I look at her huge frame and the pulsing vein on her forehead, sit down on the bench and flip the screen over, horrified to see that I am on the front header with the caption "The new face of Ultraball."

"No. No, they didn't." I look up at her heaving frame, saying, "Max, I didn't know, they didn't tell me—"

"Yeah right, *pretty* girl! Thanks for taking all the honor out of the sport. Now, because of *you*, they are going to think we are cheerleaders."

The article doesn't focus much on the technical aspects of the race but mainly on the eye candy of the girls on the field, almost as if this is part two of the swimsuit issue. Many of pictures of the other girls make them look like they are flirting and flipping the screen page and seeing my picture, I feel completely betrayed.

Suddenly angry, I yell out, "That's not fair! How was I supposed to know what the photographer was shooting!" and looking at her fierce arms, I wish I could pull my words back out of the air.

"Are you kidding me? What are you—*stupid?* "
My voice changes, "No. I didn't know. Max, I'm sorry. They tricked me... You have to believe me. I didn't know."

Turning on her heel, she coughs out, "Now that you have a huge target on your back, don't look for any help from me, *natural-girl!* "

I lean back against my locker and read the rest of the article, wondering why she just called me that and apparently, according to the article, I am the only unmodified runner in the entire Pre, in the entire sport of Ultraball, in fact. The article dedicates six entire paragraphs to this fact as if I am some kind of genetic aberration, a paradox, a freak of nature, an impossibility. They call me the "all natural girl" as if being modified is somehow unnatural or alien. Closing the cover on the screen, I realize that I am more alone than I have ever been and that who I am becoming, who they are making me out to be is completely out of my control.

As the days go by, I hear conversations stop between some of the other girls on the team when I walk in and I feel so isolated that I'd consider dropping off the team except for the fact that I am under contract and don't want to be deported back to Brazil.

I dread walking into the locker room. Clearly Maxine hates me and a few of the other girls resent me being unmodified and untrained, having so much to learn, yet making the screen header. Sidney Scott and Cyndi Battle (I call them See and Cee) are the exception; we hit it off right away and so far they are the only friends I have.

A few more days pass and today we race Brazil and I know I might face Velocity, T'mekah or Carilla and for some reason I am nervous, maybe even a little afraid and I can't seem to shake it. Tying my shoes tight, I can't seem to focus, can't seem to get my mind clear. When the Brazilian team walks out onto the field I am reminded how Velocity can somehow look mean and beautiful at the same time. Carilla Fang and T'mekah Turkah are bouncing around behind her like two puppets.

After the first half we are up by five and just before my race, Donavan says, "Okay Gabriella, you're up and Brazil is running Velocity Jones, Carilla Fang and T'mekah Turkah again, so they are probably spent and will be running as enforcers so watch out."

Great.

Waiting for my heat, I can't stop shaking, an ominous feeling of dread overshadowing me. I feel like I want to cry, but I can't understand why.

Why am I letting some stupid memory of them intimidate me?

29

See, looking over at me with a puzzled look on her face, jumps off the bench, bounds over toward me and plops down, saying, "Hey girl, don't sweat it. Just another race, right?"

Glancing over at her, I say, "Yeah, sure."

She smiles then says, "Hey! I got another one for ya!" See loves to tell jokes, even the ones that no one laughs at.

"Go ahead," I exhale.

"Okay, okay, okay," she starts, smiling broadly, "A couple of hunters are out in the woods when one of them falls to the ground, not breathing, eyes rolled back in his head. The other guy whips out his screen and calls 911 emergency. He gasps to the operator, 'My friend is dead! What can I do?'

The operator, in a calm soothing voice says, 'Calm down. I can help. First, let's make sure he's dead—'

There is a silence then a shot is heard.

The guy's voice comes back on the line and he says, 'OK, now what?' "

See looks at me expectantly so I give her a half smile and say, "Not so bad."

"Okay, okay, okay. One more then," she begins again, animatedly saying, "A woman gets on a bus with her baby and the bus driver comments, 'That's the ugliest baby that I've ever seen.'
The woman stomps her feet to the rear of the bus, plops down, fuming, then turns to a man next to her and yelps, 'That driver just insulted me!'

The man replies calmly, 'You go right up there and tell him off— go ahead, I'll hold your monkey for you.' "

I laugh out loud. "You got me, See. Good one!"

She smiles at me then says, "And hey, about you running against Velocity and her two goons... Don't you worry about them beating you. You sucking so bad will draw them back."

I smile and punch her arm as we are gathering in the staging area with Max and then we line up on the field. Even with the jokes, I still can't shake the dread, wrapped around me like a large snake, squeezing the life from my body.

At the gun, See is way out in front and for some reason a few of the fast Brazilians are holding back with me and I don't know why.

Do they want to bump me out? But why? I am not the fastest. Why would they waste their runners on me?

Rounding the first loop, Velocity, Carilla and T'mekah box me in, one in front, one in back, and Velocity just to my right, as if it had been all planned out.

What are these three doing? Trying to make me jump off the course? I can't take the disqualification without one of them going out with me.

I am leaping over a tall wall, nervously, wondering what these three are up to when Carilla cuts my legs out from under me and my head smacks the wall. *Whammm!*

I feel my body falling—
The sky is so blue—
And the clouds—

The New Face of Ultraball

Why are they so pink?—

Then—

    Blackness—

"Uuuuuuhhhh—"
I see a blurry face—
Donavan?

Then, the PAIN—
    Rushing in like a missile—
OHMYGOD!
    IT HURTS!
        IT HURTS SOOOOOOOOO BAD!
"AAAAAAAAAAAHHH!"

Lying on the tarmac, knee shredded, howling in intense pain, my eyes a blur of tears, blood and saliva spewing from my mouth, clutching my leg, it extending out sideways at a terrible, unnatural angle, I can't think about anything but stopping the pain! The pain! The pain! The pain! The excruciatingly sharp pain!

Someone is running toward me squeezing a needle.

    "Oooooooohhhhhnnnn—"

I awaken in the hospital, surrounded by Cee, See, Donavan and Mom. Cee and Mom cry when I wake.

I can barely control my mouth, "Haayyeee, avveee wwaahn!" I think my mouth is smashed. My head is spinning. Drugs are too strong probably but nothing hurts anyway. In fact everything feels dreamy, dreamy, oh so dreamy.

Max is here too, standing in the back, sheepishly, and I am so happy to see her! "Hiiiyyyyeeeeee, Maaaaaaxxxxeeeeeee*!"*

Max's face is twitching and she wipes her eyes as she mumbles, "I didn't protect her—"

Looking around I cannot control my head. It flops around but I am so happy to see everyone!

"Aaaaallllll hhheeeeerrreeeeee fooo meeeeeeee?"

Mom, crying, bites her knuckle, turns and walks out the room.

My head flops over and I am so happy to see the light on the ceiling and the white walls!

"Llooooookkkeeeee tthhhaaaaarrrrr!"

See grabs my shoulder and says, "Gabby, it's going to—it's going to be okay? Do you hear me?"

I hear Donavan say, "Sidney, don't. She's too out of it right now."

What's that noise? I am *so* happy to see the machine with the squiggly lines making the beepy noise! "Hee, heee, heeeeee*!"*

Reaching down to feel my leg through the sheets, slowly, uncontrollably, Max quickly reaches out and grabs my hand, stopping it, and lowers her face to just in front of mine. "No. I wouldn't... You don't want to see that right now." Then she squeezes my hand slowly, staring at me with soft eyes, lower lip quivering, ready to cry.

The team doctor comes in and calmly tells me it's over. I will never run again. They can modify us before birth. Of course. Shooting a DNA bullet into a zygote—that's easy. But repairing a knee that's been blown apart in a blunt force trauma—no, genetics won't help me there. They can straighten out the bones, set and put a cast on them, even inject some thermo-reactive agents to help it heal faster, but not much more than that. Maybe if I were rich, maybe if I were sponsored, maybe if someone cared about me then they could fix me up good, nice and right and I could race again. But those maybes are not options for me. I have government health-care and the team will just grab the next girl in line. No one cares about me or my leg and without a pocket full of money the doctors will only patch me up and send me away. In fact, I might not even walk again.

The painkillers they gave me are so strong that I can't stop smiling at him and I am so happy to see him! When he leaves, I howl, "Dannn Kooou!"

Meet Dr. Duggan

A few weeks have passed since I left the hospital and Mom and I are moving to a new town, a riverside town. We rented a townhouse (the realtor counseled me when I called it a row-home —*Row-homes are in the city; town-houses are in the suburbs!)* We buy a few rooms of furniture with our savings and will rent the rest. The government decided not to deport us since Mom got a job in Philly at some agency (she speaks three languages). It feels like we are squeaking by.

The first few days were unbearable. Mom blamed herself and couldn't stop crying and holding me. At first all I wanted to do was hide in my room and cry too but her being in a constant despair forced me to be strong. Somebody had to be. I kept hearing John Murray's positive, upbeat voice in my ears. I knew I would never run again, and they said I might never walk, but his voice inside of me rose up and I knew somehow, someway I was going to beat this. I was going to fight it. I didn't know how successful I would be or what the end result would be but I wasn't going to lock myself in a closet and pretend my life was over. Now I revel in tiny successes; walking to the bathroom without falling—yeah!, making it to the kitchen table without wincing, even though it really, really hurts—hooray!, bending over and picking up the morning paper off the grass without falling—alright!

Even though my leg is destroyed and so ugly—I can never let anyone see it, ever—I am somehow slightly happier than when we were hiding in the shanties in Brazil. Yes, my body is permanently damaged and it hurts terribly but at least I am not sleeping on a dirt floor, constantly trying to stop the bugs from crawling into my hair.

I don't have to use the walker anymore and canes are for old men so I have mentally convinced myself to not wince at the bone on bone pain when I walk. Well, I call it walking but sometimes it feels like I am hobbling. The doctors are quite happy with my progress so far and they say it is because I am so young but the truth is that I exercise myself all the time, not just during the therapy sessions. I refuse to become a *victim*. I refuse to see myself that way.

Mom and I are actually considering another name change, just to start fresh again. It could be a chance to become someone new, to reinvent myself, to choose who I want to be and not be defined by what has happened to me. I want something cool sounding, maybe Greek, something like Athanasiadis or Savalas; or maybe French like François. Fran-swaaah—*I love the way that sounds.* Conceição isn't our real name anyway. *Come to think of it, what is our real name?*

Sometimes I think about what my future would have been if certain things hadn't happened the way they did but mostly I am just trying to adjust and move on, become a normal, North America teenage girl like the ones on the television programs in Venezuela. *Being normal. Huh? Like what does that mean?*

Well, I am trying to fit in anyway. I go to the mall and sleep-overs. I attend high school at this typical school where the biggest controversy was when two girls wore the same dress to the prom. I made a few acquaintances at high school and maybe they will turn into friends. We talk about silly things like boy bands and online videos, how much we hate history class and Thursday's cafeteria lunch, and what we want to do when we grow up. Sometimes I like to think I'm past all the Ultraball craziness, the media storm over the *all-natural* girl and the infighting of the athletes. Other times I wish I could be right there in it. C'est la vie? That's life, right? And what happened before, my past life in Venezuela and Brazil, I don't even think about it much anymore. It wasn't me anyway; it was all just a dream. Sure, I miss Dad and I think of him, especially when I lay in bed, staring out the window at night, but that past life and all those things that happened just seem too surreal to spend much time thinking about them. What is real is what is happening right now; the fight to walk, high school, making new friends, trying to feel normal and trying to fit in. I can't choose what life throws at me, just how I react to it (Something Coach told me once). And now I know that it is so true.

Standing in the finished basement I admire my decorations (Mom let me decorate it however I wanted), my teenager zone, a place where she said I can invite friends to hang out, my own private space. Although I haven't made many real friends yet, still just Sidney and Cyndi (See and Cee); the kids here are so much colder than Venezuela. On the far wall I have a large framed poster of the cover of *Sports Illustrated*. I somehow like the fact that I was on the top of the screen now although I still become a little angry when I read the caption, "The new face of Ultraball."

Mom is getting on too. She somehow met two guys who knew Dad and her from the old country, Archibald Duggan and Smith Dinklestein, both scientists who worked on research at the university near our village when I was just a baby. At first, I was petrified that somehow we would have to escape again since they know our old name but Mom *assured* me everything would be all right. They knew us before the war, before we left the old country, before we moved to Venezuela. They speak about Dad as if he was a totally different person before I was born, a totally different person than the one I knew in Venezuela and it makes me feel like there is so much I still do not know.

I am just tidying up the teenager zone because Mom said Dr. Duggan is stopping over in a bit. *I can't call him Archibald, sounds too weird.* (And Smith? I can't say Dinklestein without laughing.) Looking at this room; the couches, wall screens and decorations; the plush, shag carpet, actual, real, painted and decorated walls, end tables with lamps on them that always turn on when I call them; so absolutely different than the shanty in Brazil; makes me feel that my life is now so textbook normal that I still don't know if it is real. *Normal. What does that mean?*

A twinge of fear shakes me for a moment as the peach fuzz hairs on the back of my neck stand on end. *Could this be real? Or am I going to wake up, roll over and look at the dirt bugs of our shanty floor back in Brazil?*

Mom yells down, "Gabby, the girls are on screen. Pick up."

I turn on the screen to see See and Cee smiling back at me.

"Hey girls, long time no see."

See starts, "Gabby, I wanted to be the first to tell you—"

"No, I'm gonna be the first—" Cee pushes See lightly with her shoulder.

"What is it?"

They both reply at the same time, "Three spots just opened on the Liberty team!"

Realizing that a couple months ago one of them quite possibly would have been mine, I say, "Wow, that's great. What happened?"

See says, "Agnes got pregnant so she left."

"What about the other two spots?"

Face changing, suddenly becoming serious, Sidney looks over at Cyndi, then they both reply, "Velocity happened."

I remember reading that Velocity, Carilla and T'mekah had moved up to the pro level.

"What do you mean?"

Cee answers, "You didn't hear?"

See says, "They were playing against Brazil last week and—"

Cee says, "Velocity and her two sidekicks, Fang and Turkey—"

See corrects her, "Turkah, Cee. It's T'mekah Tur-kah and Carilla Fang, remember?"

"Well, she's a *turkey* to me—"

See says, "Yeah, me too."

Cee says, "Those three took them out—"

See says, "For good—"

Cee says, "They won't be coming back—"

See says, "So now there are three spots open."

ChaPter six

I lean back against the wall, realizing that what happened to me was intentional. "So who is moving up? Either of you two?"

"I wish!" They both answer at the same time.

Cee continues, "Jena, Dart and Mercury—"

See says, "But that puts both of us in number one and number two spots."

"Yeah, and I'm number one!" Cee says.

"No you're not!" See says, pushing Cee lightly with her shoulder.

They both turn back toward me and reply together, "Just kidding!"

"Hey, but its good to see you two and you know it doesn't matter who is first. Don't let that get between you two."

"Of course!" they both say.

Then See yelps, "Oh by the way, I got a new one, Gabby."

Cee says, "Here we go again," looking up through her eyelids.

"Stop it, Cyndi!"

"Okay, let's hear it," I say impatiently.

A broad grin jumps across her face and she says, "Okay, okay, okay. A doctor says to his patient, 'I have bad news and worse news.'

'What's the bad news?' asks the patient.

The doctor replies sadly, 'You only have 24 hours to live.'

'That's terrible,' said the patient, 'How can any other news possibly be worse?'

The doctor replies, 'I've been trying to contact you since yesterday.' "

We all giggle then Mom yells down, "Gabby, we have company!"

"Hey girls, congratulations! You deserve it! Listen, I gotta go. We'll talk soon, right?"

When Dr. Duggan arrives in a starchy white shirt and yellow bow-tie I make tea and the three of us talk about the typical stuff, politics and current events, how different everything is here compared to back home in the old country, and how the UNA government is not addressing concerns of working people.

I try to find out more about Dad before I was born, what happened in the war, and how exactly Dr. Duggan knew them, but the topic always quickly changes to something else. Once in a while Dr. Duggan hints about some great new finding he is working on, something that he says will, 'change everything,' but science has never interested me that much although I do love technology— using it that is.

Mom steps out to heat up some spinach pies and all of a sudden I find myself in some kind of weird-tech sales pitch. Dr. Duggan slides over, moving almost too close, and looks me directly in the eyes, whispering, "Gabriella, I need your help. This is very important. Can I count on you?"

He is almost shaking and I feel like this is too weird. *What is this old man talking about?* His breath is on my face. Glancing back at the kitchen entrance, looking for Mom, I tell him, "Go on," while I push away in my seat just a bit.

He starts talking crazy-talk, too fast, excited, saying, "Listen Gabriella, the planet is rotating at about 1,000 miles an hour and the distance from Portugal to New Jersey is about 3,500 miles so if we could somehow jump out of our time and jump back in three and a half hours later we would have traveled 3,500 miles but used little or no fuel. We would have simply taken advantage of the rotation of the earth, to travel the earth—"

"Wait! Wait! Wait! Dr. Duggan, I have no idea what you are talking about or what this has to do with me but it kind of sounds like you are talking about time travel and you are *freaking me out!"*

I push further away in my seat, glance toward the kitchen doorway, thinking about joining Mom there, then decide to just make conversation until she returns. I flex my leg out, enduring the sharp pain, as I stretch it. If I don't stretch it often it tends to lock up.

"Shenanigans," he exhales, pauses, takes off his glasses and cleans them, realizing that he sounds like a nut to me, slides a bit back, out of my personal space, then continues, more slowly this time, "Shenanigans. Yes, shenanigans... I'm sorry my dear—time travel—yes and no. Time travel like on the screen, no, that's not possible. If that kind of time travel were possible, we would have met people from the future long ago. What I am talking about is more like *dimensional* travel."

"Okay, I'm listening." Okay, I was half listening. *Hurry up, Mom.*

"Gabriella, we live in four dimensions and—"

"Four?"

"Yes, that's right. Gabriella, remember your schooling, a dimension is merely a term to mean something we can measure. Weight or length can be measured and so we physicists call them dimensions. I am 5 foot 6 inches tall and my height is a measurable dimension. The four dimensions we live in are height, length, width and time."

He pauses, looks at me, making sure I am still with him, then continues, "Now if we could step outside of our dimension of time, then step back in after waiting for the earth to rotate to where we want to be, we can achieve a dramatic physical displacement with very little energy expended."

"Nice theory, I guess." I hope Mom comes back from the kitchen soon so I can escape from this conversation. I have more important things to do with my time than to talk to her old nutty friends, like go to the mall. Cyndi said eXtra is having a sale.

"It's more than a theory," he whispers hoarsely, tilting his head and looking at me over the top of his glasses.

I sit up, taking notice of the tension in his voice, saying, "Go on," and I wonder if my mother knew he was going to do this.

"Gabriella, what I am about to tell you must be in the strictest confidence. This is my life's research. No one can know. Absolutely no one."

Secrets! Yessss! Now he has my attention. "I would never tell. You have been a friend of the family since before I was born. Absolutely."

"Shenanigans. Okay, here goes. Not only is the theory correct but we have experimented with such a machine and have been using it for nearly two years. We set up two stations so far, one not far from here, in New Jersey, and another on the coast of Portugal, both on the same latitude. We are confident that it is safe, although there have been a few unexpected results."

Mom comes back with the spinach pies and sometime later she leaves again for something else. He looks at me probably reconsidering whether or not he can trust a sixteen year-old girl.

I lean forward whispering, "Like what kind of unexpected results?"

"Well, a trip through should take about three and a half hours, like I said, but we found that movement once outside of our time-dimension could accelerate the travel and reduce the time for the trip dramatically. In fact, we are now shooting people across the Void, so to speak, and the trip only takes a handful of seconds not three or more hours."

Still not sure if I believe him or if this might be some kind of prank, I reply, "Void, huh? Where is this Void, this time outside of time that you travel through?"

"We don't know exactly where it is. Perhaps, we should not use such terms as 'where' and 'when' as they do not really apply. String theory, depending on which version, says there are somewhere between ten and twenty-six dimensions. So far all we know is that there is nothing there that we have been able to measure—hence the name, the Void."

Mom returns and Dr. Duggan continues speaking about his new invention but now leaving out key details of its purpose, him becoming increasingly more animated the longer he speaks, eyes glazing over and becoming almost reflective as if he's lost someplace in there, telling us how great it's going to be, how it's going to save the environment and unite the world and all manner of other good-for-mankind type things. Of course what he doesn't say is that it will also make him rich beyond measure, but that's really the motivation of any business isn't it? I can't fault him for that.

He proposes what I have been suspecting for about the last half hour, that I be the spokesperson for this venture, "Everyone knows your face, Gabby. They love you. They don't know who you really are of course, like we do, but they all know the story. For something so radically different like this, something that will be seen as a threat to other industries like airlines, trains, trucking, and travel agencies, something those businesses will fight, I need to put a face on this that people can trust, an all natural face, a face of innocence."

I love how he drops in the, 'like we do,' when I really don't know him that well. Sure, he's a friend of the family and my parents knew him years ago, but he fled to Europe when we fled to South America. How often can you see a person that lives on the other side of the planet?

Besides, I disappeared from the spotlight after my injury and I like it that way; I am trying to be a normal sixteen year-old girl, attending a real high school, with real friends (when I start making them, anyway). I don't know if I am ready for that spotlight. I remember how quickly the media turned me into something I am not, something I didn't want to be. "Give me some time to think about it."

Mom looks at me and smiles at my new opportunity, clearly having no idea what he's talking about.

About half an hour after he leaves, I call him, saying, "Anything I endorse, I need to see and try out for myself. I won't lie to the public or anyone. If I don't like it, I'm out. No questions asked. And I need to see and approve everything that has my face or name on it. I don't want to be made into some kind of natural-girl freak again."

Tripping Through the Void

"**M**om, the girls are here—I'm leaving," I say, my hand on the front doorknob, backpack on my shoulder.

Mom yells out from the kitchen, "Have a good time... Tell Cyndi and Sidney I said Hi—and make sure you don't get too close to any of Archibald's machinery. I don't want you getting cut or anything like that."

"Ahh... I don't think it's that kind of machine. Mom, I'll be safe though."

I wobble out the front door and down the steps, leaning hard on the railing, gingerly favoring my right side. Cee bounds from the car, meets me at the bottom of the steps and grabs my arm to support me, walking me to the car. I give her an embarrassed glance followed by a thank you smile.

The plan is to run up to Princeton, check out Dr. Duggan's contraption, quickly, then spend the rest of the weekend together, catching up, gossiping and eating. It feels like ages since I've seen the girls and I have been looking forward to this weekend for a while.

It takes about an hour to arrive in Princeton which gives See ample time to practice her stand-up routine on me as Cyndi drives.

See starts, "Okay, okay, okay. Two fish are in a fish tank when one fish turns to the other and says, 'How do you drive this thing?' "

With no response, she says quickly, "Another one, a scientist and a philosopher are being chased by a hungry lion. The scientist makes some quick calculations then says, 'It's no good trying to outrun it. It's catching up.'

The philosopher, keeping a little ahead, replies, 'I'm not trying to out-run the lion, I'm trying to outrun you!' "

chaPter seven

Most of her jokes are groaners but a few have me in tears.

See continues running through them rapid-fire, "Okay, okay, okay. A man goes to his lawyer and says, 'I would like to make a will but I don't know exactly how to go about it.'

The lawyer, smiling, replies, 'Not a problem, leave it all to me.'

The man looks somewhat upset and says, 'Well, I knew you were going to take a big chunk, but I want to leave a little for my family too!' "

After that last one I am happy that we have finally arrived at the University. Looking around at the structures, See says what I am thinking, "All the buildings look like castles."

We park in the visitors' lot and wander around looking for Dr. Duggan's building.

Cee says, "Look at that one!" pointing toward a large castle with four large, militant-looking, observation towers on each corner, red brick with white stone accents, a twenty foot Roman arch entryway inviting us in. All that is missing is a drawbridge.

It doesn't take long to figure out that the campus is too big and that we aren't going to find the building without some help. I call Dr. Duggan and tell him we're lost.

"I see a building right in front of me—the sign says 'Blair.'"

"Oh... Blair is residential—"

"You mean people live in that castle?"

"Err... Yeah, we are on an entirely different campus. Go back to your car and type in 'Forrestal Campus.' When you arrive, park in the lot just past the big white building and I will meet you outside."

The girls and I are a little disappointed that this is taking so long. We ride out of the University area, over the river and into this tiny complex, surrounded by homes and shopping centers, a tiny complex of just a few buildings. One sign says Plasma Physics Laboratory and we see Dr. Duggan waving at us standing in front of a plain three-story building, nothing like the exciting castles we just left. We park in the empty lot and walk up to meet him. There is a wooden sign in front of the building, painted white with black letters, looking very temporary, saying 'Site C'. I guess the building is new and hasn't been named yet.

"Come, come, my dears. Gabriella, welcome," He says, grabbing my free hand and shaking it, "And who might these two lovely ladies be?"

"Dr. Duggan, this is Sidney Scott and Cyndi Battle, we raced together back before the accident."

"Ah... So you two are ultra-girls."

See snickers then says, "We play Ultraball. Well, we run the Pre anyway—"

Cee says defiantly, "We're *not* ultra-girls—"

See pouts, "Yeah, that makes us sound like cheerleaders—" The *Sports Illustrated* article flashes in my mind and I am momentarily embarrassed.

Dr. Duggan replies, "Shenanigans. I'm always mixing up this popular culture stuff. Please forgive me. I don't leave my lab much." I could definitely believe that, his skin is pasty white. It must never see the sun.

We enter the building, Dr. Duggan leading the way, Cee next, See and I following, me holding See's arm tight. It is a drab and boring building outside, but inside, beautiful. I think the outside must not be finished yet. Inside, the bottom floor is almost entirely open to a great rotunda with large columns rising from the base to support the roof, three floors up. The center, circular portion of the roof is domed and made of stained glass. Beautiful. We take the left-side, rounded staircase up to the second floor. The long hall has several unlabeled doors on the left and a railing on the right that overlooks the rotunda. We stop in front of the third door and Dr. Duggan pauses before he swipes his security badge.

"Now girls, what I am about to show you is top secret." He pauses, with a pained smile.

Cee and See look at each other when he doesn't open the door, him standing there, frozen. They turn their heads back to him and both say, "Yeah, sure, no problem."

Dr. Duggan turns toward the door then mutters under his breath, "Shenanigans. Off we go then."

Opening the door, we step into a buzz of activity. The room is large, too large, and I realize that all the doors on this side of the building all lead to this same room. His contraption takes up the entire left side of the building. The other doors in the hallway are false. The room has clean white walls, bright fluorescent lights and industrial tile floor, like a large classroom. There are five workstations set up on the far wall with extra large computer screens displaying all manner of graphs and numbers. The technicians seated at the stations are young, maybe in their early twenties and they wear earpieces with extending microphones. They pay no attention to us and appear to be in the middle of some procedure.

"Well now, Gabriella, girls, here is my invention!" he says proudly, extended arm pointing toward a large, blue, metal ring at the end of the far wall, a single rail track, about thirty feet long, like the kind used by trains, but a bit wider, sitting on the floor leading up to the ring and a large bundle of cables neatly snaked behind the ring, along the far edge of the room, ending at the back of the workstations.

"Great. Looks like nothing to me," I say.

A quizzical look falls on Dr. Duggan's face as he says, "Of course. Yes. It's not what it looks like, but what it does—" He turns toward See and Cee, saying, "Sidney, Cyndi, sorry but I cannot show you any more." Reaching in his pocket, he pulls out some money and extends his arm toward them. "Perhaps you two could go out to lunch, on me, while I show Gabriella how the machine works. Just across the roadway you came in on there's a bunch of different restaurants, Forrestal Village, quite good. I eat there everyday. Come back in, say, two hours?"

They both look at me and I nod, then they both say, "Sure."

ChaPter seven

After they leave Dr. Duggan becomes real serious, barking orders to the crew, almost as if I am not there. The crew becomes tense just as the blue metal ring shudders and a neon green grid pattern of lights fill the circular space, just in front of the far white wall. Suddenly air blasts my face, hard, as a large cart appears out of nowhere, seemingly coming out of the grid pattern, riding the single metal track, traveling at tremendous speed and quickly slowing down to a stop just in front of Dr. Duggan and the workstations. The cart has a single cheap metal chair strapped down to it, the kind of four-legged, stack-able chair kept in our church's recreation room. A cage with a parakeet is sitting on the chair and the bird is squawking.

Even though Dr. Duggan mentioned something like this, it still surprises me.

"Where did that come from?!"

The entire lab staff stops and turns toward me, wide eyed, and I suddenly feel like a tourist.

Dr. Duggan explains as the crew goes back to their monitors, "Ahh... It is as I explained once before, perhaps not so well, at your home. We are exiting our dimension here," pointing at the ring, "and reentering at a similar station, on the same planetary latitude, in Portugal, just on the coast."

"On the coast? Really? Like at the beach?"

"Err... Yes."

"Can I try now?"

"Gabriella... I didn't think you were serious—"

I give him an angry look and say, "Well, I guess if you don't want my endorsement—"

"Ohh... Oh... Okay. Yes, not a problem."

He turns to the crew and barks some orders that I don't understand. Turning back to me he says, "Of course you will have to go through the full battery of medical testing—" He smiles as if this will discourage me.

I reply, "No problem," and his smile quickly disappears.

He turns back to the crew and barks some more orders, wipes his forehead then whispers under his breath, "Shenanigans."

Two crew members help me onto the chair and it shocks me how rickety it feels, as if it could topple over if I leaned a little to the side. They called it the 'transport chair module' but it looks like a chair sitting on a flimsy piece of plywood and I suddenly wonder what was I thinking.

It's too late now.

I buckle my seat-belt and brace my hands on the metal side rails of the chair as the green grid pattern appears. The crew members and Dr. Duggan take their seats and strap themselves down.

"Hey! Why do you need to be strapped in?"

"You'll see!" Dr. Duggan hollers out over the loud hum.

Then, suddenly, one of the crew slams a big blue button and a black hole opens in the middle of the ring, sucking everything in the room into it. Everyone braces themselves as if they do not trust their seat-belts, papers flying all over the room, long hair pulled forward, the transport chair accelerating, being sucked into the ring, unnaturally fast, squeezing my body back, smashing the small chair cushion flat, my back crushing against the hard metal braces in the back of the chair, breath squeezing from my lungs, sound bending all around me like a rapidly moving train producing a Doppler effect, my knuckles turning bright white as I squeeze down hard on the railing, instantly traveling ridiculously fast. As I cross the ring and the plane of the green grid my body feels like it is being ripped in two and a high-pitched ringing sound pierces my mind, simultaneously in two places at the same time, on earth and in the Void. An incredibly bright, blinding white light envelops me and I can't squeeze my eyes down tight fast enough. I try to tuck my head into my shoulder to block it out.

Then, suddenly, it's over.

I feel the transport chair slowing down and stop. I hear a young man's voice, "It's okay. Just breathe. Breathe slower. It's your first time. It's natural to hyperventilate. Slow your breathing. You're in Portugal."

Looking up, I see a cute young man, my age maybe, in a white lab coat, blond curly hair just a bit too long, blond peach fuzz on his chin, his hand on my shoulder, smiling. *He's cute.*
I force myself to breathe slower, fighting off the shock of violent pain and ripping mind piercing sound.

"Can you help me up, please?"

He offers his hand, a puzzled look on his face, then seeing my scarred leg he jumps forward and gives me his entire arm.

"Take a few minutes then we'll send you back."

"You will not." I remove my seat-belt and stand.

"What? But Dr. Duggan said—"

"I don't care what he said. I want to see this place." I can't believe this isn't some kind of trick. I had my eyes closed for most of it. I want to get out of this room, see the beach, and prove to myself that I'm not in New Jersey anymore.

"Gabriella, *where are you going?"* I hear Dr. Duggan say.   Turning I see his gigantic face displayed on a wall screen.

"Be right back—going to go look around."
Before he can protest, I tug the young man's arm and we are out the door, down the staircase and out into the fresh air.
"We can't be gone too long—"

"Don't worry about it. I will take the heat from Dr. Duggan."   We walk down the sandy street and I say, "Hey, what's your name anyway?"

"Michael. And you're Gabriella. Dr. Duggan told me about you. You are going to be our spokesperson."

We walk down the sandy sidewalks along the empty streets. Tiny apartments, a few restaurants and a decaying bait and tackle shop greet us.

"Yeah, I might. I heard your name before—think he said you named that place?"

"Ohh... The Void? Yeah, I named it."

We round the corner and the beach opens up in front of us, coastline as far as I can see, and it hits me. *This is real. Dr. Duggan really did it. I am real-*

*ly in Portugal. I really just traveled three-thousand five-hundred miles in a split
second. He did it.*

"Okay, we can go back now." My voice is shallow and my eyes wide.

We return to the Portugal control room and I can't keep my eyes off
Michael. He is just a regular guy but there is something about him. I can't quite
put my finger on it but for some reason I can't keep my eyes off him.

Michael melodramatically barks out instructions as if he's in one of
those corny Star Trek movies, "Start calculations for time warp!" above the
drone of cooling fans, pumps and valves to the other three, who look like grad
students. One of them, a rigid looking lady, momentarily looks through her eyelids at the ceiling when Michael speaks, then returns to checking off steps on her
data packet on a scratched-up, dollar store screen and calling out procedure
commands to the other two.

The control room in Portugal looks nothing like the one in Princeton. I
would like so it much more if everything appeared ultra-modern and ultra-high
tech but the place is an ultra-dump. Most of the machines look garage built
from scrapped equipment. Multicolored wiring hanging out of open-topped
metal boxes runs over to racks of dusty and beaten ten year-old computers connected with tech salvage break-out cables. The boxes have a variety of differ-
ent-colored, blinking LEDs running in haphazard and crooked lines but their
purpose is unknown to me as nothing is labeled. The walls to the two adjoining
rooms have been unceremoniously knocked down with a sledge hammer, still
propped up in the corner, to allow for the laying of rail tracks leading up to a
ring similar to the one in Princeton. The framework supporting the ring was
made from standard lumber sloppily nailed together askew, tops cut to seemingly random lengths, holding the only cleanly machined object in the apartment, a
shiny, blue metal ring about two inches thick and about eight foot in diameter.
A bunch of tiny electrical coils, wires, and small shiny metal blocks with hy-
draulic lines attached to them run along the outer edge of the ring, probably a
couple of hundred in total. The wire and tube bundles snake down and across
the floor in no particular organized fashion and it is hard to find a place to put
my feet without stepping on something that might be important.

I sit in the transport chair, bracing myself, ready for my return trip,
glancing up nervously at the busted off chunks of lath sticking out past the plaster of the broken down walls, taunting me as if they were the fat teeth of a hip-
po's mouth.

*Hope this contraption stays together or I'm flying through the brick
wall just past the ring.* I remember that we are on the third floor. *Just hold on
tight. I will be home in a few seconds.*

As the last sequence kicks in, the transport chair assembly begins to
shake, a loud whir picks up just behind my head and a blue grid pattern lights up
in the plane of the ring, two rooms away. The transport chair creaks and slowly
shuffles forward a few inches as the maglev kicks in.

Just then Michael yells, "Engage!"

It is over in a moment and when I untuck my face from my shoulder
and slowly open my eyes I see Dr. Duggan smiling down at me. The pain hurts

46

more this time, being ripped in two, maybe because I am expecting it, and the residual feeling of it stays with me for a few minutes.

"Not so bad, huh? Here you are, all in one piece, " Dr. Duggan says, smiling.

"Yeah, not bad."

He helps me up and I suddenly feel like vomiting. Clenching my mouth down tight, saliva pooling in my cheeks, I stumble to the trashcan, crash into the wall and let it all out.

"Oh dear," I hear Dr. Duggan say over my retching.

When I am done, Dr. Duggan leads me to the bathroom so I can clean up. When I exit the restroom, he is there waiting for me and says, "Sorry, about that, Gabriella. I should have warned you about the first time. Happened to most of us."

Looking down the hallway this feeling comes over me like it didn't really happen. That it was somehow an illusion. *It feels so impossible.*

"Don't worry about it. I think I will do better tomorrow."

"Tomorrow! What do you mean tomorrow?"

"I want to go through again. Tomorrow."

"Gabriella, when you said you wanted to go through, I was hesitant but sure, I humored you. I understand you didn't want to endorse anything you haven't tried but now you have tried it. I thought you only wanted the one trip. I don't see the need—"

"Look, Dr. Duggan, just one more time? Okay? I want to spend the day in Portugal." I give him my sweet, little girl smile and he caves. *The smile. Gets 'em every time.*

Out of The Corner of My Eye

Cee and See pick me up and we have a fun sleep-over but I can't help feeling distracted, can't stop thinking about tomorrow. In the morning I apologize for not spending the day with them, treating them like a shuttle service, but hey, what are friends for if not to help each other out? See let me borrow her dad's old strap-on welding glasses and they drop me back off at the Site C building.

I arrive bright and early and Dr. Duggan keeps to his word about the medical testing. It's clear he is trying to discourage me as it takes about five hours but feels like all day. His extensive battery of tests include drawing several vials of blood, urine samples, a small spinal fluid sample, electrocardiogram, stress test and stress echo to check my heart, several full body scans with names like ultrasonography, others that they call by their letters as if I am supposed to know what they are like CT and MRI scans, and physical performance tests like the ability to hold air, oxygen exchange and uptake rate, and all manner of strength and speed performance measurements. I thought I would escape some of them since I can't use a treadmill but they set up some device that is like a treadmill for arms.

He checks in on me periodically, perhaps hoping that I will give up, but the more I see his smiling face the more I decide to go through with this but I am not sure why I am fighting for it. *Maybe just 'cause I'm so stubborn.*

The testing eats up half my day so when it's done I am eager to get on with it. I strap my welding glasses on tight, grab down hard on the side rails of the flimsy metal chair and happily howl, "I'm ready!"

Blasting through the head-splitting pain, not as bad this time, I force my eyes open to see light all around, in every direction, as far as I can see, endless whiteness. It is so bright that it appears hazy. Almost blurry. I see something like low lying clouds in the distance. And the smell. Like lilac. And jasmine. Faint. Wispy.

Here comes the exit. A black circle, so distinct compared to the ultra-bright white light, screams toward me.

What's that!

I break the plane of the ring, instantly in Portugal, the transport chair slowing down rapidly, me hanging on as to not fall off.

OhMyGod!

>*OhMyGod!*

>>*OhMyGod!*

>>>*DidIReallyJustSeeThat!*

"Calm down. It's okay. Just breathe, just breathe—"

Michael places his hand on my shoulder. But it isn't the trip through, the shock of the head splitting pain that is freaking me out, it's what I just saw.

"I slide the welding glasses back into my hair, look up at him and say, "Thanks. I'm okay," and force myself to breathe normal, fighting the pulsing blood in my temple.

"Do you need help?" he says, stepping back and offering me his hand.

Exhaling long and slow, the others staring at me, I look up at him, smile, and say, "Sure." I grab his arm and heave myself up, then, turning towards the group, say, "Sorry about the freak out. I'm Gabriella. I didn't introduce myself last time."

After a few niceties, Michael and I leave (he was informed by Dr. Duggan that he would be my escort for the day.)

We walk up and down the streets, looking in the storefront windows at a bunch of stuff that I would never buy, typical beach shop junk, just enjoying the walk.

I think I could become used to holding onto his strong arm.

"So, tell me about yourself, Michael, my Portugal escort."

"Err... Not much to say really. I am seventeen. University at thirteen. Built my first particle accelerator, in my parents' garage, at fifteen. Tripped the power to the whole village when I fired it up."

"Really?"

"Yeah. It was hilarious."

We laugh, and I tug his arm, leaning my weight into him, then he continues, "PhD in physics at sixteen. Obviously really smart. I spend most of my free time in the lab, although I really like it here." He looks out toward the beach and the sun, hanging over the Atlantic.

Looking at the sun, high in the cloudless sky, I remember that I shifted five time zones and it is still mid-afternoon here.

"That's cool. I really like that by the way."

"What's that?"

Chapter Eight

"The way you describe your accomplishments—not like you are bragging—just stating them as facts," I pause for a moment, looking into his deep eyes, then motioning for us to sit on a bench, I continue, "I mean I think it's funny. Athletes seem to have no problem saying that they scored the game winning point. In fact, they will run around the room screaming about it. In fact, they will tell the story to their grand-kids forty years later. But when it comes to intelligence and mental accomplishments, no one seems to celebrate too much, almost like people are embarrassed to be smart."

"I know what you mean... It's almost as if it's taboo to tell someone that you aced a test. I don't believe in bravado, but, as you said, just telling the truth."

"So I guess you know about me?"

"Somewhat. Only what Dr. Duggan told me. Said you were into some kind of sport and that you were hurt. That's all I know."

My heart warms, in an odd sort of way, heat radiating up towards my cheeks. "You know *nothing* about Ultraball?"

"I know they play it with two balls." He smiles then looks away. "Not really. I don't follow sports much."

"You know... You're kind of cute," I giggle then add, "for a nerd."

He turns to me giving me a coy smile.

I tell him all about Ultraball, about how they don't wear pads or protection, about how there are no timeouts and about how it is a constant grinding muddle of bloody and broken flesh. Then I quickly change the subject to something nice, the sunset. We talk and talk and talk. Michael gives me the scoop on the other lab attendants, especially Maryann, who seems to resent him, Dr. Duggan and the grand plans for the future, and the more he talks the more I can feel Michael's intense love for everything technology.

Later we go for a swim (my leg does much better in water) and he is a little embarrassed pulling off his shirt, showing me his thin but muscular frame. I came prepared with my suit underneath. We spend the rest of the evening together, a wonderful, fantastic evening, a Cinderella-at-the-ball evening, a lost-in-some-crazy-fantasy evening, and I have never had such a great time.

Michael helps me into the chair, my return trip chariot, and my body is butter in his arms. Maryann's red laser beam eyes are piercing. The others are gone for the night. They load up the program and send me off.

Flying back through the Void I am suddenly reminded of what I saw last time. I look around, trying to find what I think I saw last time, but it is too quick. I don't see anything except the bright light and the low lying clouds and I can't help wondering if my eyes were playing tricks on me last time through.

The transport chair slows to a stop and I see an exhausted Dr. Duggan, alone at the controls. The windows are pitch-black and I suddenly realize that it is five hours later here. *I am such a dud.*

"So sorry, Dr. Duggan, I forgot the time."

"No matter, my dear. Let me shut this down and I will take you home."

The ride home is long and quiet in Dr. Duggan's big, old-man car. Dr. Duggan is probably too tired to talk and I want to think, think about what I saw in the Void, think about Michael and just savor the moment, a moment that I will probably never have again.

"Dr. Duggan—"

"Yes, Gabriella?" His eyes are heavy, his jaw slack.

"Would you be upset with me if I told you I wanted to go through just one more time?"

His eyes grow tense and then soften, as he suddenly wakens. His voice is slow and firm as he says, "Yes. Yes, I think I would."

I plead, "Please? Just once more? Next weekend?"

"But Gabriella... Why?"

"It's hard to say—"

We are quiet for a while, then a surprised look washes over his face and he says, "Is it that boy? Michael? You know this is not a dating service! That machinery is very expensive! And we are still running tests!"

I don't say anything, looking down as we pass several exits. We sit in silence until we are a couple miles away from my house then I turn toward him and plead, "Please?"

He exhales a huff, glances at me then says, "Oh, okay. But you are going to have to go through another round of testing then—"

*****

The week does not go by fast enough and for once I am happy for my time-eating school and study schedule. Still, I lay awake at night, wondering what I saw, wondering what I glimpsed out of the corner of my eye.

Was that real? Did I imagine that? How could it be possible?

In the still of the night, lying awake in bed, staring out the window at the pale moonlight I decide something. I decide that I am going to do something radical. I decide that I am going to do something crazy. I decide that I am going to do something risky and that there is no way that I can know what will happen and what the results will be. I decide I am going to leap off the transport chair. Into the Void.

Fantasy Land

I almost can't believe where I am; surrounded by bright blinding light, like floating on the surface of the sun, low lying clouds drifting all around me caressing my skin with tingling static, and the strong smell of jasmine and lilac that takes my mind away to another place. And dead silence. An unnatural silence. A silence so strong that my ears ring, trying to fill in the absence of sound.

I am standing in the Void.

But the real reason that I am back here, the reason I couldn't tell Dr. Duggan... Oh boy, the real reason—yes, the real reason is that a figure in the distance, at the last possible moment, the tiniest of moments, a moment just long enough to see a face of the greatest importance, the face of my dead father, out of the very corner of my eye, a tiny flash, then gone, just as I passed through the Void exit and back into the dull of reality —that's what brought me back here to this lost and empty place. *Am I crazy? I can't believe I am doing this! I can't believe I jumped off the chair! I must be crazy! I am in another dimension! And for what? A momentary glimpse out of the corner of my eye? Gabby, what were you thinking?*

I know, I know, I shouldn't have done this, but I am here now—

So many unanswered questions haunt me, so many unanswered questions about the day that he died, so many that I have been avoiding that I just had to do this. *I guess I am crazy. A glimpse out of the corner of my eye and look what I did! Look where I am! This is insane!*

So here I stand, welding glasses on, eyes squeezed down to barely open slits, staring into the blindingly bright white light of the Void, looking, searching, hoping to see an apparition, the ghost of my father, hoping my eyes weren't playing tricks on me the last time, hoping that I am not going insane.

I want to know who those men were and whom they worked for. Why was my father so afraid of them? What did they have on him?

We just owned a small clothing store—what could he have possibly done? Was it something he knew? Something he saw?

Why were we hiding anyway? Are Mom and I in danger? Or was this just about him?

And why does Mom always change the subject when I ask questions? She's hiding something, I know it. But what?

I can't wait too much longer. Even though time bends here, I can only spend a few more minutes searching or Dr. Duggan might freak out and tell Mom.

It's impossible to see anything but whiteness. It's everywhere. The only thing that doesn't burn white is the dark black of the entrance and exit rings. And even the ubiquitous white light seems to shine through me. Looking down at my arms and hands, it's like they're made of thin translucent strips of paper and the white is shining through revealing every bone, artery, tendon and vein.

Distance is blurred here too. There is no horizon, no sky, no floor, no ceiling, only eye-piercing light, everywhere. Behind me, more white light. And over there, white. Over here, white. In the distance, white. I would like it very much if there was a horizon, a place where the sky touched the earth, but there is none and therefore it is impossible to know how far away anything is, even though all I see are hazy, fluffy things that look like clouds. There is no feeling of perspective. *I better stay close to the entrance and exit gates. It would be real easy to wander off and become completely lost in here.*

I have to keep my eyes open as much as possible too. Closing them, nausea hits me quickly. It's the motion. I think I am feeling the rotation of the earth, turning on its axis, traveling its course around the sun. Feels like being pulled on the end of a rope, maybe like parasailing would feel like—I've never done it so I don't know—or maybe like being a kite. Yeah, that's it.

Well, I can't tell time here; Michael told me that no watch, nothing mechanical or electrical, no machine works in the Void, but I must have been gone long enough for the others to start worrying, not to mention that the transport chair would have just came through empty, so I begin shuffle-stepping toward the exit, a small, distracting crunch of bone-on-bone pain with each step, when a white mist envelops me, reminding me of those low lying clouds I used to see running up Corcovado. Jasmine and lilac, soft and graceful, swirl around me, like the scent of the forest Dad took me to in Venezuela.

I pause at the Void exit looking through the ring at a frozen, life-sized three-dimensional photograph. Michael and Maryann, the track and the work-stations, the transport chair that just came through, everything frozen. One of Maryann's legs is slightly raised, caught in mid-step, arm extended, finger pointing, mouth ajar. Michael's brow is frozen in a furrow, lips pursed as if he is about to speak, his thoughts stuck in his mind, unable to be released. It is the most bizarre thing to see, time frozen like that. I wonder if I am aging, in here, while time is stopped out there.

Suddenly I feel something, like an invisible hand, grab my ankle, pulling, and I scream,

"Aaaaaaaaaaaaaaaah!!!"

I jump, stumble and trip, falling into the Void exit. Crossing the dimensional barrier, a force grabs my body and hurls it, my body accelerating with such a momentum that I completely lose control of myself, spinning head over heels. A mass of flying, out-of-control flesh, I am suddenly thirty feet into the room and tumbling over the transport chair module, the now-empty chair that was supposed to keep me safe and secure while traveling through the Void, the chair I jumped off so I could take a look around, crash landing on the old, dirty and cracked hardwood floor of the control room, bruising my shoulder and scraping my shins.

"Shenanigans! There she is! Find out what went wrong and call me right back!" I faintly hear Dr. Duggan shout over the wall screen through the muffled ringing of my right ear.

Some hands grab my arms and help me off the floor and into a flimsy metal folding chair.

"What happened?" Michael says, urgency in his voice.

Although I spent about fifteen to twenty minutes in the Void looking around, I arrived in the room only a few seconds after the transport chair that I had been sitting in when I left North America. *Maybe he thinks I fell off the chair. Maybe he doesn't know how long I was in there.*

"Let me clear my head first then we can talk."

"Maryann, take over the shutdown procedure and close up the control room, then all of you take a break. I am going to take Gabriella to the medical unit for some tests."

Dr. Duggan calls it the control room like it's some really cool-tech but that's kind of a joke since it's in the backroom of a crappy, rented, third-floor beach-village apartment just off the coast of the Atlantic in New London, a tiny, nondescript, hard-sand, beach village in Portugal.

She acknowledges flat and cold. Maryann Williams is the consummate professional, at least Michael said so. She knows every aspect of every machine and every control, the theoretical physics behind the testing and procedures, and every possible scenario and contingency. She even wrote some of the source code. Her eyes pierce Michael in her response but her face is cold and unemotional. She resents Michael, a seventeen year-old, stepping in out of nowhere to run *her* lab considering *her* pedigree, *her* training, and *her* experience. But Michael doesn't acknowledge her 'tude.

"Can you walk?" he reaches out to help me up, the others looking on, machines in the back clicking, blinking, flashing and chirping, his face still holding a curious expression, possibly wondering what happened, possibly wondering what was I doing in there, out of the chair, or perhaps even wondering if I was trying to sabotage his experiment.

"Of course," I say flatly, ignoring the offer of his hand, struggling to stand up, favoring my right side and brushing the floor sand off my brown suede jacket, one of my favorites. I grab his hand before he can stow it at his side and fold his arm into mine, pushing us toward the apartment exit.

Traveling down the ancient-feeling, sand-encrusted staircases, squeezing through the squeaky glass and metal building exit doors, a combination of salty sea air, gull sounds and screaming hot sun explode over my senses. Back in Portugal!

I did some research on this place last week, apparently the founders of the designer-conceived village called it New London to attract the British tourists but the idea never took so the village is mostly populated by aging, retired Portuguese and Spanish factory workers who had dreams of being fishermen in their retirement. That's what I love about this place, it's not some British tourist trap, it's filled with real, authentic, salt-of-the-earth people and the place looks used and worn, battered by the salty air of the Atlantic. It reminds me of home, my *real* home in Venezuela.

I pull Michael tighter, letting him support me, and my steps become lighter. Hiding my leg as best I can, hiding my ugly, scarred leg, I lean my left side into him, holding his arm tight, my head nearly on his shoulder. Looking around, I smile; I love this place, suddenly. It feels like an escape. There are no expectations, limitations, deadlines, and pressures like back in North America (most of them Mom-expectations.) This place is like my own private fantasy world where I can pretend to be whomever I want and have whatever I want here. I know Mom and I talked about changing our name again, after the accident, about moving, reinventing ourselves, starting over, but this, here, in Portugal, is something totally different. It is my own personal fantasy world. I don't have to fully commit to it. I can try it on like clothes at the mall and if I don't like them, I can just return them.

Finally I answer Michael, "I left the chair on purpose. I wanted to look around."

"At what? You can't see anything there anyway. And why the goofy sunglasses?"

"They're welding goggles, silly. I borrowed them from a friend." I have them tucked neatly into my hair on top of my head as if they are some cool new fashion accessory.

We round the corner and are just a few feet from the clinic entrance. Dr. Duggan has an arrangement with one of the doctors here to provide a battery of no-questions-asked tests on his subjects and to send the data to him and him only, simple stuff like blood work, EKGs, stress tests and the like in addition to more complex tests and scans followed by some psychological testing. It felt like it took all day last time and this is the one thing that I am dreading.

"Don't understand why you would need them. Haven't made the trip yet myself but the reports from the initial human trials described it as a couple seconds of pitch black emptiness, like absolute nothingness. No light. No nothing. I mean, like a darkness that none of our lights could penetrate."

"Really?"

"Yeah, they said it was black, black, black. I mean that's why I called it the Void. Like it was the nothingness. They actually said it was more than just the absence of light. They described a feeling, kind of hard to describe, but it was as if the light was being sucked out of them, if that makes any sense."

He glances at me sideways, head tilted, "Their description. Not mine."

He continues, "But these were full grown adults, mind you. Mostly educated men and women, grad students, PhD students, mostly in their late twenties and early thirties, and they said it was scary-dark."

"Yeah, they're probably scared of roller coasters too."

He smiles.

We enter the clinic and walk into Dr. Borges' office, no one stopping us. Michael has probably been here many times.

"Will you stay with me?"

"Well, I need to hear more about what happened. Dr. Duggan wants my report, to know what happened and how, or I should say why you got out of the chair, so I need to know what to tell him. Give me your story, let me go contact him then I'll be back as soon as I can. I have to run your psyche anyway."

"Not much to tell really. I wanted to look around a minute, that's all. Time doesn't really move there anyway, like you said. A couple minutes in the Void is like a split second here, right?"

"We still don't know how time works there, you know that. But you shouldn't have been walking around in there anyway. I mean what did you step on? What did it feel like? We don't know what that place is really made of. What if we lost you?"

Something in my heart wishes he asked that question because he cares about me. I wish he cared about more than just running Dr. Duggan's tests and experiments. I can't read his emotions. *So smart and such a nerd, but where's your heart, Mr. McAllister?*

"I don't know, Michael. I'm not a physicist like you. I'm just the face on the box. That's all."

"Stop it. You're smart. You're inquisitive. You're the toughest girl I know. I mean, I don't know many girls—" He turns red then says, "I know why Dr. Duggan wanted you for the job and all, but there's a lot more to you than that." Michael's probably just trying to put me at ease so I will give him more information but I am enjoying the compliments anyway.

"Well Michael, let's just say that I don't know what I was standing on but it supported my weight just fine and I didn't see anything. I looked around for a while, didn't see anything then I jumped through."

"So why the scream?"

"I think maybe my foot caught on the ring edge and I fell when I came through."

Dr. Borges steps in saying, "Gabriella, so good to finally meet you. You know I think things would have been different if you would have competed for S.A. I would have loved to see you out on the field wearing my blue and yellow." Apparently, he has ties to Brazil.

"I know. I know. I get that a lot. But you can't turn back time can you?"

"Michael, same tests, right?"

"Yes sir. I'll be back to run the psyche though. Gabby, I think I have enough for Dr. Duggan. I'll be back in a bit, okay?"

I nod, noticing that he called me Gabby and not Gabriella.

Dr. Borges' extensive battery of tests is about the same as the previous ones in Princeton so I brace myself for a long drawn out day. I fill out some stupid forms (the same ones I filled out last time) and a nurse takes me into an area with gurneys, beds, patients, nurses and orderlies. An immense woman pours off a gurney that three nurses are clustered around and a few other patients are waiting, some standing, some sitting, another on a gurney moaning, connected to IV bags. The nurse throws back a curtain showing me to my bed area. After she leaves, I draw the curtain and put on my hospital gowns, one in front, one in the back (I'm not letting anyone see my butt!) and those thick socks that have non-skid rubber stuff on the bottoms. The nurse returns and bleeds me for a long time then hauls me through ice cold, dimly lit corridors that remind me of some B-grade horror movie. They scan me several different ways and attach tubes to my arm. In the distance I hear police radios and I remember that people die here.

The next several hours are an endless stream of pokings, proddings, needles, arm-style treadmills with air tubes in my mouth and sticking various body parts into large, pulsating machines. A variety of different doctors examine me. A number of hours later I am bored, tired and worn-out. It didn't help that I had just shifted five time zones. I am ready for the Gabriella body inspection to be over.

Dr. Borges comes in and asks me how I am doing in his native tongue, "¿Ta boa, Gabby? We're almost done."

"Yeah, just not my idea of a day at the beach."

"I'll call Michael. After the brain wave testing, he can take you."

Before he can call, Michael pops in. Dr. Borges says all my tests were perfect so far, identical to the tests taken before I entered the Void. No one expected any changes anyway. Dr. Duggan had been sending a variety of objects, animals, and people through the Void for over two years now and not one test had indicated anything abnormal, or so they told me.

Dr. Borges hooks up a spider web of electrical disc sensors all over my face and head to measure my brain's electrical activity. The little needles drawing squiggly lines on the electronic chart paper say that my brain is still functioning fine, identical to before, so we finally move onto the last test.

They inject me with some form of radioisotope and my head is placed in another large scanning machine. Michael shows me a series of different pictures or asks me different questions, some easy, some hard, some without a concrete answer and the monitor displays a three-dimensional colored picture of my brain, different areas glowing red, green, yellow or blue depending on what or how I am thinking. The harder questions, harder for me anyway, make my whole brain light up. Simple questions cause tiny, specific areas to fire brightly. They can see what areas of the brain are being activated, how I am thinking, and they map those areas to know if there have been changes from previous tests.

"Okay Gabriella, our tests are done. Clean up and come into the office."

Dr. Borges, seated behind his cheap metal desk, and Michael, facing him on a hard wooden chair, stop talking as soon as I enter, both of them staring at me as if they don't know what to say.

I'm tired and ready to leave, "Everything's fine, right?"

Dr. Borges starts slowly, "All your physical tests were outstanding."

I detect a hint of caution in his voice. "And?"

Michael blurts out, "Your brain scan was different," his face pale, clearly concerned.

"What are you talking about? Speak plain."

Dr. Borges interrupts before Michael can continue, "Your brain scans are all normal. It's just that you seem to be thinking differently. Different areas of your brain lit up than the last time these tests were run. Your way of thinking, which is different with every individual, has somehow changed."

"And that's weird? I mean, have you seen that before? Maybe I'm just tired?"

They are both silent for a minute, looking at each other, choosing their words, then Dr. Borges says, "No. But it's probably nothing to worry about right now."

Feeling perfectly fine and ready to leave this dingy clinic, I turn to Michael saying, "You hungry?"

Face a little red, he seems to be a bit embarrassed at his outburst. He replies, "You buying?"

"Sure. See ya, doc."

"Ciao." He watches me as we walk out, screen containing my results still in his hand.

Michael and I pop into the restaurant with the best food in the whole village, *Gloria's Place*. It sits right on the beach sand about one-hundred meters from the shore line and is the size of a typical North American backyard shed, no more than three meters by three meters, constructed from grey cinder blocks built up about waist high with four wooden poles in the corners supporting a roof made of palm tree branches. The chairs are old stump-sized chunks of driftwood sitting on raised piles of sand and the counter is made from rough cut wooden beams, reclaimed from a decaying and abandoned house that fell down a few years ago.

"¿Que desejas, lindo?" the owner asks Michael what he wants to order in a flirty kind of way, happily smiling, her weathered and worn face peeling and covered by an abundance of medium-sized brown spots that merge together creating an odd looking yet somehow attractive large brown swath across her cheeks, the results of too many years of sun and salty air.

A playful smirk steals over my face at Michael's not knowing what to say considering this place has no menu. I look at him, my eyes twinkling. The sunset shines lightly, across the rippling waves, through the knee-deep fishermen casting long shadows, highlighting the right side of Michael's face, the light accenting a thin straight nose, cheeks that slightly dimple when he smiles coyly, and a strong chin, chiseled with a tiny cleft and slightly fuzzy, but too fresh and innocent to be regularly shaved.

He sees me watching him, smiles then says, "Whatever she's having."

"Gloria, just whip up whatever moves your heart," I respond in her native tongue.

She smiles at that and calls out in heavy Portuguese, so much different than the Brazilian dialect I am familiar with, to one of the fishermen down in the surf.

As we wait, the gulls sing to each other and I look back at him as he begins to speak of his passion, better living through technology. His face is young and lively, shining with the aspirations of bright new things, bright eyes and a bright passionate mouth that speaks with an excitement, no, a zeal for the future of mankind that I know I will find difficult to forget even when I haven't seen him in a while: the technological salvation of mankind, a united society, the promise of a continuously improving tomorrow, of new, different and exciting things just so near that we cannot see them or necessarily know what they are or how they will change us yet they are so close that we can almost touch them.

I wonder what Mom would think if she saw me sitting alone with this boy. *I know what she would think.*

She would—

Lose—

Her—

Mind.

"So Michael, tell me more about the time-line. When is Dr. Duggan going to unveil this thing, his technological miracle, to the public?"

"He hasn't said, but pretty soon I think. He's working on mapping out some of the other routes. After we test enough routes that have a demand, we will let the world know and apply for a license to operate, I guess."

I laugh, "You mean there's no demand for a route from New Jersey to New London. I like it here, I get to see you."

Why did I say that? This is all a fantasy, just play-acting, but Michael doesn't know that. I like flirting with him but only because he has never taken the bait. He has no idea that this isn't real for me. What's real is what I am running from, the fact that I have no choice. I could never choose who I want to be with. It's our culture and I can't escape it. My family's culture would never allow me to choose an outsider and after what happened with my father, I could never hurt my mother by disobeying her anyway. The hard truth is that we would one day, when I finally gave in, go to a match-maker, mother and I, and they would show me to a bunch of different young men as if I was a new suit to be tried on for fit or a new car to be test-driven and tires kicked. We could never be alone together—not until we were married. Both families would make excited, decided and deliberate sales pitches as to the quality of their respective blood-lines and the great honor of the family's name, and a formal vetting of the entire family line back to great-grandparents would be performed such that a prospective suitor could be disqualified for what a great uncle had done eighty years ago. Eventually family approval would be received and one or more would take a fancy to me and with their parents, aunts, uncles, cousins and siblings in tow, would ask for my hand in a big, dramatic meeting in front of everyone. If I agreed, and I would eventually have to agree to one of them, the two families would meet and come to some financial arrangement then the suitor and I would be married in the traditional way, in traditional clothing, with much traditional fanfare, blowing of traditional horns and riding gallantly into a rented hall on traditional animals like camels or donkeys wearing traditional saddles, the groom carrying a traditional sword, the men stomping the floor violently, dancing a traditional dance, and the women yelling a shrill traditional victory call. If we fell in love sometime later then that would be nice too, but it never comes first and it is never guaranteed; at all.

An old fisherman, grinning broadly through a few missing teeth, brings over a large red fish hanging from a short hunk of fishing line tied to a piece of driftwood. It's still alive! You can't get any fresher than that.

Gloria begins cooking the fish, head, tail and fins on, in a giant pan full of olive oil, spices, and local vegetables, shaking the pan to the rhythm of an old folk song she's humming, singing and tapping out on the worn block-wood counter.

"So tell me about your childhood, Gabby," he says with a matter-of-fact tone, not looking my way, as if he is probing somewhere he is not sure if he is allowed to go.

That took me off guard. *Is he interested in something about me that isn't a data point he can graph?*

"Well I didn't have one," I say plainly.

"Everyone has a childhood—"

"I have no memory of mine—"

I pause wondering if I can open up to him, wondering if that will mean that I am losing control, then decide to do it anyway. "My earliest memory, and I have only one, I was like six years-old, maybe. I clearly remember my aunt, maybe she was fourteen or so, dashing into my bedroom, screaming, 'the soldiers are coming!' and violently scooping me up. It was night. Not stopping her run, she dropped me down just outside of the house and I nearly fell as I stumbled into a full run behind her, holding up my bed skirt in one hand and my ZuSha doll in the other. My ears were stuffed full with the surrounding gunfire. It was everywhere. We couldn't tell what direction the screams, yells or gunfire were coming from. There was smoke and the smell of burning things. We ran into the field. She held my wrist, tugging it. 'The winter wheat is high,' she said. 'They shouldn't see us.' We ran and ran and ran. The sound of my hard breathing and the pulse of my blood coursing through my temples was in my ears. We heard screaming in the distance and more angry gunfire. After a while we reached a meadow then the ground got real muddy. My aunt, just a child herself, picked me up and carried me until we reached the river."

"And?" softly, genuinely interested, he questions.

I find myself staring at the soft waves of the Atlantic, "And that's all I remember. My next memory is about two years later. We are living in South

America. Venezuela. I have no idea how I got there, I somehow have already learned Spanish and it's like I just wake up from the darkness. I can remember everything from that moment on, but before, no, just that one memory. A few images that make no sense, maybe if I concentrate real hard, but they are smudgy, like there's Vaseline on the camera lens. "

Michael reaches down and squeezes my hand and says, "Wow."

Interrupting the moment, Gloria announces, "Food ready! You gone like Cutey!" walking toward Michael and laying out a five-course meal displayed on a mismatched variety of scratched and worn plastic plates.

As we eat, Michael tells me his story, "As you already know, I'm a genius." He smiles coyly. "But what you probably don't know is that's not what my father wanted."

"Oh no?"

"No. He contracted with Human Genomics to test-tube me. You know, take away all the flaws from his and mom's genetic code, and remove all the precursors to genetic disorders and diseases, along with the standard battery of strength, speed, and longevity enhancements."

"Must be rich, all that stuff is very expensive."

"He works for a bank in London. But yeah, I was a disappointment. He wanted to sue them when I turned out weak and sickly but my Mom stopped him. It wasn't until a few years later that they found out I was really smart."

"Well—and this is a compliment—you don't look modified."

"Okaaay," he drawls it out long and slow, looks at me, pauses, and then smiles his smile, a smile that only he could smile and, I hope, only at me. We both laugh.

"Do they think the genetic modification made you smart?"

"The company would love to claim that, I'm sure, but they never have and I am not convinced either way."

"So do you think you will live to be three-hundred like on that goofy commercial with the old bald guys sailing with Speedos on?"

"Only time will tell, but I guess I don't think about it. What's a long life if you are not happy?" He pauses, contemplating his fish, forking his vegetables, then says, "And what's being happy if you don't have someone to share it with?"

Thank God he wasn't looking at me when he said that. I am suddenly becoming uncomfortable on this driftwood stool. "You mean in general, right?"

"Oh yeah, of course."

The Silence in the Halls

The wall screen buzzes for a moment then Dr. Duggan's face appears, "Okay Gabriella, Michael and I spoke and I understand what happened. That's not going to happen again." I am pleased that he left his statement vague enough. He clearly doesn't want my actions spelled out to the rest of the crews on either side.

"No problem, Dr. Duggan," my voice is sheepish but reveals nothing to the others. I hope.

"Michael, load up the return trip program and let's get her back home." Dr. Duggan's face fades from the wall screen. I resolve to do as Dr. Duggan asked, not leave the chair; just hold on tight and this will be over in just a few moments.

The transport chair blazes forward followed quickly by the mind numbing pain, the ear ringing silence, then, *Crash!!*

"*Ugggghhhhh!*"

The transport chair runs into something. I know I promised Dr. Duggan I would stay in the chair, but I gotta check this out. I leap from the chair.

The transport chair module moves on and exits about forty meters away, as I shakily stand over the creature lying in the white mist. He stands up fluidly and easily, almost as if he has no bones.

OhGodOhGodOhGodOhGodOhGodOhGodOhGod!

"Hello, Gabriella."

"Oh my God, are you my father?" My voice trembles at the thought of this moment finally arriving, the moment I haven't been able to remove from the back of my mind for the last two years. The shiny white man looks like my father, at least a younger version of him, a version I've seen in pictures, maybe twenty to twenty-five years old with perfect skin, clean and clear, an unnaturally perfect version of my Dad, like one of those animated characters in a 3-D cartoon.

"Why have you come to me here? What is it that you seek?" He doesn't talk like my father. The intonation and word choice is all different.

Why doesn't he hug me? Why doesn't he say he loves me, that he misses me?

He is at arms length. I want to be closer. To grab him. To hold him. *But is it really him?*

My voice trembles, "I wanted answers from my father, if you are him, about the day he was murdered. Whether or not Mom and I are in danger." I consciously note that I used the word 'murdered.' I have suspected since he died, but this is only the second time I say it out loud.

"In the end, everything is fine. In the end, everything is always fine." His voice has a weird internal echo, as if two voices are blending together. The man is wearing a tunic, something like all-white pajamas and I can't see any feet for the mist. His hands, his face, they look normal, human anyway, but once in a while a hazy wrinkle of distortion passes across his face almost like it's on the wrong channel.

Confused, suddenly, I am not sure how to proceed, how to trick this *creature* into telling me if he is really my father. I want to grab him, to hold him, but is it really him? "Can you at least tell me who those two men were?"

"Is it vengeance you seek or deliverance?"

"I seek knowledge and safety," I say confidently. Surely Dad would understand that, he always tried to protect us. All the hiding, even him sacrificing himself, was to protect Mom and me.

"What is the feeling of safety but a false crutch to support unaddressed fear?"

"My father would never talk like that and especially not to me." My head is starting to spin. It's like the top of my skull is removed and someone inserted a mixer set for mince. Suddenly I cannot think straight. The soft, fluffy white clouds surround us and it is as if they are not only around us but also in my head. I feel like I need to escape, to move, to just find somewhere that I can think straight. I begin to walk away dizzily, almost stumbling, toward the exit. Something's going on in my head. I just now remember what Michael said about my thinking having changed. *What's this place doing to me?*

Ready to exit through the ring, I pause for a second to look back. I'm holding my forehead so I don't immediately notice that the spirit-man, ghost of my dead father, alien, figment of my imagination or whatever he is, stands suddenly next to me, too close.

He reaches down in a instant, unnaturally quick, his hand flashing pure neon-gold, brilliant, gold lines of light streaming from his fingertips, a railroad spike full of pain striking my knee like a four-inch thick surgical needle thrust into my flesh. I gulp a mouthful of air and dive crookedly for the exit.

The time shifting vortex sucks my body out through the round ring, throwing it awkwardly across the room. As my body flies through the air I remember the man who was ripped off the ground and sucked into the plane turbine engine when he walked too close to the intake. I land in a misshapen pile of flesh on the cold tile floor, my cheek resting on Dr. Duggan's shoe.

"*Shenanigans!* Gabriella! You promised you wouldn't exit the chair!"

I scramble up to the echoes of his shouting and plead, "I know, but—"

"No buts! That's it! I've had it! No more Shenanigans!" The professor turns his back to me and addresses the crew, looking on in shock, "We are shutting down the experiment until we can secure the chair such that no one can exit it! Strap it down! Do something! We're not having this again!"

Dr. Duggan turns, throwing down his screen, it sloppily bouncing on the floor, as he storms out of the control room.

The rest of the crew observe me for a few moments, most of their eyes full of contempt, some eyeing me with pity and others looking on in shocked disbelief, then turn back to their control panels as if I am an unwanted house guest, overstaying her welcome. They methodically begin the shutdown procedure.

Following Dr. Duggan out into the hall to stop him, apologize and explain, I realize that my knee doesn't hurt like it should. *Let him go. He's really upset anyway.*

The long university hall, dark and doors locked, appears eerie and still as I pass my hand on the cold eggshell-colored plaster, lightly supporting my left side, crossing the great darkness, pensively testing out my knee.

Slowly moving up and down the halls, up and down the halls, the creaking of the wind in the trees outside echoes through the silence of the halls as it is beginning to hit me. Up and down the halls, up and down the halls, as the quiet descends on me, calm and content, giving me pause, I listen, far away, far away, I listen; silence. Releasing my hand from the wall, more and more, I try; don't fall. Lift the leg. Stop. Step. Lift the leg. Stop. Step. Lift the leg, step. Lift the leg, step. I hear the quiet silence echoing through the halls and down to the base of the rotunda.

Suddenly I realize, something really just happened, just now. *What was it?* I wonder if it could be true, no more stumbling, staggering, tripping, looking away from their gaze, hiding my eyes, lame; no more.

I have heard of people being cured by just thinking happy thoughts, some kind of new-age-y, mind-over-matter, 'you can heal yourself' business, and maybe that was what just happened. My leg was busted up and I imagined the person I wanted to see, my father, and I imagined the thing I wanted so badly, to run again, so it happened. It was all in my head. Wasn't it?

Keep believing that Gabby. No way is that what just happened.

But it's just so incredible! Could it be that I actually saw my father's ghost, no matter how weird and different he looked, and that he touched my leg and now it's cured? *No way! Too much!*

Maybe it wasn't my father at all. Maybe it was some creature that lives in this Void place, wherever it is, this different-dimension-stringy-place that the doc talked about. *Maybe. Maybe that's it.*

Maybe it was God. Maybe the Void is heaven. *Woah, that would be weird right?*

How could a person go to heaven without dying? I sure would like to think that if there really is a heaven that Dad would be there. Of course he would, but that specter sure didn't act like Dad. Nothing like him. There must be some explanation.

Pondering, thinking, wondering, looking down at my shoes for a while as if they mean something that I can't yet know, suddenly, involuntarily moving, starting down the great staircase of steps, cautiously at first, I step; one at a time, one at a time I step; remembering how difficult this had been just a few minutes earlier, holding my hand just off the railing, just in case, just in case, I baby-step down the steps. One at a time first, one at a time, then, wow let's do this, wow, two now, walking at first, then faster, running them up and down, running up and down, bouncing my hand off the hand rail, intentionally, to the top and bottom, running up and down, I go. I don't know what's going on; up and down, up and down. Wondering, wondering, amazed; what's happening? Now three at a time, now four, now five, bouncing up and down, bouncing up and down, running as fast as I can, leaping, jumping, I fly. To the top of the staircase I jump and roll, flip over a bench and leap, touching the ceiling and somersaulting over another bench parked in the hall.

Stopping, panting, sweating, looking down at my sky blue Brooks, smiling, then laughing, I take off my shoes, socks and wriggle my toes. "I can feel my feet!" I think, "I can wriggle my toes! I can wriggle my toes!" One by one I try to lift up the toes of my left foot, eyes closed, tears leaking out as I realize that I can feel and control each and every one of them. They are no longer numb and dead; the nerves are somehow restored, as if it never happened, as if time had somehow rewound to before the accident.

My breathing slows as I stand there staring at my wriggling toes, calm, withdrawn, as if the beat of time, the clock on the wall has stopped and I am suddenly in it again; the zone. I fall down into the starting blocks, there in the University hallway, as the roar of the crowd falls silent. *Ready? Go!*

I take off at full speed down the dark hall, arms pumping, hands straight, closed and locked doors blur by, panting like a wolf, six days hungered, eager for the chase of a freshly spotted hare, as I reach maximum torque, maximum velocity. The end of the hall accelerating toward me, I leap with both feet pointing toward a large round column that supports the center of the rotunda, bouncing off of it, the friction spread across the width of my feet, back-tuck, spinning around, my full momentum sent into the opposite direction. Landing at full speed, I accelerate faster toward the staircase, swooping, swerving, leaping in the air over the first flight of stairs, hand-springing the landing, both bare feet slamming down on the base of the second flight of steps, in full motion, smashing through the exit doors, down the exterior steps and out into the quiet, cool night air, each hand holding a shoe, bare feet running full speed. I am like a bird, in my mind, a very small, powerful and fast bird, flapping, swooping, spinning, turning, dashing past every obstacle, in and around, with an unreal quickness, the wind in my face, wings back, dive, dive, rolling, swerving, flinging, in and out, round and round, in perfect control of every ounce of wind under my wings, faster, faster, faster. Speeding down the sidewalk, I hurdle a car, then another, vault an old, blue, free-standing mailbox, must have been one of the last in the state, crossing the imaginary finish line, slowing down and coming to rest in front of a row of tall stoic elms, the sun just setting; dim light peeking through its leaves.

I grab hold of the moment and squeeze, spellbound, mystified, scared to release it lest the magic be broken and all the pain, disappointment and heartache suddenly reappear as if it's a sleeping giant awakening from its wintertime hibernation, belly gnawing, insatiably for food.

I wish the sun would stop setting. I wish time would stop, don't let it advance; I want to stay right here in this moment, afraid this magnificent feeling might drift away like the soft droplets of fresh fallen rain around me are sure to dry up and disappear in a few short minutes under the fading summer sun.

A small leaf falls down toward me from somewhere above, touches my forehead and I suddenly realize that this is not some kind of freaky dream. I am not sleeping! I am not dreaming! I am not still in the Void! This is REAL!

"WOOOOOOOOOHHHHH
           HHHOOOOOOOOOOO!!!!!!"

"WOOOOOOOOHH
       HHOOOO
            HHOOOO
                HOOOOOOO!!!!!!"

Matchmaker Mom

"**N**ow here's a cute one. Look at this one," Mom says optimistically as she slides another head shot across the table toward me, yet another picture of a prospective match. Long before she slid this photograph across the table she would have spent countless hours with her various contacts from the old country, a bunch of old cows on the gossip-network, keepers of the dirt, those who know where the skeletons are kept and secrets buried, who have no greater passion than meddling in the lives of teenagers in the ancient art form of matchmaking that would have died centuries ago if I had my way. Since this photograph now sits eighteen inches from my nose she must have determined that this was a "good boy," secret code for one who has an acceptable, honorable family.

"Not another one, Mom." Leaning away, I let whiny distress punctuate my voice. I am just out of bed. It's morning and the first thing she throws at me and already the subject is making me tired. I feel the blood drain from my head and I want to go back to my room. I don't want to look at the pictures, especially after what happened last night.

I am fighting to stop from constantly smiling, thinking about all the crazy events, the trip through the Void, Portugal, Michael, the Void-man, my leg getting healed, all of it so unreal. *That didn't happen, did it?* I still can't believe my leg is healed. I could barely sleep. This is so surreal that I don't know what to think and I can't bring myself to tell Mom just yet. No one knows.

Suddenly upset, she flashes, "Then when, huh? When? You gonna wait 'til you old maid!" Mom's hard to place accent comes fast and thick when she's mad. She still thinks my leg is busted and that my only future, the only way that she can help me, is to marry me off.

"Old maid! Stop it." I have no plans of being married off to some stranger when I am eighteen like she was, or sixteen like mi abuelita, her Mom before her. *God no!* Even if my leg was still mangled, I am *not* being sold off like cattle.

She looks away, out into the thickness of backyard trees leading into gangly woods of pine and gum, a wall of vegetation, an entangled mass of branches, leaves and trunks. Wild turkeys are just revealing themselves, stepping out of the dense leaves to claw for worms in the sparse opening.

"Just look, Mija. Please." There is pleading in her voice and I suddenly feel sorry for her. No matter where we live some things are too hard to let go. Growing up in the old country she was brainwashed into believing that a woman's life wasn't fulfilled unless she was married and had lots of children—preferably boys. Being barren, for them, is a curse, something caused by some past sin or wrong. But being unmarried is a fate far worse than being childless because it is seen as being the poor girl's fault. Being barren could at least be blamed on some past generation, something someone did in the family long ago. If a girl's not married it's not because she's ugly or stupid either, there are plenty like that and the matchmakers still find them someone, it's because she has some kind of crazy rebellious attitude, don't know how to respect, or she, God forbid, doesn't want to. In any case, it's the biggest shame on the family to have raised such a daughter. I can feel the distress in her voice. In her generation it always comes back to blame. Whose fault is it? Everyone has a finger and it needs to be pointed. Maybe she wants to blame me, but deep inside she is internalizing it, blaming herself. And my leg doesn't help things either. She probably still blames herself for that too and in her mind no one wants to marry a woman with an ugly-looking leg. She obviously feels responsible for finding me a mate no matter how many times I tell her to stop.

I try to steer her mind away, "Mom, tell me how it was with you and Dad." I know they loved each other, I could see it. And I know, eventually, I would like to get married, maybe not now, but someday, and I need to know that I can somehow find someone in this caged up system they have me in.

She glances at me then looks back out into the woods, blankly staring for a time, rolling waves of plants piled up, vines full of life growing into and on top of each other. "You know this story. I have told you many times. We were matched."

"No, Momma. Tell me. Did you fall in love? How was it?" I never dared ask such a question before.

She glances back at me again then quickly away, water pooling in her eyes, exhales a long deep breath, then opens her mouth, "He was so handsome. Dashing. He came to our small village, a pile of cottages really, rough hewn stone walls with flat cement roofs, our precious water tanks on top, him wearing a beautiful suit and in a very nice car that looked so out of place among the donkeys on our dirt roads. He was there to attend a wedding of some distant relative so far removed that they only sent him, one representative from his family to attend. I was just a poor dirty, village girl at the market for some chick peas and cucumbers for my mother when I saw him. I hid behind the edge of a crumbling block wall so he wouldn't see me and I followed him. He looked so foreign and exotic, nothing like our local boys. Overhearing where he was going I ran home and begged my mother to allow me to go to the wedding. The village was very small and we were almost all related; most of the village would be there anyway. I spent the rest of the whole day trying to clean up as best I could but the only passable dress I found in mom's chest was an old one that had been in the family for several generations, a traditional black heavy-velvet dress with ornamental stitching and sequins, a leftover from the days of the Bedouin. It was nice, don't get me wrong, it just wasn't made to fit my body."

She goes on, looking directly at me now, speaking more and more quickly, excitedly, lost in the moment of her memories, "I put my long dark brown hair up on top of my head in big curls flowing down to my shoulders and got one of my cousins to paint up my face bright and lively like the hand of a harsh cold wind had smacked my face red. I tried to keep my feet under the table most of the night because I only had my old, terrible shoes, but when he saw me, and the way he looked at me, I forgot all about them as the strong scent of wedding flowers, jasmine and lilac, yellow roses and cinnamon, clove and sandalwood, seemed to suddenly float around me."

She stops talking, looking down at her hand resting in her lap, her wedding ring dull, the pattern worn away in parts; many years full of hard work had taken a toll.

"I thought you were matched?"

"Well, yes. Of course. We never spoke that night. Oh no, we couldn't. It would have been scandalous. Neither of us was properly represented. The next day word got around that he might be interested and the matchmakers started checking him out. About a month later, the longest month of my life, a month of longing and expectant but fearful hope, he came around with his family and asked for my hand. It was the first day that we spoke. But I loved him already."

"Loved him? How could you love him? All you did was look at him from across the hall?"

"I can't explain it, Mija," She says, standing, exhaling, caressing my hair softly as she heads off to the kitchen, "Love is strange like that." From the next room, more optimistically, "Don't worry, we will find you someone."

It sounded magical, almost hypnotic, the way mom's voice rose and fell telling her story, yet I still can't visualize it happening to me. Someday I will have to agree to someone and the longer I wait the less choices I will have. I know that. They marry young in my culture and the ones who wait until they are twenty-five find no one left. No one except the left-overs. Yuck! And the longer I wait, the less chance of finding someone at least halfway close to being a soul mate.

Soul mate. *Yeah right.* About all I can really hope for is to find someone who will respect me and treat me right. Maybe give me a little freedom. The intertwined vines in the woods, strangling tree trunks, strangling each other, fighting, struggling, reaching for the light of life, stare back at me as I realize that I don't want to face this. And what about Michael? That would all be over, of course.

I don't want to think about it anymore. All I want to think about is my leg being healed. All I want to think about is running. Running away. Just putting on my shoes, blanking out my mind and run, run, run. I need to prove to myself that last night was real, that I am back, that I can really run. I barely slept last night as I was up all night staring at the ceiling, smiling. I still can't believe this but I want to run soo bad and this is just sooo cool! Whatever happened, I don't know what it was, but who cares? I am about to run! Yeah!

Getting back in shape would be nice too. Maybe even competing. Most likely the type of husband that I will be stuck with is going to want children right away and that will certainly not mix well with competing in Ultraball, even at the amateur level.

And how would competing work with seeing Michael? I put my shoes on wondering; *what do I do know?* If I try to go back to competing will I lose my excuse to be with Michael, him holding me up because he thinks my knee is busted up, me grabbing on tight to his arm to support my weak body? *How will he see me? How do I explain this?* And if I'm somehow able to make it back on the team, actually make it back to that life in the spotlight, constantly bothered by advertisers, harassed by drug companies, the endless bickering of the athletes; *do I even want that?*

What type of life do I want? Who do I want to be? I don't know. I really don't know.

I pause after I finish tying my shoes as the drunken race-euphoria begins to rise in my belly and I realize that I have to run no matter what. It's who I am. I can't do without it, the fire in my lungs, the exhilaration, the burn and the passion. Electricity is in my veins and I am already sweating just thinking about my feet hitting the pavement. That Void-man touching me was like the hand of God as far as I'm concerned. I am restored. It's who I am and I'm back. I just know I am. I can feel it. I can feel it. I can feel it! Wow! Yeah! I will have to worry about the consequences later.

I sneak out of the house and pull my hoodie up and over my head so no one will see me. I have to know if this is real. Here it is, here it is, here it is. Run! *Go!* I have to know that I didn't imagine last night. I run a nice tight loop, about five quick miles around town, no obstacles or jumps, just run, and it's as if neon-blue is flowing in my veins, pure ecstasy. I sneak in the backyard, cautiously checking for Mom sounds, then duck in the back-door, jumping into the downstairs shower. The reality strikes me hard and fast as the water drips of my still sweating body. Looking down at my leg I try hard to find the scar and there is none. It's as if it was never there! Tears form in my eyes and I sob uncontrollably, hysterically. I am so happy and I can't control my emotions. I stay in the shower until all the hot water is gone and the cold water forces me to leave. *I can't believe it! I am healed! I am back! My leg is back!*

A few hours later I have worked up my nerve. I dial on voice only, the screen rings loudly and my shoulders tremble at what I'm about to say.

"Hello," John Murray's voice says.

I want to speak. I want to tell him I'm back. I want to tell him that it was all a big mistake. I want to ask for a second chance.

"Hello? Gabriella? Are you there?"

Horror grips me as I realize that my number is in his screen and he knows that it's me even though my face is not there. I can't hang up now. I eke out, "Hi, Coach," turn on the video, and look at his smiling face.

"What's up? Long time I haven't heard from you," he says slowly.

"Yeah. Not since after the accident—" My voice is cracking uncontrollably.

"Hey, hey, don't worry about that. You did good. You did your best. I just hope your leg is doing better." That was Coach Murray, always optimistic, always bringing people up, uplifting, encouraging and positive. I can tell he really means what he says.

"Coach, about that."

"Yeah?"

I pause, here goes nothing I think, then let it all out, "I want to compete again. Can you help me?"

Silence. Then, "What about your knee? And... Gabby, I mean... The modders have been getting better and better and with you being all natural. That's cool and all, I mean the fans love that, but even at your peak—" He doesn't finish his sentence, but I know where he is going. All the pros are genetically modified, designed at conception to be the best athletes. Their parents were great athletes and the drug companies cooked their DNA to make their children that much better and it works. I was the only one. Was. But no more. The Cinderella story. The poor girl from nowhere, unmodified, all natural, something I prided myself in, who could somehow compete with them. A freak. Someone the fans loved, the fans that couldn't afford the modifications, the poor people who wanted to think that they could somehow compete with the rich, the people who wanted to convince themselves that this life wasn't so unfair, the people who needed something more desperately than any other thing, hope. Yes, I was their hope. The unmodified girl who could somehow keep up and maybe even win. A freak.

"Coach?"

"Gabriella, I... I don't know what to say." I could hear his desire to hang up, yet he still cared about me. He was such a good coach.

"Coach, for old time's sake. Just let me know how to make it back."

"Tell you what—" He pauses and I hear clothing rustle, then his voice is suddenly a whisper. "You have to build up some points in the amateur field again because you lost your ranking, of course. Run a bunch of amateurs. Make *sure* they are qualified and sanctioned races. And you *have* to win. Don't come in second or third. You *need* to win. Do that at least four or five times. Try to pick a few of the bigger races at the end, something that might be televised or catch some media attention."

He is putting an unaccomplishable goal in front of me, a goal that he knows I can't accomplish. "If you make it that far then call me back, maybe I will be able to help you then. That's the best I can do. You know I'm under contract and only allowed to coach the NuGen athletes."

The hairs on the back of my neck bristle at hearing the name. NuGen. I hate that name. They always played rough and dirty. It was Velocity Jones, and her two goons, Carilla and T'mekah, NuGen girls, who bumped me off the track, intentionally I think, the day I shredded my knee, tearing both ligaments, medial and posterior, a complete blowout, unrecoverable.

NuGen Biotechnics, all their athletes are signed to lifetime contracts by their parents before they are test-tubed. It means money for the parents, and kids for that matter, but a life always under the microscope, owned by the company. NuGen runs their athletes regardless of what team they are on and in effect they run the teams more than the coaches do. Sure the coaches coach them, but NuGen runs their strategy and their strategy is dirty.

I hear my mother yelling my name.

"Ok, Coach. I will see what I can do. Hey, one more thing... Don't tell anyone, Okay?"

"Sure."

"See ya," I hang up quickly, "Ma, what is it?"

She yells down to me, "Smith is coming over."

"Great," I mutter under my breath. Smith Dinklestein seems to be sweet on Mom, and he treats her real nice, but I can't fold my mind around the fact that he works for NuGen, even though he's only in research. I bound up the steps, heading toward my room to dress, then quickly stop myself and take the steps much more slowly, like I did before, not yet ready to reveal anything.

When Smith arrives the polite family of smiles suddenly appears. My mother's favorite phrase can be heard hundreds of times in her most syrup-y voice, "Oh, that's niiiiiice!"

The three of us sit there, in the decorated living room, the one only used for special company, the one no one is allowed to enter on any other occasion, us sitting on clear plastic-covered couches, trying not to stick to them, talking about a bunch of nothing, then Smith says, "So Gabby, have you seen any of the pictures I sent over?"

There is a faint indefinable expression on his face, lips almost curved into a smile, but not a smile, somewhere in between, as if it is an uncontrolled, unconscious punctuation mark to his question; the question, then the short quick flash of an almost-smile, as if he knows something that only he can know.

My mother's face freezes, looking forward; she doesn't turn toward me. "What pictures?" I say casually, my mind racing.

"I sent over a few pictures of young men who work for the company. Your mother told me you were having a hard time meeting someone with all that has gone on. Eligible bachelors. Good boys with good jobs," then that flash of a half-smile, there for an instant then fluttering away.

Good boys! Does Smith know the code word I wonder? I huff, " 'All that has gone on?' 'All that has gone on?' What do you mean, 'all that has gone on?' " There is an edge in my voice that I try to hide.

Defensively he answers, looking to Mom for help, her eyes straining, "Well, you know. You moved here not long ago... and it's hard to make new friends. You didn't speak the language at first—"

He's trying to buffer, to put a soft spin on it. I give him a little credit for trying anyway. It's not really his fault that the athletes his company sponsors play dirty, even though I can't help but hold it against him.

"Then with you being a bit famous from competing in last year's games. Some boys find that intimidating." His punctuation mark, flashing smile returns.

Famous! Ha! If the press hadn't found out I was "all natural," no one would have known my name. How many players in the Ultrabowl can anyone name? Maybe one or two, the lead strikers or goalies. Maybe. I ran the Pre on a farm team, coming in third in my best-ever race and Coach Donavan was only hoping for me to come in second anyway. It was only because I was different, a freak, the *all-natural* girl, that I made headlines. The unmodified girl. The drug companies hated me. Especially you-know-which-one. If an unmodded girl can beat a Nugen modder then why spend the money for their test-tubes anyway?

Mom finally wakes from her trance and speaks slowly and carefully, "The picture I showed you this morning, Gabby? That's Kyle—Kyle Conrad. He works at NuGen with Smith—and his Grandmother is from the village just west of ours."

Calling it, 'ours,' Mom still lays claim to the old country village that she grew up in and I find that ridiculous. The only people that stayed when the soldiers came were the ones who couldn't make it out in time. We know almost no one there now. It's only a memory of hers and I have no ties there. If I were to call anywhere home it would be Venezuela.

"He's cute." I don't know why I say that. I must be distracted, but it is true.

Mom smiles at Smith and jumps the gun, her mind probably racing ahead to the riding of donkeys, wearing of traditional clothing, stomping of feet and shrill victory yells, then quickly on to a multitude of babies on her lap. "Smith? Invite him over then. We must meet this *nice* boy."
Smith's punctuation mark smile morphs into a leering grin.

I want to protest but the words are stuck in my mouth. I know eventually I will have to marry someone; I want to be married eventually anyway, and with the culture I am in and the way Mom is, I will have to choose someone from a very small set of suitors. I know this has been coming for a while and like those tangled vines in the woods behind our house, I'm trapped.

Kyle Conrad

How good I've become at sneaking around is really starting to bother me. Enlisting Cee and See to help me work out, train and attend competitions without actually revealing what I am doing, I'm developing into a full time master of misdirection; I'm afraid. I don't lie, I would never lie to my mom, I just don't volunteer information that isn't asked.

"Mom, I'm going over to Sidney's." True. That's where I'm going but from there See's going to drive us to a beautiful, wooden park called White Clay Creek in nearby Delaware where we will run a bunch of miles through the wooded paths, across streams and around dense vegetation, leaping over felled trees, swinging from hanging vines and zigzagging up and down steep hills, all under cover and away from curious eyes. See bought an eight year-old Wrangler that I love to ride in with the top off. I jump in and we speed off.

"So what's next, girrrrl?" See says smiling, wind in her hair. She loves the secrecy as much as I hate it and in her mind everything we are attempting is going to be a success. I will just train hard and somehow make it back onto the farm team, shortly thereafter we will find ourselves running for the Philadelphia Liberty, then one day win the Ultrabowl—easy as that. She obviously hasn't lain in bed late at night wondering what happens when my leg gives out again or what to do if I fall and split my head open in the middle of nowhere.

"The New York Open is next. Do you think you could take me?"

"Of course, of course. Me or Cyndi will take you. New York, really? But don't you have to sign up for that in advance?"

"Yeah," I say despondently, looking at the passing trees. "Could we do it later at your house?"

"Sure."

I ran in three small races so far, tiny ones really, all local affairs, couple of hundred competitors at most, some high school and college girls that were a little quick but not a real challenge. I was terribly nervous at the first one but by the third race I was really ready to move up. I chose those three because they had walk-up registration. But the New York Open is something entirely different. I am going to have to register in advance and the organizers will see my name—it might even make the news. I know I'm going to have to tell Mom soon.

The run in the park is great. I feel like I'm back, like I'm at least as fast and strong as I was when I made it onto the semi-pro Philly team. The work is starting to pay off and I appreciate Cee and See helping me train; they are so great to me. The last few weeks have flown by amazingly fast, what with all my time going to training and racing, sneaking around and developing alibis, and school and studying; it feels like just a giant blur.

We sit on the car hood talking, letting our bodies air-dry and See takes advantage of her captive audience.

"Okay, okay, okay, a couple are going out for the evening so they put their doggie outside. When the taxi arrives, and as the couple walk out of the house, the doggie sneaks back in so the man darts inside to chase it out. The woman, not wanting the driver to know that the house will be empty, explains, 'My husband is just going upstairs to say goodbye to my mother.'

Several minutes later, an exhausted man arrives and climbs back into the taxi saying, 'Sorry I took so long, the stupid idiot was hiding under the bed and I had to poke her with a coat hanger several times before I could get her to come out!' "

We both laugh, me crying at the image of that one.

"Okay, okay, okay, last week a squirrel slipped into my house so I did the logical thing and called my mom at work and asked her, 'How do you get a squirrel out of the house?'

She told me to leave a trail of peanut butter and crackers to the outside. And guess what? It worked! The squirrel ate his way out of the house. Unfortunately, he passed another squirrel eating his way in."

I smile and say, "That didn't really happen. Did it?"

She giggles, "Got ya!"

Joke time is over so we jet over to See's house to sign up for New York. I don't want to take the chance of Mom walking in on us. I don't know how to tell her and I want to delay to the last moment.

We enter See's home, a typical river-side ranch, and I greet See's mom, a load of laundry in a basket pinned to her left hip and large wooden spoon in her right hand.

"Gabriella, how are you today?" I'm not exactly sure what she might be more interested in using the wooden spoon for, stirring her pot of soup or keeping her three sons in line.

"Great! And you?"

"Oh, you know... They keep me busy!" Ms. Scott says referring to the triplets, Jonathan, George and Scott. The last one's name, Scott Scott, was a mistake at the hospital that she never got around to fixing. Sitting around the dinette table they smack each other whenever she looks away.

"Keep your feet off the table!" Mrs. Scott yells at Scott Scott, then turning back to me says softly, "And what did you girls do today?"

"Sidney and I had a nice time at the park today, it's really beautiful this time of year. I love how the light streams through the leaves."

"Keep your mouth shut while you're eating!" Mrs. Scott snaps at George, "Oh, that sounds beautiful, Gabriella. Do you want anything to eat?"

I quickly calculate the calories I have already taken in today. "Thanks, maybe just a banana."

"Stop poking your brother!" Mrs. Scott bellows at Jonathan. The only possible explanation for how she saw him is that there really are eyes on the back of her head. "Sure, take whatever you want."

As I grab the banana, Jonathan waves excitedly at me and starts quickly bouncing his eyebrows and fluttering his eyelids then sticks his tongue out at me and licks his lips.

"He's going to want your autograph and a kiss from you next," See says with a grin. "He does that to all my girlfriends."

Mrs. Scott glaringly scowls at him and he quickly stops, frowns and points his face down at his plate.

"Oh that's alright. I'll give you an autograph, Jonathan." He smiles up at me, bouncing his eyebrows.

"Stop shooting peas!" Mrs. Scott snaps at George, "What else do you girls have planned?"

Scott Scott, the terror of the bunch, is watching his Mom carefully, apparently waiting for an opportunity for mischief.

"We're going to go use the screen for a bit then maybe shopping," See says just as Scott Scott tosses a frog in mom's laundry basket. See and I can't believe it so we turn and leave the room not wanting to be witness to what will happen next.

See and I open the screen and I register for the New York Open and a feeling of finality falls on me. I am really going to do it.

After cleaning up, we go out to the mall for a while and the day slips away. As we arrive at my house I see Smith's car parked on the street and looking for shelter I convince See to come in for a bit. Opening the door, I am fairly surprised to see Kyle sitting there next to Smith, across from my mother, drinking tea, Mom acting as if she is the one looking to marry, but I am not sure to which one.

"Gabriella, Sidney, come in, sit, have some of this *nice* warm tea. This is Kyle Conrad, the *nice* young man Smith has been telling us about."

Turning back to the two men, she says, "Sidney is one of Gabby's *nice* new friends she has made since we've moved here. She's very *nice*."

Then she turns back to See and says, "Sidney, Kyle works with Smith at NuGen. He has come here to meet Gabriella. *Isn't that nice?"*

I look at See as if to apologize with my eyes, then turn to them and say, "Hey Smith, how's it going? Hi Kyle, good to meet you." I extend my hand, shake, then walk around to sit on the couch that Mom is on. "Sidney, you can sit here if you like." I point to the spare chair at the end.

"No, I better be going."

Before I can stop See from abandoning me, Mom says, "Okay then. Have a *nice* safe drive."

The door closes and Mom turns to me, "So how was your day?"

I want to say, '*Nice*,' but that will probably make her mad. "Fine. We had a good time milling around at the mall. You know, girl stuff."

"And that's it? You *only* went to the mall?" Mom's eyes are twinkling and her smile is frozen on her face as if someone painted it there.

"We went to Sidney's too. Hung out for a while. Why?" I look over at our two guests and they are clearly becoming uncomfortable.

Her cheeks are suddenly pink. "Oh, I don't know. I thought that maybe you might have been out running again, that maybe Sidney has been helping you to train."

Fire blasts my neck as if a furnace kicked on under my shirt pumping heat out of my collar. I look over at our two guests who won't meet my eyes, then back at Mom. I can feel my cheeks flashing red. "Okay Mom, what's going on here?"

"How long did you think you could hide this! You know Smith works at NuGen and they track every athlete registered for every major race in the country. How did you think you could register for New York and not have anyone know?"

Kyle is fidgeting in his chair, looking down at the wisps of steam coming from his tea. He looks better in person, dark hair and dark eyes, thin, but not too thin, and tall, about 6 foot. I wonder if he's modified; he looks so perfect.

I turn to Mom. "What do you want me to say?"

"Smith, I'm sorry about bringing this up in front of you. Kyle, you too." Smith flashes her his stealthy smile then looks back down when I glare.

Her voice grows softer. "Gabriella, what about your leg? You hurt yourself last time, so now I guess you are feeling better but I thought you were done with this? I mean it was great... It got us out of Brazil and where we were, but now we don't need that anymore. I thought we talked about this. I thought we were past all that."

Mom and I always hated Ultraball and she was terrified that I would get hurt but I begged—pleaded really—to let me race. I told her I would be safe. I told her it would be different. I wasn't going to be on the field with the three-hundred-pound, genetically-modified monsters hurling, smashing and crashing each other on and off the field like charging wildebeests. I promised. Then my leg was destroyed. The doctors did the best they could but it was still scarred and ugly and what was really important to Mom was in jeopardy—me getting married.

ChaPter TWelve

I know where this is going, the same place it always goes, so I decide to cut straight to the end, "Mom, the purpose of my life is not to give you grand-children. You understand that, right? This is my life, right?"

"Oh, Gabriella, I love you, you know that. I just want you to be safe. I don't want you to get hurt again." That's always her cover when she wants things done her way, protecting me from some unseen evil out there that's going to grab me. Being safe. I'm tired of that story.

"Whatever." I look at Smith out of the top of my eyes for a good two seconds as I stand making sure he doesn't mistake my stare for anything else but contempt. I grab a glass of water and go out to the back deck.

I don't want to argue and especially not in front of those two. Besides I'm afraid if I argue long enough I might back down, I might not show up for the race. It would be much easier wouldn't it? Just keep going to high school, eat-ing french fries whenever I wanted instead of counting and rating every calorie, spending time doing whatever I felt like, socializing with friends or attacking the clearance racks at the mall instead of dodging eyes in order to run until my legs fall off, sleeping in on weekends and milling around in fuzzy bunny slippers instead of stretching, balancing, running, leaping, jumping and climbing all day long, days on without end.

"Do you mind if I join you?"

I turn to see Kyle standing there. "Sure. Free country."

He sits on the bench across from me and peers out into the woods in the same direction my eyes are headed, perhaps trying to see what I am looking at, but I am looking at nothing in particular. "Sorry you had to see that. I'm sure that wasn't the impression Mom wanted to make on you."

"I think you running is cool." His voice has an odd texture to it, he would probably make a good singer.

"You think?" I look at him.

"Yeah, I mean, why not? If you want to compete and you can make the team, why wouldn't you? I mean, why live with the regret of not doing some-thing you really wanted to do?"

I exhale long and slow and look back through the sliding glass door, across the dining room at Mom sitting on the living room sofa, her sitting at just the perfect angle to keep her eyes on me over Smith's shoulder. I think she will be alright with us out here, alone, talking, as long as we don't sit too close. I look back out into the woods. Tapping the wooden bench next to me, I say,

"Come over here, Kyle, and tell me about yourself."

He sits next to me and tells me that he is modified, a NuGen test-tuber, and he has been with them all his life. "They sent me to college, helped me pick my degree program, offered tutors in school when I needed them. Yeah, they're all around just great. Almost like a second family there."

There is something intriguing about Kyle and it's not just the way he looks, although he is beautiful, but the confidence that's radiating from the pores of his skin like some subconscious flower pheromone attracting bees, rippling around him. There's such an intensity in the air and being there, next to him, makes me feel, somehow, more calm, relaxed, and even, *comfortable*.

His description of NuGen is a completely different perspective and because the words are coming from *his* mouth I somehow believe them. I only know the ultra-competitive, win-at-all-costs NuGen, the NuGen that doesn't consider it cheating as long as they're not caught, but he makes them sound so good.

"And what do you do for them? If you are modified, why aren't you involved in sports?"

"Oh, yeah. About that... not really supposed to say—"
I slowly place my hand on top of his making sure Mom won't see, "You can tell me."

He pauses for a moment, probably trying to figure out how much he can say, then answers, "Not everyone is modified with the goal of running faster or being stronger. NuGen has all forms of modifications."

"That's nothing new. Most of the companies offer health and longevity modifications and some offer non-sports related biological changes like hair color or increased height. I have heard of that."

"Yeah, everyone has that stuff but NuGen has been perfecting what they call task specialization. It's really just an outgrowth of what we are already doing in sports. Modifying genes so that a person would be really good at a certain task."

"Give me an example."

"Well, I hate to give you too much detail. Most of it is proprietary or still in the research phase."

"C'mon, Kyle." I smile and slide closer, but not too close.

"Okay. Well, for example, take a lawyer. A great lawyer is going to have certain characteristics, a certain disposition and personality. NuGen has isolated most of these characteristics to genetic markers and we think that we can alter a given person's DNA such that they have most of them. Of course conditioning plays a large factor also, so we offer those services as well."

That doesn't sound bad to me so I am wondering what he is really hiding. "So you were modified, but not for sports? Is that what you're saying?"

"I have never actually seen my own profile, not that I would know how to read it anyway. I don't actually work in research like Smith."

Smith opens the sliding glass door, saying, "Gabriella, didn't mean to interrupt but your Mom and I are doing the dishes, are you done with your glass?"

"Sure," I say, passing it to him.

Palming the glass, he flashes his smile-not-smile, almost a momentary smirk. If it had stayed on his face any longer I'd call it sinister.

I turn then quickly glance back to see him wiping the rim of my glass with his handkerchief and stealthily stuffing it in his pocket as he walks back into the kitchen.

Turning back to Kyle, wondering what Smith would want with whatever tiny residue my mouth left on the rim of the glass, my saliva, my DNA, I say, "What do you do?"

"I'm what they call a Technical Specialist. Kind of a generic term for a middle management, do-all, out-in-the-field type person. When they have a job that requires traveling somewhere and interfacing with the public, they send a Technical Specialist. The two guys you met in Brazil who discovered you at the stadium, they were Technical Specialists."

"Really? I never knew that. I thought they were scouts for the Philadelphia Liberty. So those two worked for NuGen?" Now dominoes are falling in my brain and Kyle looks to be straining to prevent his face from flushing red.

"Err... Yes, We scout all the major competitions."

"But why would NuGen be interested in me? And how could two NuGen scouts offer me a position in Philly. Isn't the team independent?" I know I am playing dumb here. Everyone knows the sports teams are controlled by the media outlets who in turn are controlled by the advertisers and NuGen is one of the big three spenders of advertising dollars so that is probably the link, but I didn't think it was so overt.

"I don't know all those answers. I'm just a Tech Spec, but I can say that one of my roles in the Philly area is to advise the team actually. Quite a number of NuGen athletes are on the team and we advertise pretty heavy in the Northeast region since our corporate office is here."

Pausing for a while, trying to sort out all this information and the obscure links to what I already know, wondering how much of what I think I know is true and how much is either lies or my imagination, I say, "Tell me this. When you go out 'in the field' as you say, do you wear one of those shiny, blue-black suits?"

"We all do," he says plainly, having no idea what the answer would mean to me.

Suddenly I am back there, in the clothing store, and I am watching the two men with the blue-black suits explain to my father how he has to die and there is no other choice. *Die, die, die! You have to die! There is no other choice! You have to pay! You have to give back what is owed!* Their suits shimmer in the fading sunlight and bile floods my mouth like it is water cascading off a falls crashing on the rocks below, a never ending stream of thick, course fluid. It's rushing to my head, too hard, too fast, the blood, pounding, my heart suddenly racing unbearably fast. I am just a lost, little girl, unable to stop it, unable to stop them, unable to reach my father, so far away, on the other side of the room. I see him explaining something to my mother, saying something about something he has to give them. I can't quite make it out, the sounds are muffled then he bellows loud and clear, "I WILL BE RIGHT BACK," and my ears ring painfully and it is as if he yelled it directly into my ears. Then we are running, mom and I, and then on the bus and I am crying, mom is holding me and people are staring. *Why are they looking at us? Why don't they leave us alone?* I don't know what is happening and don't know how to stop it. *How to stop time? How?* Pause, pause, pause. *How can I stop this crazy thing? How can I stop it for just one moment so I can figure this all out?*

"Excuse me... I'm not feeling so good." I stand up to go to the bathroom and seeing the most beautiful light pink and baby blue neon sparkles, like thousands of tiny hummingbirds, I pass out.

Friends and Enemies

"**H**ow did you know your Mom was gonna be cool with it?" Cyndi asks as I just finish the last of my packing.

"A reporter called. Guess they saw my name on the registration list. I overheard her say, 'Yes, it is the same Gabriella,' then a few seconds later, 'Yes, she is running the race.' I scrambled downstairs before she saw me, but from that... Yeah, I guess she's cool with it."

Admiring herself in the mirror mounted to the front of my closet door (Cyndi just got her hair cut yesterday) she says, "Kind of weird though. I didn't think it would go down so easy."

"Yeah, it surprised me. You know, I wonder if Smith had anything to say about it after I... maybe he changed her mind."

Looking my way as she grabs one of my bags, "Why would you say that?"

"Well Kyle seemed to like the idea."

"Yeah, Sidney told me about seeing him in your living room. We know him from the team. He's a cute one, isn't he?"

Heading down the stairs and out to load the car, I say, "Of course. All the modders look perfect."

"I *thought* so! He is modified, isn't he! His skin is just so sweet!"

"Yeah. It is," I pause, wondering the same thing that is probably in Cyndi's head right now, 'What does Kyle want with me?' The modders typically marry their own kind since they are so focused on positive eugenics, improving their blood-lines through science and breeding. "Mom is trying to match us and Smith is in on the whole thing."

"You're kidding! I wish my Mom was out searching for hot guys for me!"

"It's not like that, girl, and you know it!"

We put the bags in the back of mom's car. "Do you think it will work out?"

"Who knows. Mom just wants grand-kids. I mean, she wants me to be happy, but in her head, everything just works itself out, just like it always has. For some reason I just can't buy that."

"So what are you going to do?"

"Well, I convinced Mom to let us see each other for a while, to back down on the pressure, and she agreed to escorted dates. We'll see from there. I am really trying to take it slow."

Mom comes out and Cyndi quickly changes the subject, "Yeah, that science test was hard. Ms. Con-sec-cow, I guess we're ready to go now." Cyndi can't pronounce our last name right; no one here really can, one of the reasons I want to change it.

Mom looks at us with a smirk, no fooling her, she knows we were talking about *something*, she's an old hand at subterfuge.

We head out and quickly make our way to the New Jersey Turnpike, one of the more boring highways on the planet, and I try to doze off to prevent Mom from asking me any questions.

Too late. "So, Gabby... I guess this means your knee is feeling better?"

"I think so."

"You're not going to push yourself too hard are you? I don't want to see you hurting yourself again. It's not worth the risk."

"I know."

She lowers the radio, passes a few trucks, then continues, "So how did that happen anyway? The doctors said you would never run again. Did it just heal itself?"

"Maybe."

Mom blows her wind out long and slow, then raises her voice, still not looking my way, "You're not going to tell me anything?"

"Mom, I don't know exactly how it happened. It just happened... I'm still trying to figure it out myself. All I know is that my leg is better and I'm taking advantage of it."

"I mean, Gabriella... I just don't get it. The doctors said your knee was shredded—not in so many words—but now you are not only walking perfectly, but running, and not only running, but running in a race... I don't understand how this happened and I don't understand why you want to go back to racing."

"Mom, I don't know, I just need to do this. I told you that you didn't have to come with us." That stung more than I meant it to.

She pauses for a minute, hurt, then says, "But, what were you doing when it started to feel better? When did you notice?"

It takes me a while to answer. She is looking at the road, Cyndi is trying to act like she's not paying attention, slouched in the back seat, screen on, and I am looking at the passing trees out my side window. I let it out soft, almost whispering, "The last time I went through Dr. Duggan's machine."

"What do you *mean* 'went through'?"

She pauses for a few seconds, then like some slow motion special effect, it hits her. "You actually rode in his crazy contraption! I thought you were just going to look at his lab! You didn't tell me that! Wait until I... I... I get a hold of Archibald's ear. I'm gonna tear that thing off—"

Fighting to hold back a smile, I visualize Dr. Duggan's ear in mom's hand, him squealing, her yelling, him pleading, her twisting it, him bouncing on the balls of his feet.

"How dare he put you in one of his crazy contraptions and not tell me! Doesn't he realize that you're all I have!" She stops ranting then ends with a "Huff!" and I suddenly feel bad about not letting her know.

I look at her. "It was me, Mom. I pushed him to let me try it. It's not his fault."

"But Gabby, why? Don't you know those scientists... they mean well... but not all their experiments... They don't always know *all* the consequences."

Personal experience echoes through her voice. I know that Dr. Duggan and Smith were both in research before I was born, in the old country, and that Mom and Dad knew them but I always assumed they just lived in the same neighborhood but now I am beginning to wonder.

Mom says, "I just don't want you involved in that, you don't know what might happen."

I don't answer and the car becomes quiet except for the drone of tires on pavement. A few minutes later I play with the radio station tuner.

About two hours later the congestion becomes real thick. North Jersey is like one giant continuous city with multitudes of decaying row-homes right next to oil refineries belching white smoke and trash incinerators belching tainted steam and it reminds me of the build-it-right-on-top-of-your-head construction attitude of South America. We cross the George Washington Bridge, spend a few moments in Manhattan, then quickly enter the Bronx.

Cyndi bangs the back of my chair accidentally with her knee so I know her eyes are darting back and forth like she just landed on Mars. There is a fair amount of graffiti on the walls, vandalism to road signs and buildings, trash on the streets and little micro-deserts, piles of sand and stone where old buildings were knocked down, but it is nowhere near as bad as I thought it would be considering the Hollywood depiction I held in my head. And nowhere near as bad as where we were in Brazil. The highway quickly dumps us at the entrance to Van Cortlandt Park and we find parking in a grass field among what feels like thousands of cars and the landscape is full of racers, fans, friends and families walking around everywhere like ants.

The race is split into two races, an "open" and an "invitational." The open race is first and anyone who pays the fee can show up and race so there are boys and men running too which feels really odd. There are about a few thousand recreational racers who just want to complete the course along with all their families, friends and general spectators so there are people everywhere. The invitational race will follow the open and to enter it a person must have received an invitation from the race organizers by being either an "elite" or by submitting a fast enough qualifying time in another sanctioned race. That is what I did. There are about one-hundred others who did the same as I did and another fifty or so elite. I chafe at the term as if it means they are somehow a superior human and it drives home what I know I am; an all-natural freak. The course is one large loop twisting and turning through open fields and patches of woods with different obstacles all over the place. Many of the recreational runners are in costumes, Viking helmets, baby-blue ballerina tutus, face paint and wigs. Some are drinking large amounts of beer and yelling loudly at apparently nothing. I enjoy watching the recreational runners and saddened at the same time because I remember when it used to be so much fun. My first race, back in Brazil, comes back to me for a moment, then I shake it off and let the importance of the race bleed into my joints.

Once the first race is over, an announcer calls out the names of the top fifty or so runners and the fans scream for their favorites. The Vikings are really drinking now. Goose-bumps ripple across my flesh when I unexpectedly hear my name. Just as the one-hundred and fifty or so of us gather at the front to applause from the mass of partiers I notice that Smith, Kyle and some other guy who is with them are with Mom and Cyndi. Smith seems to have the ability to text whole paragraphs without looking down at his screen. Kyle and the other guy are real serious looking in their blue-black suits that make me nauseous and are looking around intently, I have no idea at what.

We line up and everyone is eying each other. A lanky blonde painted in a lime-green body suit, neon white gloves, a too-tight swimmers skull cap and odd looking knee-high athletic shoes that lace up the back with tassels hanging out, prances like a boxing pretty boy across the field and out to the start line. Two more with red suits join the line near me, one quite short and stocky, and the line is bursting. Expectation drowns most of the audience into silence except for the drunken Vikings who won't stop hooting. We bend down into our starting poses, my knees flexing, legs spread, blood pumping with adrenaline.

The announcer has an Asian accent and speaks softly, not yelling out, "Go!" like he is urging us on, but real soft and casual as if we had an option.

We jolt out of the blocks full of pure naked acceleration, arms pumping, backs arched, running straight ahead, afraid to turn our heads the slightest, angling our bodies into the oncoming curve. The first obstacle comes quick, my leg flicking forward and I'm airborne for a second, a bird again, then my heel swings for the dirt like a home-run batter. We speed up toward the next, a deep under, and I dive as if a propeller pushes me, both arms pointing forward, under the barbed wire, into the mud, some splashing in my mouth, the crowd screaming, loving every moment. Scrambling through, covered in mud, I launch myself out of the pit, my hands not out in front fast enough, and skid my jaw across the rough dirt, cinders and a few small stones. Up as if it's nothing, continuing to the next wall, blood trickles down my neck and shirt and I am suddenly mad.

I pump harder, elbows, knees, feet. Hands balled into fists, I careen around three large round barrels filled with sand. The other girls and I are all close, too close, some in front, some in back, a mad gaggle of pumping arms and legs, flexing, flicking and flying, seemingly intertwined. It feels dangerous and a lump forms in my throat. I pass the stands that Mom, Cyndi and the men are in and I see the fear on Mom's face. Cyndi is screaming her head off. Kyle's lips are an immobile straight line, eyes focused like he's looking through a gun scope, his partner looks like his clone and Smith is texting, a play-by-play maybe, without looking down.

Rounding the next curve we come up on sixteen thick ropes hanging from a large wood framework like a row of Old West hangman's nooses. The pack surges, everyone trying to be first to the ropes. No one wants to wait. I grab my rope with one hand and immediately fling both legs and my free arm as hard as I can, trying to reach the peak of the far wall, and barely make it. Falling over the wall I am quickly back at full gallop, trying to make up distance. My rhythm is off, like my heart only beats when my feet are in the air. Or maybe it's the crowd; so big, too many.

Just go girl! Just go! Ignore them, be free, just flow! I focus on my breathing, trying to block out the noise, trying to focus on what's next, but the winding paths of woods and trees prevent me from being more than a few seconds prepared.

I am a leaf on the wind, I am a leaf on the wind, I am a leaf on the wind.

Slowly I start to catch the front pack and as I reach the end of the third section I realize that nearly half the field has dropped out already; the rope leading to the large wall is too difficult and they lost too much time. About two miles to go, closing in on Lime-Green and Red, a section of stands erupts with, "Go Gabby Go! Go Gabby Go!" and goose-bumps ripple my flesh. A surge of energy powers me and I feel like I must run for them, must win for them. They are suddenly my people. *They came to see me run; I cannot disappoint them.*

I throw away caution as if it is fetid trash and unleash raw, unchecked aggression toward the obstacles. Dry sand smacks the backs of my calves as I lean forward letting my body weight propel me as if I am falling forward.

I am a leaf on the wind, I am a leaf on the wind.

It is all I can do to come up even with the two, Lime-Green and Red, and glancing over at them a twinkle of fear looks back at me and I know I have already won. As we break the final clearing a growl escapes my throat unnaturally and I push forward, hard. It is an all out dash for the finish line and the Braveheart crowd is screaming, leaping and dancing in their kilts and Viking helmets, wigs and face paint, most still covered in mud like it's a badge of honor. Crossing the line, winning, I feel the tiniest twinge in my knee, as if it says, 'Hello! I'm still here!' and the joy is wiped from my face. People are screaming, cheering and high-fiving me as I walk dazed toward Mom and Cyndi, Kyle and Smith, and the other guy.

I mentally check myself, making sure I am not limping and smile broadly, hiding my fear inside, as I reach the group.

"Alright Gabby!" Cyndi yells as she hugs me.

I give Mom a big hug and say hello to the three men. Kyle doesn't treat me special and I guess it is because he is actually at work. Smith congratulates me, flashing his mystery smile, and introduces Kyle's partner, Sebastian Roberts. We chat briefly and the three go off for some business.

Cleaning the blood off my chin and shirt, Mom says, "Gabriella, I am so proud of you! You did good! I am so glad you have your running back. I know what it means to you." *I wonder if Mom knows what Kyle said to me on our back porch.*

"Thanks, Mom," I hug her again then whisper in her ear so Cyndi can't hear, "I love you," and I really, really mean it.

Looking over Mom's shoulder I see Kyle and Sebastian speaking with Lime-Green and Red. Maybe they are new farm team prospects?

After I grab my trophy and take a few pictures with the race organizers, we head toward the hose off zone and Kyle and Sebastian meet us with Lime-Green and Red in tow.

"Gabriella, could we have a minute?" Kyle says as if he doesn't know me.

"Sure, what's up?"

"These two girls you ran with today, we are scouting them and they asked if they could ask you a few questions."

"I guess so."

Sebastian continues, "This is Qi Tan," he says, pronouncing her first name like 'key,' pointing his arm gracefully toward Red, "and this is Nomi Franklin," motioning to Lime-Green. "They are both local here to New York City, and we thought you might have some words of advice. They say they know everything about you." Sebastian winks, but the two don't see.

I smile at that. Fans. They know *nothing* about me. "Sure, ask away."

Lime-Green starts first, "Like, I've read everything about you, and it's, like, such a plea-shure!" She grabs my hand to shake and won't let go and I am not sure if she is real or plastic.

Then it's Red's turn. She is more serious. "I wondering how you got on team? What you did. You no finish best in Brazil. I read it. Still you picked up." Her jet-black hair is pulled straight back, tight, and ends in a tiny tail and her skin is an odd-textured olive.

"I don't know to be honest. Maybe my fight? I tried to not show any weakness, especially when running by the judges. Always look strong, even if you are losing. Always look like you have more to give, more fight."

I stop for a moment, contemplating the question myself, then turn to Kyle, "You have access to the NuGen records, you could find out why they picked me, right?"

Lime-Green finally lets go of my hand but she still has that goofy smile on her face.

An odd look comes over Kyle's face, then he says, "Err... Maybe we can talk about that later. Sure."

Sebastian's brow furrows looking at Kyle, then he turns back and says, "How 'bout you, Nomi, any questions?"

"Are you trying to get back on the team 'cause that would be, like, awesome? Maybe one day we will be running, like, together on the same team?"

Poor girl, hope that's not contagious. "I just love to run—to compete. It's in my blood. I can't describe it. Something inside of me just needs to do this. Like that old fable of the Scorpion and the Frog, I just have to do it."

"I don't know that one," Lime-Green says with a confused look.

"Ahh... The story goes like this. This frog gives a scorpion a ride on his back across a stream on the condition that the scorpion doesn't sting him since, of course, if the scorpion stings him they will both drown. All goes well until the scorpion stings the frog. As the two begin to sink to their deaths the frog asks the scorpion, 'why?' to which the scorpion replies, 'I couldn't help it; it's in my nature.' And I kind of feel like that about running. I just have to. I can't explain why."

Qi howls, "Frogs? Scorpions? You killing me!" then starts laughing.

Nomi has a spacey-dazed look in her eyes, we are all standing there, no one saying anything and just before it becomes awkward Sebastian says, "Okay girls, let's let Gabriella shower off, she has a long drive ahead of her."

As Sebastian walks them away, Kyle finally drops his guard and says, "It was great to see you today, running I mean, back at it. It made me feel good to see you doing what you love." He smiles and my heart grows warm, strangely, and I can't help but smile back at him.

He stays with me in the hose-off line of muddy warriors. "Thanks so much Kyle. By the way, I wanted to apologize to you for passing out like that the last time I saw you. I just came back from a run in the park and I must have overdone my training."

"No problem. But hey, I'm just glad you were alright and it was nothing."

"Thanks. You know you are totally different than I expected."

"How so?"

"Of course a good chunk of my family—cousins, aunts, uncles, went through match makers. Especially the ones who left the old country, as matching up once the family left the villages was difficult. People stay together, make lives you know, make due, but I have never seen anything magical." I blush. "I mean, I didn't mean to say—"

"I know what you meant. It's okay," he says, smiling.

"It's just so weird, I mean, we don't even know each other and we are being pushed together with the idea that we might marry. Doesn't that make you uncomfortable having that kind of pressure?"

"Yes, I think there is an expectation, but my pressure is nowhere near as severe as yours."

I am next in line for the water. "Really?"

"My family is much more liberal than yours. At least half my cousins have married outside and my father says it's up to me. Mom would love to see me marry someone from our culture but she would never force me."

"So then you are going along with this—why?"

I step into the water, and mud, dirty old shoes and left behind clothing are all over the ground.

He stands back as to not wet his suit and says, "I can't say exactly—your picture interested me, of course. You are beautiful," he smiles, looking down at me, "and I am in the business so I knew your story—your background anyway. I liked your spunk. And even though my parents are not so interested in cultural pedigree they are definitely interested in genetic pedigree. I guess it was the weird combination of hometown village-girl, super-athlete that intrigued me."

I towel off nice and dry, look for signs of Mom and not seeing any nudge closer to him, looking up into his strong face, "And are you still intrigued?"

Looking down deep into my eyes with his perfect orbs, hazel with a light tinge of wintergreen, he says, "Of course I am," then smiles.

I smile and pull back. "Walk me to my car?"

"Sure."

Strolling along, I say, "Can you do me a favor?"

"Maybe, what is it?"

"Take me out on a date."

"But what about your mom?"

"Tell Smith to suggest a tour of your facility in Philly, you can show me around. We could spend the day together, maybe get to know each other better, Smith would be our cover," I giggle up at him and say, "Please? I'll hold your hand."

He chuckles, "I'll see what we can do."

As we arrive at the car, Mom is smiling and I see her holding babies in the reflection of her eyes. I feel like I should give Kyle a peck on the cheek to say bye but Mom is right there and I just squeeze his hand and off we go and as he turns to leave I regret not doing it.

On the ride home I want to sleep but Mom, excited that Kyle and I are hitting it off, sings all the songs on the radio, poorly.

As soon as we arrive at home, I sneak into the backyard and call Dr. Duggan to prepare him for Mom's eventual call, hear him say "Shenanigans" three times, beg him to not tell Mom anything about Portugal or Michael then beg, beg, beg him to let me ride the machine again. He agrees, says "Shenanigans" two more times, and we hang up.

The Secret

Now it's back to the endless loop of school, studies and training. An endlessly repeating Groundhog Day owns my every waking minute and there are nights when I am so exhausted that all I can think about is sleep yet I don't want to go to bed because I don't want to wake up and start it all over again.

I find myself texting Michael far more than Kyle, all the time in fact, and even though I know I can't ever be with him, I can't stop myself. It's like I am living two separate lives and I know that one of them must die. Like the baby bird that fell out of its nest when I was ten, holding it all day, knowing it would soon die, I can't stop myself from holding onto it just a few moments longer, loving it passionately, even as I watch the life ease out of its body.

*****

About a week after the New York race I receive a package, unmarked, unlabeled, and opening it, find a couple items. One is a tiny parachute with a belt, supposedly to provide resistance when I run. *Boy am I going to look weird with this on!* The other item is another belt with two short stringy bands that are to be tied to my ankles, supposed to help with vertical leap and explosive power. See thinks they are both hilarious and is already trying to make up a few new jokes about them.

The only card in the box has one word scrawled on it, *"—Coach."*

After I register for my next race, Madrid, an invitational, I call Michael on the screen and ask him if he can drive me to Spain but I tell him that I can't tell him why just yet. He asks a lot of questions that I dodge and then finally agrees. I can't wait to see him again but I am not exactly sure why since I know we can never be together.

The Secret

When the big day comes, hoping my training is enough, hoping I am really ready, I ride the bus to Princeton and nervously glide through the University hall, remembering the day I was cured, the day I ran this same hall in utter shock at what had just happened. I knock on the door, Dr. Duggan lets me in, and I see the crew already in action, already sending things, animals, and people back and forth through the Void. The transport chair has been rigged with a seat belt and metal bar, like a roller coaster, all thanks to my actions last time.

Dr. Duggan distractedly runs through procedure steps as the last transport chair comes through, barks out a few orders as the whir of the machines dies down, comes over and greets me, saying, "Gabriella, you know I am against this, but, shenanigans, you have me over a barrel."

"Sorry about that. But I have my reasons."

"Alright, we will make this quick and painless. No more shenanigans, okay?"

"No problem, Dr. Duggan."

I slide down the welding goggles, strap myself in nervously, expecting the suction vortex and the momentary head-splitting pain and close my eyes down softly. If there is something in the Void this time, I don't want to see it.

The chair reverberates through my spine, and I am off, acceleration knocking the wind from my lungs. The pain comes quickly, like a mesh of needles across my flesh, then I'm in. Unable to stop myself I open my eyes and see him standing there, as if he is a passenger standing on a train platform, bags in hand, waiting for the train to stop so that he can board. Moments later I exit through the ring and see Michael's smiling face.

I can't believe I saw him again! He must be real or I must be crazy. No way!

I unbuckle and slowly step off of the transport chair module. Michael's smile erases and his brow furrows when he notices my limp's gone and my leg is no longer scarred. I want to grab his hand, his arm, and pull him in close and tight, resting my head on his shoulder, but now it would mean something different.

"You ready to go?" I want to be closer to him but I don't want to do anything in front of this crew. And what I just saw, oh my God, I can't start freaking out in front of everyone. I need to get out of here.

"Yeah, just give me one minute. Maryann, could you take over for me now?"

She gives him an odd, slack jaw look, then replies, "Sure."

Leaving the room and heading down the hall, he immediately says, "Gabby, what happened? Your leg—it's cured?"
Nonchalantly, I say, "Yeah. It is."

"Oh my God! I thought the damage was permanent. What doctor?"

Like a gentleman, he opens the car door for me to an old convertible Karmann Ghia. "I can tell you but it's a secret." I shake my finger at him and say, "No blabbin' "

"Okay, okay, just tell me." We pull out of the parking garage and out into the hot Portugal sun, heading towards the highway.

"No really though. I'm serious. You can't tell anyone."
The wind is blowing my hair all over the place, so I roll up the side window and it calms down.

Face straight and even, he says, "You can trust me," and it's as if he means it in a completely different way.
I tell him the story of the man in the Void. I tell him how the Void is bright white when I go through, not pitch black like it was for the others. I tell him that I don't know who the man is, or even if he's real or something from my head. I tell him that I don't know if I am crazy. I tell him that all I know is that my leg is healed, cured, like time rewound to before the accident. I tell him my leg is not fixed; it's *like it never happened.* I tell him that I am competing again, and that he is driving me to a competition in Madrid. I tell him that I might be able to make the team again.

He is quiet for a long time, listening, contemplating, a pained expression on his face. Sitting there silently I can't help but wonder where his mind is wandering. Is he trying to put together the Void science? How could two people *possibly* have completely different experiences in the Void? Or maybe he is remembering my test results in Portugal and that my thinking had somehow 'changed' in there. I know I have thought a lot about that and sometimes I am still not sure if I can trust my own eyes. Maybe he thinks I am crazy. I am not so sure myself.

And me talking about the man in the Void, that has to make a data-driven, hard-facts, science-freak like Michael crazy. Well, the most obvious answer is that I imagined him so that is what Michael is probably thinking but how can he explain the miraculous healing of my clearly damaged leg? He can't push that away as mental magic. Or maybe, hopefully, he is thinking about me. Just me. Maybe he is wondering where we go from here, seeing as I just changed the entire basis of our silly little fantasy relationship.

I feel like he is becoming attached to me. *I know he is.* And I suddenly feel terrible for it, like I have been leading him on, and that I have been using him for a ride. And not just this ride. I feel like I have been playing with his emotions and it's all just a game for me. *It's not my fault. I am just a silly six-teen-year-old girl and I don't mean to hurt anyone.*
Gabby, that's no excuse and you know that!
No. I know I am hurting him. I just don't know what to do about it. And I can't stop being with him because I think I love him.

Some hours later, we pull into the packed parking lot of the Vicente Calderon Stadium, Michael buys a ticket and I head to the locker rooms, packed with strong girls, beast women, and I cannot stop staring at their intense bones, sinewy muscles and the wild, savage looks in their eyes as if they are cannibals and I am on the menu.

We exit the locker room and head toward the stadium entrance. The hall, long and wide, stretches up toward the field and I see the stands in the distance, as if looking at a different planet through a telescope. As the other girls and I take the final steps out into the open, bright lights suddenly beaming down on us, the nearby crowd erupts into applause, a contagious applause that ripples across the home team side of the stands, then practically the whole stadium population begins shouting excitedly and I see a mother holding a crying baby and she looks at me and smiles like she knows me. I am vaguely uneasy.

As we finish the warm up, bodies streaming with perspiration, I notice a section of the stands holding up large letters that spell, G-O-G-A-B-B-Y-G-O, and I begin to shiver uncontrollably.

The fans howl rhythmically, "Ooohhhh, yeeeeaaaahhhhh, ooohhhh!"

I see Michael, there in the stands, not too far from our pit area. He must have paid a good chunk of money for that seat. I smile at him uncontrollably and wave. I can't help it. Looking at him, I can't stop myself from smiling. His eyes hold my body in a warm embrace, following me as if they are attached by cords. I see longing in his face and I force myself to look away. *Focus girl! You have an important race to run!*

I am warmed up already but trying to set my mind right, to focus, so I start running the outside loop alone, the one with no obstacles. After a few slow laps my head comes together so I blast off with a full-on sprint for two-hundred meters in front of the stands and they lose their minds. It is an immense crowd, a packed stadium, at least 40,000 and a good portion in section near me chants, "Go, Gabby, Go!"

I stop for a moment, allowing the sweat to bead, and look at them, placing a fake smile on my face and waving, waving to the sea of faces wearing Philadelphia red, faces happy and excited as if something momentous is about to happen and they are going to be able to tell their water-cooler friends where they were when it happened. They're watching me as if I am some kind of magician who is about to perform a trick. I can suddenly sense forty-thousand wills pressing me forward, irresistibly, fantastically, win, win, win. And suddenly I realize that I am not free. Whatever these people expect of me, I must do or die trying. A sinking feeling grips my heart, an extreme hollowness, a feeling of futility, that I am merely a ridiculous wooden puppet, pushed, pulled, controlled, by the will of this manic mass of faces in the stands. After the *Sports Illustrated* debacle I dreaded the thought that I might become some form of role model, that I would lose the tiny morsel of freedom that I had if I came into the spotlight. But instead of a role model, someone who people look up to, someone young girls would imitate, me influencing them, I am a puppet and I must do what *they* expect.

Shaking off that dreadful thought and looking down from the crowd to the other athletes I see some old familiar faces. It is Ultraball off-season and many of the top Pre runners are here from both farm and pro teams, some probably trying to gain more exposure, making names for themselves so they can demand more money in negotiations, others probably wanting to grab a slice of the substantial prize money from this event, and others, the marquee names, are paid by the race organizers just to show up since it helps to fill the stands. A few girls I know from the Philadelphia Liberty are here, Jena and Mercury; and my two girlfriends from my old team, Sidney and Cyndi (See and Cee); and a few from Brazil, Velocity Jones and her two pets, Carilla and T'mekah. Velocity's eyes fling daggers at me as she curls half her upper lip in disgust.

I walk over to the three of them, saying, "What is *your* problem?"

"My problem. I don't have a problem. You have the problem."

"Alright, so I guess I'm stupid. You're the one who broke my leg yet I am the one with the problem. Tell me what it is Velocity."

"Your problem is you don't belong here."

Carilla sneers, "Yeeaaahh!"

"Apparently not. I qualified, I'm here," I reply.

"Only because they absolutely couldn't believe that someone as inferior as you would even try to be in our league."

T'mekah sneers, "Yeeaaahh!"

A large curved vein presses itself through the dark skin of Velocity's forehead. "Face it, it's your DNA. You will never be as good as us. The only reason you should be here is to sit in the stands or mop the floor."

Carilla sneers, "Yeeaaahh!"

"You don't deserve to be on the same track as us."

T'mekah sneers, "Yeeaaahh!"

Velocity turns on her heel, walking away. The other two follow, giving each other high-fives and laughing.

I am ready to squash her right there, even though she towers over me, but thank God See and Cee run up and place their hands on my arms, saving me from being killed. "C'mon, Let's go, Gabby. It's not worth it," they both say at the same time.

"I know, I know. But can you believe that! The nerve of that girl!"

See says, "Just stay away from her, Gabby—"

Cee says, "She just wants to ruin your chances—"

See says, "You don't want to get disqualified for fighting."

I blow my air out slow, looking at Velocity's back, her talking strategy to her coaches as she occasionally looks back at me and smirks. "You're right. It's good to see you two. It's been a few weeks, huh? How's things?"

See starts. "Great here—"

Cee says, "Me too—"

See says, "I've been keeping up—"

Cee says, "Leading the pack is tough—"

See says, "AZ-PG is great—"

Cee says, "No problems so far—"

See says, "Just hoping to move up to the bigs—"

Cee says, "You know that—"

See looks at Cee, then says, "Cee doesn't have it so good though—"

Cee's eyes dart to See, then back to me, then says, "Well, you know NuGen is a lot more aggressive than AZ-PG. They have a new test and it is such a pain."

"What is it?"

"They inject you with some junk—I think they call it nanobots or something. A quick finger prick in a little machine before the race then a blood test after the race and their screens spit out all these graphs showing exertion levels, oxygen levels, all kinds of stuff—basically they can tell if you're running

The Secret

at full potential or if you're slacking," she exhales, then continues, "At first I thought it might be a good idea—You know I'm a data freak, right? But then they started really using it against us, punishing us for being *just* under threshold—like 99% isn't good enough. It just really sucks right now. Sometimes they act like they own me which totally rubs me the wrong way, but what can I do, right?"

"Yeah," pensively, shallowly, I say. Then changing subjects, "Listen, my heat's up next, can we talk later? I have someone I want you to meet."

I glance back up over Cee's shoulder at Michael, him staring at me lovingly, tilt my head slightly and give him a playful wink. He smiles broadly and gives me a thumbs up.

Cee says excitedly, "Yeah, me too! I want you to meet my new boy-friend!"

Gathering with my heat at the staging area, waiting for the announcer to call our names, looking for Michael out in the stands, the blood drains from my body as my eyes touch on the translucent Void-man sitting there, just behind Michael, in the audience, hands on his knees, back unnaturally erect, face pointing forward, staring as if in a trance. *Can't anyone see him?*

I frantically wave to Michael. He waves back and I begin jumping in the air and pointing behind him. He turns his head, scans behind, looks back at me and shrugs his shoulders. Just then the Void-man turns his head toward me mechanically, like slow gears, cogs and pinions are in his neck, his eyes momentarily flash my way and the scent of cinnamon and clove surrounds me. *What's going on?! Did he follow me out?!*

They call us up to the starting blocks and my wobbly legs carry me to the field as if I am floating on a cloud. The gun fires and I am off, barely able to run, and I want to cry.

I am a good fifty meters behind the last girl. I shake my head vigorously, trying to focus and speed up. At the half point I catch the back of the pack and Carilla and T'mekah seem to be slowing down for me intentionally. As I pass them they smile at each other and form a wall right behind me, too close, forcing me to speed up or be mowed over. Trying to pull away from them, we become a three person arrow, darting ahead, and we three catch the front of the pack becoming a jumble of seven runners; too close together. Velocity Jones slows and moves directly to my right. A flashback of blood, spittle and knee shredding pain spikes my brain and I realize I have to get out of there NOW!

At the next obstacle, they make their move, one of the two in the back kicks my foot out from under me as Velocity slams into my shoulder, my body uncontrollably spinning. My head suddenly turned toward the stands I see Void-man staring directly at me, body glowing neon white and a sudden flash blinds me. Cloves. *Why do I smell cloves?* I unconsciously reach my hand out toward the ground, feeling my body falling and my hand hits the short obstacle wall and I somehow, miraculously, cart-wheel over it landing in front of Velocity, pointing in the right direction, me speeding off, Velocity crashing into Carilla and T'mekah, taking them out of the race. The crowd explodes into fierce applause.

Crossing the finish line, winning my heat, the Void-man in the stands on my mind, I barely slow down, run off the course and straight towards Michael's section of the stands and he's gone. The Void-man is gone.

Suddenly, like being shaken from a daze, I notice the fans all around so I smile, wave, then trot off toward the pit area.

Was he really there, in the stands? Did he disappear? Why can't anyone else see him?

Out of the corner of my eye I see several Tech Specs in Blue-black suits at the NuGen pit hovering over screens with charts and graphs. Sebastian is one of them. Another is barking at two girls for not meeting quota. John Murray is there, not saying anything, hand grabbing his chin, forehead creasing, clearly uncomfortable. I would love to go talk to him.

Stretching my hamstrings on a bench I watch See and Cee race then stand and scream my head off when they take first and second. Celebrating as they walk toward our pit, arms around each other's shoulders, waving at the stands, they stroll toward me. We hug and hug and hug.

Sebastian Roberts walks up and I am wondering why a NuGen Tech Spec would be over here when Cyndi turns, jumps on him and says, "Gabby! Here he is! My boyfriend!" then plants a big kiss on his cheek.

Sebastian extends his hand, saying, "We met at the New York Open, remember?"

"Sure, I remember," I say, shaking his hand.

"I saw your name on the list, but I wasn't sure if I would see you here since you weren't booked for any of the flights to Madrid."

Wondering why he would check such things, I reply, "I came in through Portugal."

"Oh..." he answers slowly, as if something doesn't make sense. "Well, it's nice to meet you again. Just stopped over to say Hi. I have to be back at my screen. Duty calls, you know."

As he walks off, Cyndi says, clearly smitten, "Isn't he the cutest, Gabby?"

"Sure. Hope it works out. Yeeeooohh!" I jump as someone grabs me from behind and spin around, saying, "Oh, Kyle... You scared me!"

As we turn back to face the two girls, Kyle reaches for my hand, but I move it then he looks toward See and Cee and says, "Hey girls. Good job out there. The three of you are the top three seeds for finals so far and the next couple qualifying rounds don't have anyone threatening. Congratulations, solid races all around."

"Thanks Kyle," they both say at the same time.

I don't have to look up into the stands to know that Michael is watching and I could not be more uncomfortable right now.

"Gabby, I totally didn't expect you here. If I would have known you were coming I could have arranged for us to ride the plane together, you know, we could have spent some time together."

The Secret

"I didn't know you were going to be here either." I flash a glance up to the stands, where Michael is sitting and I catch his eyes then he quickly looks away, back out at the race.

"How are you getting back?"

Before I can answer Cee blurts out, "Ooooh, is this the one you wanted us to meet? Is this your boyfriend?"

"Err... Not exactly. It's complicated," I say, looking to Kyle for help.

"We've only just met recently actually and are going out on our first date soon," Kyle replies, placing his hand on my shoulder for a few moments then sliding it off.

See turns to me, saying, "I wanted to tell you when I saw him at your house. We've known Kyle for a while—"

Cee says, "Yeah Gabby, of all those NuGen pencil pushers—"

They both looks up at Kyle and say together, "No offense—"

Then they turn back to me, See saying, "He's the best—"

Cee says, "He's always there to help—"

See says, "And doesn't beat us down like some of the others." See looks at Cee, tilting her head to the side.

Cee jumps in, "Stop it Sidney! Sebastian is not like that!"

"I know, I know, I'm kidding."

Looking out to the field, the next qualifier just ending, Kyle says, "Okay girls, have to run."

"See ya," See and Cee says simultaneously.

As he walks away, over See's shoulder I see him rolling up something with two fingers of his right hand, the hand that was on my shoulder, and it looks like it might be a strand of my hair. He tucks whatever it is into his pocket.

See grabs my attention and says, "Gabby! Listen to this one!"

I look at her.

"Okay, okay, okay, looking down the stairs at an Ultraball game, a fan spots an open seat close to the pits. He asks the man sitting next to it if the seat is taken.

'No,' he replies. 'I used to take my wife to all the games, but ever since she passed away, I've gone alone.'

'Why don't you invite a friend?'

'I can't. They're all at the funeral.' "

I smile, mercifully, saying, "Now that was terrible!"

With Velocity and her two goons not advancing, the finals are relatively uneventful and first, second and third fall out to Sidney, Cyndi and myself. It feels great when they place the third place medal around my neck, standing next to my two best friends.

After we clean up, I say bye to the girls, congratulate them again and sneak off. I text Michael to meet me at the car and when I arrive, he's not too talkative. In fact he is a brick wall, expressionless, cold and dead.

As we pull to the lot exit, I try to make conversation as if everything is the same, even though I know it is most certainly *not* the same. "So what did you think of your first Pre match?"

He pulls out of the parking lot, replying coldly and in a low voice, as if I am a distraction, "It was okay."

What do I do? What do I say? Michael, Michael, can't I have you for just a few moments more?

"Did you see that crash between Velocity and those two girls? They almost took me out." I lean my shoulder toward him and smile, to, maybe, make him look at me, pay attention to me, like before, but he doesn't acknowledge my movement.

"Yeah, I saw that." He makes a sharp, quick left, bouncing my body away from him, against the car door.

The smile is erased from my face but I haven't given up yet. "And what did you think? How did it look from your angle? Did it look intentional?" My voice cracks, just a little, and I notice it myself. *Control, Gabriella, control. Keep control of yourself. Control the situation.* I choke back and vow to not let my voice crack again. I refuse to cry.

"I guess," he replies as if I am a tiny flying insect distracting him from some deep thoughts.

Forcing my happy voice back, full of rose petals and lavender, I sing, "You guess? That's it?" and tilt my head playfully.

His voice doesn't antagonize. It has no rage, no anger. It is just cold and dead and that is the worst of all. "I couldn't tell." His voice doesn't say he is mad, it says '*I don't care.*' He turns onto the highway.

"Wait! You're jumping on the highway? Don't you want to go out to eat or something?" I can't help it, the panic shows as if it was a giant fluffy pink dress with sixteen petticoats.

"I have to be back at the lab."

"Ohh—"

I pause for a while, trying to think of what to say, desperate for just one more morsel of time with him, desperate to not lose my fantasy. Portugal and Michael are my escape from reality and today my *fantasy* and my *reality* collided and I am in no way ready to lose either one. There must be somehow, someway to separate them, to salvage this. *Maybe just air it out, tell him the truth.*

"Michael, I know you saw me with that guy. Are you upset?"

"Yes I did see you and no, I am not upset."

I find it hard to believe but it really appears so. He is so calm and resolute. Not speeding, not driving angry, hands on the wheel as if all is well in the world of Michael McAllister.

I know I have been too selfish, trying to salvage my little fantasy when eventually it must disappear and anyway it is not only about me and what I want. *I know that. I don't* want to hurt Michael. I mean, I never did, I just wanted a little escape, a little fun, and I know I am hurting him, but perhaps I can somehow make it all better.

The Secret

"Michael? What's wrong? Please? Why won't you talk to me? Can't we just talk?"

Now it's his turn to be quiet. The road noise echoes in my ears and then, after a long moment, I see a soft shudder cross his face then it disappears.

"Nothing's wrong. You have your life back... That's great... Really, I am happy for you. Really—" His voice is back to being cold and unemotional as if he is standing among his physicist peers stating facts in some scientific seminar.

The moment I have been dreading is here and it hurts. My insides are thrashing and it hurts. The muscles in my jaw are tense, too tense, and it hurts. I don't know how to deal with this and it hurts. I can't seem to breathe enough, as if the air doesn't provide enough oxygen, my lungs are struggling, and it hurts.

"Michael? I, I, I don't know what to say—"

He cuts me off, cold and short, "Then don't say anything."

His voice, coated with ice-cold daggers, stabs me, stabs me smooth and slow because it has no venom, no bite. He just says it matter-of-factly and unemotionally, as if we never had anything, as if we never had a moment in paradise, as if those moments never happened, as if they really were a fantasy, not real. 'Don't say anything' he says, as if those fairy tale days and magical evenings in Portugal were nothing. Forget about them. They are gone, lost forever.

"But, but, Michael? I don't want you mad at me." I turn my face away and wipe my tears, over and over, I wipe my tears.

"I'm not mad at you. I'm mad at me—mad at me for dreaming, thinking a beauti—" He stops midsentence, shakes his head quickly then says, "Nothing. Don't worry about it. I'm not mad at you."

I want to tell him something, to say something, anything, to say that he has a chance with me, to say that I enjoy myself so much more with him than Kyle, to say those words that I can never say, the words that would destroy my reality, my mother, and everything, to say 'I love you' in the most passionate way, pouting my lips, winking and smiling as I throw my arms around his neck. But I can't say anything because I know we have no future together. I can't say anything because I know this is just a fantasy. I can't say anything because my heart hurts too much. I can't say anything because I know that anything that would come out of my mouth would be leading him on and I can't hurt him any more.

My hair is flying again so I roll up my side window and my hair falls down, dead.

Liberty

"It is my pleasure to invite you to join the Philadelphia Liberty's farm team! The Philadelphia Freedom!" Smith says, handing me a recognition certificate hidden in two pieces of stiff cardboard along with a multi-page contract.

"Hooray!" Mom howls, hands clapping baby-sized mini-claps. "Ooohh, Gabby! I am soo happy for you!" But I think she is only happy because of Smith.

Cee hugs me, saying, "Good job, Gabby! I knew you would do it!"

See says, "It's so great to have you back!"

Kyle gives me a quick, emotion-less hug then says, "You deserve it, Gabby."

"Now for the cake!" Mom announces as if I am at my ten year-old birthday party.

I am happy and having a great time, but it is more because I am surrounded by all my friends than being offered the contract. I secretly wish Dad were here. Michael too. But I try not to think about them; I am trying to close the book on that part of my life.

After everyone leaves, I read through the contract and consider not signing it, still unsure if I want that life back. I still don't know who I am or who I want to be and being on that team with all its rules makes me feel like I am some pre-packaged commodity. In the end I sign it.

On Monday I report to Coach Michelle Donavan and with most of the girls on the team it's like I never left; some love me, some resent me. Qi Tan and Nomi Franklin are the other two new girls who make the team.

"Okay girls, gather around!" Coach Donavan barks out. "We have a tough schedule this year and with three new girls," Donavan glances at me, but not Qi or Nomi, "we have a lot of work to do!"

Elektra, the girl who replaced me last year after my accident, hoots out, "We're here to work, Coach!"

Elektra Silver is sponsored by AZ-PG, like See, and she really helps to unite the girls in a common bond against Donavan according to Cee and See. I think Elektra is being sarcastic but Donavan doesn't pick up on it.

"Don't worry, girls! Work you will! I want to make one thing clear," Donavan glances at me again, "I don't care how many tickets you sell, if you are not pulling your load, you're gone!" I am the only one still in high school and Donavan does not seem to appreciate the fact that she has to make special allowances for me again.

Elektra and Maxine both look my way as if I am diseased.   Max growls, "Don't worry, Coach, we're going to work."

Elektra hoots, "We're going to win!"

See and Cee roll their eyes.

"Last year, I am now willing to say, I tried something that really didn't work. I was very cold and hard on all of you. My goal was to take a bunch of different girls, from all different backgrounds, and with different abilities and mind-sets, yes, to take all of that and meld it into a unified team. The method I chose, for those who were not here last year, was to be a total jerk in hopes that the team would unify against a common enemy—me. I was hoping that all of you might dislike me enough that it would bring all of you together. It was actually starting to work until a few things happened, well I won't get into that, but in the end we had two groups not one."

Donavan pauses, scans the group, then continues, "This year, I am not using that strategy, thankfully. We have some new faces and some old, but I still want to unify the team so we are going to establish a mentoring program for the new people and I want to ask the people who have differences to put them aside for the benefit of something higher than individual needs, put them aside for the team, be a part of something greater than yourself. So for you new girls, I want each of you to be mentored by one of the others until you learn the ropes. Qi, you're with Sidney."

Qi howls, "Sidney? You killing me!"

"Okay, enough chirping! Qi, you obviously don't know how I operate. You are excited to be on the team so that's good. And you are obviously fast or you wouldn't be here. But I make the rules around here, so obey my orders or you're gone!" Donavan's hard eyes stab Qi, then she continues, all business, "Nomi with Cyndi. And Gabriella, you probably think you know what you are doing, but just in case I want you with Elektra."

Elektra lets out a sigh.

Donavan's eyes pierce Elektra and she sits up taller. Donavan pauses again, looks down at her screen, then looks up and tells us all the boring details about team behavior emphasizing that we represent the team even when we are not in uniform. The same stuff I heard last year so I zone out to most of it until she says, "And we are going to try out having two team captains. I want you all to have someone you can go to besides me, maybe handle problems internally if needed. The captains for now are going to be Sidney and Maxine."

We all clap. Max looks embarrassed.

Donavan continues, "Now one more thing, there has been a rule modification, new for this season, that is going to affect our training so pay attention."

The room grows quiet.

"Most of you know the Pre rules, at least you better, or you're gone, and so far that is all we train for, but due to the Sacramento game last year—most of you remember that one—a ruling has come down that the Pre runners can also play on the field."

"*What?* Coach, that's ridiculous!" See and Cee yell out and I wonder how they always seem to speak at the same time.

"I know, I know. Right now only one female plays the field on any Ultraball team, the Galaxy team, and she's one tough cookie."

"She's a man, I tell ya," Cee yells out.

Donavan's eyes dart to Cee saying, "Cyndi!"

Cee looks down sheepishly and says softly, "Well, she is."

Murmurs dying down, she continues, "Alright. If I can continue. The teams wanted the flexibility of using their fast Pre runners on the field in the case of—injuries maybe—or, who knows—distracting the men. I don't know, but anyway, of course you know that to be tackled on the field you have to be holding the ball, so as long as you don't have the ball, you should be fine. Okay? Let's begin!"

It is base-training time and a few weeks before our first matches so we start with slow pace distance runs and run them day after day, everyday, but it doesn't feel tedious because I know what comes next; the pain. After a long summer of hard long-distance runs up and down White Clay trails, I push, showing that I am ready to get to work.

The days fly by and my ledger already has me up to ten miles at recovery pace, about six minute-miles for me, but I stay with See and Elektra who are running 5:35 average. I refuse to fall into that same rut I was in last year. Qi pulls off the road, heaving, hands grasping her shorts, and looking up she says, "I feel terrible! I thought I was in shape, but this is impossibly hard!"

Cee stops with her and cheers her up, "Don't worry. You can do it! We all went through the same pain last year. You can make it!"

Later we are in a stretching circle and we talk quietly amongst ourselves, catching up on our summers and getting to know the new girls and I can feel a completely different vibe from See and Max. Apparently Donavan has been grooming them to lead the team for awhile. In the circle I ponder how everything is becoming a giant blur. Being in High School and being a semi-pro athlete at the same time leaves me almost no time for anything. My life is composed of school and the team with nothing in between. The training is harder than I remember it and I feel at a distinct disadvantage with all the special treatment that the NuGen girls have. To run six miles in just one round during the game, at top speed, we have to run countless miles at a variety of different paces and tempos during practice. Since I am the youngest and still in high school, I am only putting in about eighty miles a week. The top runners, See, Cee and

Elektra are putting in around one-hundred miles a week with one-fifth on the long Saturday morning run. For me that is an unbearable sixteen miles and I have no idea how they do twenty after the intense weekday schedule. One thing that certainly does help some of the girls is the Nugen techniques. Sebastian and Kyle are in almost daily to do nanobot monitoring to Qi, Cee and Maxine and I almost feel jealous to not be one of them. Qi quickly becomes much faster and one of the top runners and it is all I can do to not be the slowest. Last year the NuGen girls would travel out to their site once a week. This year, NuGen has an office right at our training facility.

*****

A week has gone by since the day I made it back on the team and pushing hard in those first few days is coming back to haunt me now. I am really sore. There is a major difference, I am finding out, between being in shape and being fit. I can blow a hole through a course and win a race on any given day, but to do that consistently, day after day, takes an entirely different level of fitness and I am not there yet. Today we all run a two-mile warm-up out to the grass field with a ¼ mile track, stretch lightly while See divides us into three groups then run from eight to sixteen 200 meter pick-up sprints at lactate threshold pace with no more than 60 seconds rest in between, rest being defined as running at recovery pace.

Donavan seems to enjoy pointing out that I was on the *Sports Illustrated* header as she often says things like, "C'mon, pretty girl! Let's see *the new face of Ultraball* put out some effort or you're gone!"

After that blistering workout, my head is in a cloud, intoxicated with race endorphins, and I can't wait to enter the stretching circle. As we stretch, with Donavan several paces away watching, See and Max take turns goading us, asking us what each of us wants out of this season, as if it is now somehow up to us.

"Last year, my only goal was to perform the best I could, as an individual, so that I might make it to the Liberty." Looking around at the group, See continues, "This year, after not being chosen, I realized that they are looking for much more than an individual. They are looking for a team member. And that is now what I am. I am willing to do what ever it takes, including sacrificing myself and my own goals, to see the team win. What do the rest of you think?"

One by one we come around to the idea and make a decision, a collective decision.

"It is going to be tough," Max says, "but we have to learn to lean on each other."

Glancing over at Donavan, her hiding a smile behind her hand, I realize what she is doing, empowering us, trying to make us take ownership of the team. Once we each take ownership of such a high altitude goal, a goal of winning at all costs, we are allowing Donavan to train us as hard as necessary to achieve that goal.

I look over at Kyle behind his screen, studying graphs and realize that seeing him almost everyday is different than I expected. He is great at his job, but I couldn't tell you anything that he likes. He is all business around me. I notice Sebastian and Kyle whisper or pass notes to each other quite a bit. I understand that not all the athletes are sponsored by NuGen so they have secrets, but it still makes me suspicious.

Trying to start up a conversation later, I say, "Hey Kyle, how's the monitoring going?"

"Quite well, Qi is up seven percentage points."

"Good for her. Could you give *me* any pointers?"

"Of course. I noticed that you could twist your left hip a little more on your hurdles. If we recorded you in motion capture I could draw some lines on the screen and tell you exactly how many degrees your hips are off." His response seems strangely unemotional.

"Sure. That would be nice."

"Ok, tomorrow then," he turns to walk away.

"You won't get yourself in trouble?" I say, wanting more connect time with him.

Not breaking his stride, he leans his head back saying, "No, not for you."

I wonder if he means he is willing to risk trouble for me or maybe that he is somehow authorized by NuGen to help me. It seems I can never decipher exactly what he means.

Kyle leaves and I am the last in the locker room when I hear something fall over in the conference room. Tiptoeing slowly across the room I put my ear to the conference room door, hearing muffled noises that sound like people wrestling.

Flinging the door open, I surprise Sebastian pressing Cyndi up against the white board.

"Oh... It's you two."

Sebastian backs away from Cyndi, a worried look in his eyes. He knows that fraternizing with the players is prohibited.

I start to close the door saying, "Don't let Donavan catch you—or you're gone!"

We all laugh.

Sebastian says, "Gabriella wait—"

Cee giggles, tickling his ear.

I stop and say, "Don't worry. Our secret," and close the door.

*****

About a week later I wake up from the weirdest dream. I go to the bathroom, sweating. *Ooof! It's the middle of the night!* I hate waking up in the middle of the night. Staring in the mirror, I think about what I just saw in the dream. A little scary. In the dream I am sleeping and wake up, in the dream, to see the Void-man hovering over me, staring at me, whispering something at me. I can't quite make out what he is saying. He repeats the phrase over and over but I can't make it out. *Weird.*

The alarm goes off; Groundhog Day all over again. School and training, school and training; I want to strangle that ground hog. Today's run is a fartlek, a constant run with no stopping but varying paces and speeds that constantly change through out the run. We each have a cue sheet of paces to run and for how long. See and Max like to set up things by time not distance. My sheet says, "two mile warm-up, 90 seconds A T pace, 4 minutes at steady pace. Alternate. Do this for 55 minutes." A T pace, or anabolic threshold pace, is about how fast I would run for a 3.1 mile race, a standard 5k run; right now that is a little faster than a blistering 4:45-minute mile. Steady pace should allow me to recover for the next 90 second run, but is not slow either, about 6:45 for me. It is a terribly hard work out.

After my run and shower, I catch Kyle alone just before leaving, grab his elbow and pull him around the corner so we won't be seen if someone walks in.

"Hey, I want to talk to you."

"Sure. What's up."

There is an unexpected hardness to his eyes. Blinking, they suddenly become soft. *Strange.* "Are you still interested in me? I feel like you treat me cold here."

"Just don't want the other girls to think anything. Sebastian doesn't treat Cyndi any different here."

That's what you think. "So where are we?"

"I've been very busy getting the team off the ground with the rule change and with the new girl, Qi, but I definitely like seeing you here, even if it has been on a professional basis. How about we go out on our date? Say, next week?"

He is so robotic, unnatural, like a preprogrammed automaton sometimes, like his charm can be turned on and off depending upon the situational need and it creeps me out.

"Yeah. Can Smith call my mom?"

"I will take care of it."

Mom drives us home and I zombie my way to bed. I don't know what day it is. I blink my eyes and the alarm goes off. *Groundhog! Where are you!*

It's another day and another different style run is thrown at us. Donavan drives us out to Lancaster, Pennsylvania, an area full of Amish people driving horse-drawn buggies and really old-looking, wooden covered-bridges. We run a moderate length course that has several steep 100-meter hills. The tempo is 90 seconds hard, real hard actually, with a slow, full recovery pace for 60 seconds. For me I almost have to walk to recover that quickly. On my second walk, Nomi catches up to Cee and me, and says, "This sucks. My ankle hurts. It's just too sore from all the hills."

Cee says, "C'mon, you can do this. We'll stick together, okay?"

At the end of the run, we ride back to the practice grounds and everyone is quiet and battered. Cee has been bandaging her right knee for about a week now and she has been rubbing it the whole ride. Elektra and Nomi both have bandaged gashes from falling when missing jumps, Elektra's on her thigh and Nomi on both shins. I am beginning to wonder if this is worth it.

Cyndi and I are last to leave practice so I grab her to talk.

"So how are you coming along, Gabby?" She says as she packs her bag.

"Good. It's tough but I'm making it. Donavan is different this year but I still think she could be more supportive."

Closing her locker she looks up saying, "Well, maybe I shouldn't say, but—"

"What?"

Cyndi looks around, comes closer then whispers, "She didn't want you back. Said she didn't need any *picture girls.*"

"Ha! Well she certainly doesn't hide it."

She steps back, grabs her bags and keys, saying, "Well, we love you."

We head out toward the parking lot.

"Some of you anyway."

"Don't mind Elektra and Maxine. They're okay. Just takes time for them to grow on you."

"Like mold."

We both laugh.

"Stop it, girl. We're all on the same team."

Sometimes I wonder about that. "I know," changing the subject I say, "I see you and Sebastian are getting close."

Erasing her smile, she looks right at my face, saying, "I think I love him, Gabby."

"And how does he feel?"

She pauses a moment, considering the question, "I hope he feels the same way. You know those blue-black suits are so hard to read. It's like they train their emotions away."

"What's *up* with that? You know Kyle is the same way."

We stop at her car. "How is your relationship with him?"

"Honestly? I don't know." And it was true, I really didn't.

"Well he certainly is interested in you."

"Why would you say that?"

"I hear him and Sebastian talking about you all the time."

"Really?"

"Yeah, sure. Mostly work stuff. He has been helping you, right? I saw your graphs on their screens once."

"Yeah, he helps me," I say hollowly, but it isn't true, not to the level I would like anyway, "What kind of graphs? The same graphs like your graphs? The NuGen graphs?"

But doesn't that require nanobot injections?

She puts her bags in her back-seat. "Sure... Hasn't he showed them to you? Sometimes I wish they wouldn't show me mine. I see them too much."

"I guess I should ask to see them."

"Oh, I just remembered—so the other day they were looking at your charts *again* and I hear Kyle mention something about taking you out and getting closer." She winks and gives me a knowing smile.

"We are going out on a date soon. Taking me on a tour of the science labs at the main office."

"Cool! Get to see where the babies are test-tubed?"

"Hope so."

"That's where I came from!" she says like it was Mom talking about 'back home' in her dreamy voice.

I hear a noise so I say, "Alright, getting late."

"See you tomorrow."

Cee drives off and I head toward Mom's car then see Kyle.

"Hey Kyle, didn't know you were still here."

"On my way out. By the way, how's next Saturday. Available?" His voice seems cold.

"Sure."

Suddenly his eyes flash warm again, his body language shifting, standing there like a department store model. He sure is gorgeous. "Smith passed it through your Mom and she's fine with it, said he would escort us."

"Cool. Saturday it is."

I jump into Mom's car and she drives us off. I confirm with her about Saturday and she is more excited about it than I am. I pass out on the ride home and she shakes me awake when we pull into the driveway. Straight to bed and I am so tired that I can barely undress and I consider lying in the bed with my clothes on. I fall onto the mattress and am instantly asleep.

It's the middle of the night and I wake up in a puddle of sweat. It's the dream *again*. Every time the same thing; I am sleeping, in the dream, and wake up to see the Void-man hovering over me, staring at me, whispering something at me and it's always the same words. He repeats the phrase over and over. I made out the first two words so far. "Watch out—" Then I wake up. I mean really wake up. And he is not there, of course. *Thank God.* I would totally freak if he was *really* hanging over me while I was in bed, but since I know it is just a dream, I'm not so scared anymore.

NuGen Biotechnics

It's Saturday morning and Mom is worried about what I am going to wear like Kyle hasn't seen me sweaty and covered in mud so I finally cave and put on my long boots, leggings, brown suede vest and lace scarf.

Smith and Kyle show up and I am glad that Kyle is not wearing his blue-black suit. Smith has a nice silver SLK Daimler and I snicker because he looks like a chauffeur with Kyle and I sitting in the back.

Smith pulls us out onto the roadway and I say, "So what are we seeing today?"

Smith begins, "We can't show you everything, but I have authorization to take you on more than the standard tour."

I can't see Smith's face, but he is probably flashing his punctuation mark smile-not-smile.

Kyle continues, "We are going to take you back to Smith's lab, show you some of the research NuGen is working on."

"Cool." I try to sound even, maybe only mildly interested but I really want to know what these two are up to.

Driving through downtown Philadelphia, Smith pulls up to a newer building, twenty or so stories high and all black glass. He parks and we take the lift up to Badging where I am given a visitor's badge with my picture on it and my hand is scanned.

We pass through several of the boring lecture and display rooms. *All this stuff I already know. Hey, I am living it already.*

Once we leave the main floors, every door has hand scanners next to them and dome shaped mirror cameras above them. We go through several botanical rooms and Kyle tells me about the crop modifications, "We inject corn and soybeans with fish DNA so that it can be grown in salt water." He goes on talking about how it is done, using some sort of weird DNA bullet, and that it takes a lot of experimentation to do it right.

Looking at the tall, stalky corn with twenty or more ears, I say, "Can I ask a question?"

"Shoot," Smith says.

"This is kind of philosophical, but how much fish DNA can you put in the corn and it still be corn? I mean when does the corn stop being corn?"

Kyle and Smith look at each other then Smith says, "We have heard those arguments from the conservatives for years but I can assure you that everything we do here is perfectly legal and moral." His smile flashes.

We pass through rows and rows of various plants, obscenely large apples and oranges somehow growing on the same tree, other plants with roots hanging from cords like clothes on a clothesline, apparently not needing dirt, and others with unnaturally odd shaped and colored leaves.

"Of course, I understand that. But there is something bigger here isn't there?"

Walking past enormous, purple-leafed eggplants seated in a thick, salty, brine solution, parsley with full, thick leaves the size of lettuce and a tiny cherry tree only about two feet tall with enormous cherries the size of cantaloupes, Kyle says, "Yes. The bigger question is one of definition. Why do we have to define anything so rigidly?"

Smith holds his hand up to Kyle, "It's like this Gabriella. Every creature on this planet has been changing for eons due to environmental stressors. We are merely accelerating that process. What we do is perfectly natural." He holds his punctuation mark smile a moment too long and it morphs into a leering grin, then it's gone just as quickly.

We leave the botanical area, enter the hall then ride the lift up a few floors. The lift stops but the doors do not open. Smith runs his ID at the lift controls. I didn't notice the scanner before. Kyle and I run our IDs and scan our hands and the lift door opens to an immense room with a ceiling that is at least twenty feet high. The room probably occupies at least two whole floors. There are people in lab coats everywhere running various experiments on different sorts of animals, looking into microscopes and scanners while large robotic arms move tubes around, squirting various solutions into them. We leave the platform and take the staircase down to the main floor.

"I know what you are saying Smith, you see your work as merely accelerating evolution but let me ask you this—"

"Go on," Smith says as he leads us through the maze of lab-coats.

"Supposedly humans came from chimpanzees, right?"

"Not really, the theory of evolution states that humans and chimps diverged from a common ancestor, but I know where you are headed, go on—"

We stop in front of a set of cages, animals inside with extra appendages, arms, ears, eyes. One chimp has two extra arms, like little baby arms, coming out of the top of his head. Fully functional, they are peeling a banana.

Looking at these odd creatures, I continue, "Well, chimps and humans are different in many ways. Chimps don't have human rights, for example. I mean, a chimp can't sue me for hitting it with my car. But if we *alter* a human's DNA—"

Kyle interrupts, "Gabriella, you can't compare what we are doing with human DNA to chimps. C'mon, that's not fair. We are not making people into animals."

"I know, I know, bear with me—"

The next aisle has tanks of fish and amphibians, frogs, toads and newts, and several of the fish, having tiny arms and legs, walk out onto the rocky gravel of the tanks.

Smith jumps in, "Kyle, Gabriella has a point. It's like this... A chimp has somewhere in the neighborhood of 96% similarity with human DNA, but they certainly do not have 96% of the rights, of course. And they shouldn't, they aren't human."

"I agree with that," I say.

Smith continues, "Of course you do. Most everyone would. What we are doing at NuGen is not the same though. Even on the most modified humans—even the fourth gens are 100% human genetically. In general what we are doing is keeping all the best human DNA and removing all the worst. But Gabriella, keeping in the spirit of your question, let me ask you this—"

"What is it?" I say, looking up at the two of them.

"What if you could change your DNA, making yourself only 99% similar let's say, but making yourself superior in every way; faster, stronger, more disease resistant, smarter and longer lived—would you do it?"

We continue on aisle after aisle of tubes, machines and creatures, Smith stopping right in front of me.

"I, I don't know. I guess—"

"What if you had to go down to 98% but it would add a few hundred years to your lifespan? What then? Or what about down to 97% and you would be immune to all diseases and ultra-intelligent, able to instantly learn any language, calculate differential equations in your head or have such heightened perception that it is almost as if you can see things before they happen. "

"I think that might be cool. But we are losing something, right? When do we lose enough, change enough that we stop being human?"

Kyle jumps in, "Human? See Gabby, that's the whole problem. Why do you keep labeling things and putting them in a box? Who's to say what it really means to be human?"

"I see." *And maybe I see more than I want to.*

Just then Smith steps out of the way and I see a young boy, maybe nine or ten years-old, on a treadmill, running impossibly fast, insanely fast.

I didn't know treadmills could go that fast.

"What the?"

His extra long legs are a blur and he does not appear to be sweating or even trying hard. His torso is so short compared to his long, lean legs, legs that comprise about 75% of the height of his body. His stomach is sunk in and flat and his chest cavity bulges out like a wine barrel.

"How is this possible?" I ask.

"Just watch," Kyle replies.

Smith waves at a group of lab-coats and one of them hits some buttons on his screen and I see the display go up to twenty.

The young boy speeds up and the strain of the increased speed crosses his face ever so slightly.

"Kyle, is he really running twenty miles per hour?"

"Yes," he says, smiling widely.

"That's... that's... that's like a... three minute mile!"

"Yes, that's exactly what it is," he says smiling even more widely.

"That's impossible!"

He looks down at me, turns serious and says, "He can run faster."

"But how is this possible?"

Smith says, "That, my dear, is classified."

Smith waves his hand and they slow the young boy's treadmill then we move toward the back of the room and I wonder if what Smith said about the fourth gens having 100% human DNA is true.

An incredibly ancient looking man in a lab coat comes forward, wild-eyed, looking like a cross between the mad scientist who created Frankenstein and the Crypt Keeper. Long stringy grey hair, his gap-toothed mouth smiles as he opens it and hisses, "Gabriella Conceição, we have been expecting you!"

I shake his scary looking hand, then he turns his gaze toward Smith hissing, "Is she ready?"

Smith looks at me and says, "Gabriella, I thought you might want to see your profile. We could look at your DNA, give you some ideas about what your children might have to look forward to."

I look at Kyle, feeling betrayed and say, "I don't know about that."

Crypt Keeper grows oddly animated, hissing, "It is nothing Gabriella Conceição, just a tiny blood sample. We put it in the machine then all the magic happens!"

I wonder why he repeats my last name. Maybe he is proud that he can pronounce it correctly.

"Er... Maybe another time." This sudden feeling of being trapped, of being too far from the exit comes over me.

Kyle, sensing my panic, says, "It's okay. Another time perhaps."

Crypt Keeper looks immensely disappointed. And so does Smith.

The tour concludes and Smith leaves Kyle and I to eat lunch. We spend a couple hours together and he is suddenly sweet and caring. I still can't understand how he can turn on and off his emotions, almost like he can become a different person at will.

Smith picks us up, we walk to the car and head out on the highway toward home.

"Smith, can I ask you something?"

"Shoot."

"How did you meet my father?"

He pauses for a while, passing a few cars then settling into his lane. "We worked together."

"Doing what?"

"Your mother is going to kill me for telling you this, but here it is. Your father didn't sell clothes back in the old country, he was a research scientist, just like me. We worked together, gene spliced together, wrote papers together. Your father was a brilliant man."

I am suddenly aware of my skin when I say it. "Then why did NuGen want to kill him?"

"What? Gabriella, no. Where did you get that lie. NuGen would never—"

"Tell me why he left the lab. What happened? I know you know, Smith."

"Gabriella, I thought you knew this. You were a small child, but you were there. The soldiers came; we all left. It wasn't NuGen, the university or any one else. It was the government... It fell apart."

My only childhood memory comes flooding back. I quietly choke back a tear and say, "I'm sorry. I didn't mean to sound like I was accusing."

"No need to apologize my dear, we know what you went through was traumatic."

The car grows silent and I let Kyle hold my hand and it feels cold to me.

We ride the rest of the way to my house not saying much then Smith drops me off at home and Mom meets me at the door.

"So how was it?"

"Revealing."

I enter, knowing that Mom is not going to stop until she has soaked me for every useless detail at least three times.

"And?"

I tell her what she wants to know, "We're getting on fine, Mom. It's about what I expected. I mean, how can two people fall in love like this? There is no spontaneity."

"I know, I know, dear. It's hard for you, but don't worry, everything will be fine."

A chill runs down my spine as the hairs on the back of my neck stand on end.

"What did you say?"

"I said 'everything will be fine.' You know that Mija, everything is always fine. It will all work out."

"I, I just never heard you say that before."

"Oh, I don't know. I think it was something your father used to say long ago, when we lived back in the old country. I don't know why it just came to me now."

The Void-man said it too. But it couldn't have come from my mind, could it? If I didn't remember it, he couldn't have stolen it from my head, right?

"I think I want to go to my room and rest for a while. This is the first day I've had off and I think I want to waste the rest of it being lazy."

"Sure, Mija. Get some rest."

I walk toward the steps, grab the handrail then stop for a moment and turn back. "Mom?"

"Yes, Mija?"

"Does it ever get any easier?"

"What?"

"You know—all this—stuff," I pause for a moment, looking for the right word, then say, "Life?"

She stares at me for a moment then looks away and says, "No."

I start to go up the stairs then halt when she says, "Yes. Yes, it does. When you find out who you really are... and what's important to you, it becomes easier. Easier to choose, I mean, easier to see the right path."

The Kiss

Donavan barks, "Gabriella, in my office!" then walks away before I have a chance to question.

Following her in, she says, "Close the door behind you."
I close the door and stand in front of her desk, saying, "Coach?" as she looks down at her screen.
"Where do you see yourself in this organization?" she asks.
I have no idea what answer she is looking for. "Ah... I know I'm not the fastest, but the fans seem to like me. I fill a lot of seats. And sell a lot of merchandise."

Still looking down, she starts, "You are right. The fans do like you and the team owner likes the fans' money, so that is good. And you are also correct, you are not the fastest. Out of seven girls, right now I would probably rank you fifth, maybe sixth," she pauses, looks up from her screen and continues, "Maybe if I didn't count Max and Qi, who both can be enforcers, I would rank you fourth out of five. The only runner behind you is that dimwit Nomi—and I don't think she is going to last long, which would put you right at the bottom of our runners." She is staring up at me and I don't know what to say.

Looking back down like she still can't believe what she is reading, she says, "Today I received an odd request from one of our sponsors. NuGen. They are offering to add you into their program. Do 'bot performance monitoring, everything that all the other NuGen girls have. I have no idea why they would offer this, it makes no sense to me, but frankly, I don't care why. All I want to do is win, which means making you faster, and if this can improve your performance then I am all for it. Of course, it is up to you, not me, so if you refuse, I understand. Some of the girls feel like the monitoring is an invasion of privacy, and I get that, but seeing as you are someone who could really use the performance boost, I think you should consider it."

She stops talking and the room is silent except for an old-style clock that ticks. I become uncomfortable, standing there, then say, "Okay coach. I guess I will think about it." I chew my lower lip and say, "Is that all?"

"Yes."

I turn to walk out then she says, "And Gabriella?"

I stop, hand on the doorknob, not turning around. "Yes, Coach?"

"I think I was wrong about you—and I know you have it in you—to be faster. It's there, I can see it now. You just have to find out how to unlock it."

Well, that was uncharacteristically supportive of her. "Thanks, Coach."

I walk out and see Kyle and Sebastian whispering to each other on the other side of the hall. As soon as they spot me, they stop and Sebastian walks away. Sebastian doesn't look too happy. Even though they were whispering, I think they may have been arguing.

Walking out onto the practice field I see, finally, that Donavan is introducing obstacle running and technique drills. It is what I am best at and I am eager for an opportunity to shine. Standing on the field, blocking us from the course, I can't wait for her to finish another one of her little speeches.

"Listen to me now because I am going to teach you something that applies to all of your life, not just running these courses! In order to succeed, you need more than just speed! Much more, in fact! You need a sweet combination of talent, physical durability, meaning that your body doesn't break too easily, courage, and mental fortitude, meaning that your mind can overcome that voice screaming in the back of your head, that voice that constantly screams, 'Stop! Stop! Stop! Running hurts!' "

We all smile at that then she continues, "Now all of you have some amount of talent, or you wouldn't be here. But now we are going to find out about the other qualities, because without the others you will never make it! The most talented Pre-runner here will die if she has no courage, if she is afraid. When the moment of truth comes, if you become petrified with fear, unable to act, no amount of talent will save you and you will lose!"

As she speaks, I wonder how durable my body is. *Velocity broke me. Am I weak?*

Donavan continues, "The nice thing is that courage and mental fortitude are things you can learn!" Stepping out of our path to the obstacles, she adds, "And I *aim* to teach!"

Qi's ankle is sore so she sits out and spends the day water-running in the pool and alternately heating it in the barrel Jacuzzi but the rest of us are hitting it full force. Donavan is yelling out at us, "Own your energy! You control it! Don't feel negative about your results! Make yourself feel how you want to feel then the results will come based on those feelings!"

Max is hitting it harder than ever. Lines of salt crystals form crooked hieroglyphics all over her shorts and top. Elektra's and Nomi's gashes are mostly healed and leaping obstacles, swinging on ropes, and ducking under wood bridges feels great to everyone. The workout is strenuous but all the long distance base training at the beginning of the season is really starting to pay off as we are not fatiguing and our recovery times have shortened dramatically.

We start off cautious but after the third pass the pace inches up and everyone looks smooth. By the tenth lap, the pace is murderous and no one can catch See or Cee, although Elektra is trying hard. Nomi and Max have fallen off the back but both appear pleased. At the break Nomi exclaims, "I have never run that fast!" and Max, scribbling her log onto the team screen, says, "I am 30 seconds faster than this time last year! Pretty good!"

After practice, I catch Cee in the locker room. "Hey Cee, can we talk?"

"Sure. What's up, girl?"

"NuGen is offering to monitor me and I was wondering what you think of that."

Cee's face is normally overly optimistic smiles so I am surprised to see her flat-line. "Well, huh... They did, did they?"

"Yeah. Weird, huh?"

"I guess Kyle might have pulled some strings for you? Maybe he likes you more than you think?"

"Maybe."

"Well, it's a mystery to me why they would do it. I can't see how it would benefit the company to have you of all people, do well... but as far as the monitoring, it does help. They show me charts, graphs, and hard data that display my performance and it is laid out against a video of my race so that at any point in the race I can see exactly where I can extract more energy. Even a tiny tweak makes a big difference in this game. It has definitely helped me improve. But of course, and you already know this, the oversight can be irritating. I don't feel like I own my own body sometimes."

"I remember. You told me something about it before."

She pulls the last of her gear out of her locker then turns. "Hey! You didn't tell me how your date went!" The old excitable Cyndi is suddenly back.

"Great. Saw some really cool stuff there. I definitely think NuGen has the future of athletics wrapped up."

"Really?"

I tell her about the kid running the three-minute mile and we talk mindlessly about what the future holds then, after a pause, she asks about Kyle.

"Oh, I don't know. I mean look at him. He is gorgeous, successful and with a promising future—everything I should want, right?"

"But there's something missing?"

I sit on the bench and lean back against my locker, "I'm trying, really I am, but I just don't feel the connection."

She sits next to me and puts her arm around my neck, "Maybe give it some more time and if it doesn't work out, then I guess... move on?"

We are quiet for a few moments then I say, "Do you think people can fall in love after they are married?"

"Err... Maybe. Sure. Yes. My mom told me she fell in love with my dad all over again, once. They had been fighting, back before I was born, about the whole test-tube thing."

"Yeah... Maybe."

"Hey, speaking of that, you didn't tell me about the test-tubes!"

I smile broadly and turn to look at her little face. "Yeah, I saw where you were born! The test-tube area. It was cool, I guess."

Donavan turns off her office light and walks into the locker room. "Girls, I'm leaving. Don't forget to lock the door when you leave."

"Got it, Coach," Cee says and now we are alone.

Cee leans to me and whispers, "Maybe I shouldn't say this but I heard something Sebastian and Kyle were talking about." There is an eagerness in her voice and I begin to stare at her intently, watching her mouth move. I want to know what she is going to say so I move in closer, whispering, "Tell me."

"Kyle said something about needing your blood which really freaked me out. I mean the way he said 'need'. I don't know, just sounded weird—like one of those horror movie vampires. Later Sebastian mentioned something about checking for traces. I would love to just ask Sebastian about it, you know, just out in the open but I don't want to mess anything up with him right now. Do you know what that means, checking traces?"

I lean back against my locker and say, "I have no idea," faking disinterest. But I'm lying. It was something Smith said on the tour. Genetic modification leaves traces on the DNA strands. Almost like a signature. Some Trace-Checkers are so good at identifying traces that they not only can tell that a person is modified but also by which company, which lab and even which technician who did the procedure. They must think that I am modified and I am not so sure myself. Ever since I did so well at the tryouts in Brazil I have suspected something. *How can I be the only one that is not modified?* It doesn't make sense.

Just then, Kyle walks in.

So we are not alone.

I lean back again and say, "Thanks for the advice, Cyndi. I guess I better be going."

Kyle looks our way, "Leaving Gabriella? I can give you a lift."

I call Mom and she is okay with Kyle giving me a ride, but I don't know why. She never let me be alone with a boy before. She must really think this is *the one*. No way would Dad have allowed this. I know she trusts me, but with them it is never about trust, it's about appearances.

I nervously walk to his car and get in and I feel excited and nervous at the same time. It is just a ride home but... wow! Anything could happen! We are alone!

Riding along the highway, I can't believe how quiet his car is. For me, a really good car blocks out all the road noise, but in here, it's almost too quiet.

"So, Donavan told you about the NuGen offer?" he says.

"Yeah, how did that come about?"

Being alone with him and the thought of what might possibly happen is frightening but at the same time exciting. *Maybe he will stop the car and try to kiss me.*

"I can't say exactly. I did help it along though. I want to see you succeed."

"And that's all? NuGen wants to help me out of the goodness of their corporate hearts?"

"Noooo." He drawls is out slow and long, then says, "There was a fair amount of pushback actually. But in the end we got our way."

"We?"

"Smith helped."

"I see."

Kyle keeps both his hands on the steering wheel at ten and two, eyes straight forward. He looks so rigid. "So, what do you think?" he asks and I let his words hang in the air.

"I don't know." I want to know. I mean, I wish I knew, but I am not sure. This is the man that might be, one day, my husband, the man who could, right now, stop the car and kiss me and I wouldn't fight him too much, yet I don't know if I can trust him with my blood sample. *Oh, what to do?* I wish I could be certain that NuGen is not going to us my blood for something weird. I wish I could somehow separate NuGen and Kyle in my mind. I wish I could stop thinking that two goons wearing blue-black suits, working for NuGen, killed my father. I wish I could stop thinking about Kyle wearing one of those same blue-black suits.

His voice suddenly raises and it shocks me, *"You don't know? I went out on a limb for this... for you... Can't you see I just want to help you? I mean, we are considering marriage. Don't you trust me?"*

"Yes, Kyle. I do." And it is the second time I have lied today. "I just need more time to think about it."

"But why?" The frustration in his voice is building. "I just don't get it, Gabby. You say you trust me. Your Mom seems to like me. We are getting on well. I think so anyway..."

Suddenly, he slows the car and pulls over, quickly flipping on his hazard lights, and I am terrified. The car comes to a complete stop and I can't take my eyes off his strong hands as he shifts the car into park then slowly turns his body toward me.

OhmyGod! OhmyGod! What'sHeDoing!

Fearful at what might happen next, I look up into his face and relax slightly when I recognize his uncertainty. Our eyes lock and he reaches for my hands without looking down, fumbles for them in my lap, then, finding them, pulls me in closer.

"Gabriella Conceição, will you marry me?"

I try to prevent my face from showing a shocked expression, as if that might somehow insult him. But *this*, no way did I expect *this!* A little kiss, okay, maybe... But *this!*

What do I say? What do I say?

Then, suddenly, I realize that... *OhMyGod!* He is looking for an answer right now!

"Err..."

The Kiss

WhatdoIsay? WhatdoIsay? WhatdoIsay?

"Kyle?"

He draws me in a little closer and I can feel his breath on my cheek. "Yes, Gabriella?"

Stalling, I say, "Tell me again how it will be."

His big eyes are barreling down on me and I see love in them, suddenly. He answers slowly, letting each word hang in the air, "We will love each other... take care of each other... respect each other. You can do what you want. If you want to run or compete, you know already I am all for it. I will support you whatever you want to do. Freedom. You will have freedom. And that's something that, I think, you won't have with most of the others that the matchmakers will find."

Nervously I squeak out, "Okay."

"*Okay?* What do you mean 'okay'? Do you mean 'okay'? Or '*okay*'? " He smiles, a little worried for a moment, then I giggle and throw my arms around his neck, nibble on his ear, slightly, like I saw Cyndi do to Sebastian, and whisper as my lips caress his ear, "You have to set it up, do it official, with the family representatives, in front of my mom, and I will say 'yes.' To you, Kyle Conrad, I will say 'yes.' "

We kiss for the first time, awkwardly at first.

Then better—

Then much, much better.

He takes me home and I can't stop smiling. I don't love him, but I think I will, eventually. And I think this is the best I could ever hope for.

Cyndi Battle

The weekend finally arrives and I sleep in a whole extra hour. My body has become too programmed to lie there much longer. Sundays are rest days and we are on our own but still expected to put in a run. My "rest" assignment is an easy pace for 60 to 70 minutes followed by eight 100-meter striders. I blow through it no problem then shower.

Over breakfast, I casually ask Mom about Dad's relationship with Smith before I was born. She must be in a moment of weakness because she actually gives me a little information, "We knew Smith for four or five years before you were born. Back then, everything was different. It was a different time, a different place."

"But mom, how did you know him? How did you meet him?"

She sighs and I know sharing time is ending with her. She sips her coffee, rubs her temple then says, "I'm not sure I want to dig up all that old history right now, first thing in the morning. Maybe we can talk about it another day?"

Staring at her, I reach over and touch her wrist lightly. "When? You have been dodging this forever. You never want to talk about it. Why?"

"I'm just not feeling so good right now." She pulls her wrist away and nibbles on more of her breakfast.

I don't want to pull out my trump card but she is giving me no choice. "Smith already told me anyway." I stand up to go upstairs.

"Wait! He told you what?"

"Everything. How they worked together in the lab. Everything."

"He told you." She looks away, out through the sliding glass door, out into the woods that she stares at too much, then whispers, "I'm gonna kill him."

I take a few more steps away, slowly, hoping she will add more, then she says, "He actually told you—everything? How they worked together—in the lab?"

"Gene splicing, yes, everything."

"Wow," she stares at the woods but I know she no longer sees them. "Your father was brilliant. All the top drug companies wanted him. In fact, that is why Smith was in the old country, to work with your father. I mean why else would he be in that backward place?"

"Backward? I thought you loved it there?"

"No. Soon as we were married I was ready to leave those dirt roads, for the EU or UNA or—anywhere, really. But your father, he thought it would allow him to do his research without so many prying eyes."

I walk back toward the table. "Prying eyes?"

"Your father and Smith were working on something, I don't know what exactly. I am sure Smith won't tell you. He would never tell me. Archibald knows about it too, but try to get him to talk? Huh! All I know is that they had a falling out over it about a year before you were born and things were never the same between Smith and your father."

"Really. What kind of falling out?"

"It was so long ago. They argued over—not exactly sure, but it seemed to me that your father didn't like the way that NuGen was going to use his research. I think he felt somehow betrayed—like maybe they were using him for something different than what he was promised."

She pauses, concentrating, then continues, "I don't remember exactly what all happened or why but I do remember that Smith, he didn't agree with your father about NuGen and even seemed to think that your father figured out something that he didn't want to share, that he was holding something back. But no matter. After you were born, all was well. Smith came to your dedication and they were friends again. Although they never worked together after that."

"NuGen? Huh?"

"I thought Smith told you? Well, I guess it's too late now. Your father's contract was with NuGen."

Blood pulses in my temples. "I guess I didn't figure that out. The way he said it." *It's all starting to make sense. The NuGen goons that came to visit Dad the day he died wanted something from him. Maybe some information— who knows—and then, finally, he decided to give it to them, and they killed him after they got what they wanted.*

No, I don't think they would have done that. Maybe he changed his mind after he left us standing there. Maybe they were chasing him and it really was a car accident. But why would they push him so far that he would crash? Then they really wouldn't get the information.

Mom turns to me, smiles softly and I think I can ask a little more.

"Mom?" I think about telling her about last night, about the proposal, but I want to surprise her. No, that will come out later. When I am ready.

"Yes?"

"I was all natural, right? No test-tubes, right?"

"Gabriella! Of course! Yes, you were formed out of love. I remember it like yesterday. I had been sick that month, in the hospital for some tests. Your father at my side the whole time, ignoring his research—it meant a lot to me. And the week after I came from the hospital, it happened, we got pregnant. Don't know why you are such a great athlete, but sorry to break it to you, you are all natural."

"Thanks, Mom. I just had to ask."

Dad could have done something to Mom in the hospital, couldn't he? Now I am more unsure than ever! Am I modified?

I leave the table and grab a moment alone down in the basement teenager zone and call Michael.

"Gabriella. What can I do for you?" His voice is cold and it surprises me.

"Two things. First, I wanted to apologize to you again—"
He cuts me off, "Don't bother, I'm good."

"Ah... Okay then."

I really wish I could somehow make it up to him, at least talk to him like before, but no, that probably wouldn't work. I don't think Kyle would accept it.

"I was hoping you could find out some information for me."

"Maybe. Like what?"

"Apparently my father and Smith worked together back before I was born, and Dr. Duggan, I think, knew something about what they were doing, what they were working on—not sure how much he knows but I was hoping that you could somehow ask Dr. Duggan what they were working on—back then—without tipping your hand of course. I mean, don't tell him that I want to know."

"Maybe... No promises, but I'll see. Is that it?"

I don't want to hang up. "Michael?"

"Yes?"

Like holding a dead flower that brings sweet memories, I don't want to let it go. "How are you doing?"

"I'm fine. Do you need anything else?"

Realizing that there is no way to unfreeze his coldness, I say, "No, I guess not," and the screen goes black.

That night I ease into my bed looking forward to the dream. The Void-man dream has become more regular now. I look forward to it like it's a puzzle that I can't stop thinking about. I want to figure out what he is saying. I feel like I am playing detective to my brain, a little self-psychoanalysis. *It's just a dream, right?* It must be either some kind of random firings of the neurons in my brain or maybe the message is just something that I am subconsciously worried about. *It's just something in my head, right? Curious to see what it is.* Tonight I figured out a little more. "Watch out... Don't trust..." I have that much. Just a little more and I will have it all figured out.

When the alarm goes off I slam it off the night stand and curse the ground hog again. I am up and off to practice and it is another week gone and the sun is rising across the field as we prepare for our Saturday morning run and some of the runners, especially the new ones, Nomi and Qi, are starting to fall into the mid training-camp blues. It doesn't help that the high volume of miles is starting to expose any physical weaknesses that we each have. See's calves are perpetually tight and Donavan lowered her weekly mileage to a paltry 80 miles a week. Max has a nagging plantar fasciitis problem on her left foot and Nomi has severe shin splints. I have been avoiding injury, but I haven't been giving my all out effort either. It goes back to what Donavan said about courage. After being hurt last year, I am being cautious, maybe a bit too cautious and I wonder if it is not caution but really fear.

Today we don't run in packs. We race.

Donavan says, "The only purpose of today's run is to race. You are going to race each other, using whatever strategy you want! Don't wait for anyone! Just run your race and try to win! I will not say anything, just watch!"

Going all out feels glorious and even though we are trying to beat each other, we are still on the same team and the competition is fun and somehow brings us closer together. Max throws in the towel halfway through due to her foot, no one can beat See and I somehow take second, but no one is discouraged, because our efforts were full and we are beginning to learn another lesson; when to push our bodies and how hard.

*****

On Monday, I wait for practice to end, hoping to find Cee alone again, to ask her some more questions.

Sitting in the locker room, I listen to a few of See's jokes then she leaves too. Just as Maxine is leaving, I say, "Max, have you seen Cyndi?"

"Uhh... I think she's in the conference room."

I open the conference room door and scream, face frozen in shock. Cee is lying on the floor, face down, in a pool of blood.

Max pushes past me, running into the conference room. Reaching Cyndi, she snarls, "Go get Coach!"

I stand there, frozen, and Max screams, "NOW!"

Running through the halls, passing the NuGen office window I see Kyle sitting there behind his screen. Turning down the corridors, running, I scream, "Coach! Coach! Coach! It's Cyndi! Coach! Help!"

I find her and we hustle back to the conference room, Kyle joining us.

Max turns Cyndi over and blood is in her mouth. Cyndi looks like a small broken doll in Max's big arms. Max presses down hard on her shoulder, covered in blood, trying to stop the bleeding bubbling up from a puncture wound.

I'm in shock as the paramedics come in, strap her to a gurney and wheel her out. Max is upset, wiping tears from her cheeks. Donavan is visibly upset, but mostly angry. I am upset. Even Kyle appears upset.

What happened? And where is Sebastian? Did he hit her? How could this have possibly been an accident?

She was in the conference room. The same room that those two were meeting in, like everyone didn't know. Now she is hurt and he is nowhere to be found.

We pile into the team van, rush off to the hospital and arrive at the same time as Mom and Sidney. They meet us in the hospital waiting room and the doctor comes out and addresses us, "Cyndi has a mild concussion and a puncture wound on her lower shoulder. Looks like something blunt stabbed her pretty hard. We are going to hold her for at least a day."

Coach asks, "Doctor, what do you think would have caused the injury?"

"I have no idea. Something blunt, not so sharp. Maybe she fell into something after she whacked her head?"

We look around at each other, questioning looks on every face as the doctor runs through several of the possibilities then talks about running more tests then shuffles off.

I give Max's hand a squeeze and thank her for having her wits when I froze. She seems the most upset of all of us and it is kind of odd looking to see the biggest of all of us tear up. I give See a hug then Mom and I leave for home.

The next day we find out that Cee will be out for at least a few days and that means more race time, much more race time, for the rest of us now that the season is just opening. At least one of us will have to run twice in the next race and it feels like a tremendous weight has been added to our already jam-packed saddle bags. With the season just starting and Cyndi expected to be out for only a few days the front office staff decided to not pull in another runner to replace her. Donavan enters the locker room like nothing happened. "Alright! Gather round!" Donavan sure knows how grab the attention of a group. She isn't screaming but it sure feels like she is.

"As you know we are down one runner so I am going to ease up on practices around games. Don't need you girls burning out. As far as Cyndi's recovery, she is coming on fine. We still don't know what happened, but apparently she fell down so the doctors are going to run some tests to see if maybe she passed out and they are ruling out a lot of things. There are some circumstances that might seem suspicious since she was found alone, but I don't want any of you speculating on your own or talking to the press about it. We clear?"

I look around at the others, wondering what they are thinking. Their faces look worried.

"Okay, now back to business! Heard from some sources that our first match, against DF, is going to be a little different! Looks like they may be throwing up a wall that is too big for one person to climb over so we are going to start practicing throwing each other over! Maxine, looks like you are going to be learning a new role!"

I've never seen Max smile quite like that.

"What?" See yells.

"I'm too big to be thrown," Nomi says.

"I get over wall. No problem. No help," Qi says, waving her hands erratically.

"We'll see! We are erecting a practice wall. If you can make it over—fine. If not, you get thrown over!"

Donavan walks out, our mouths hanging open.

Trying to go over that wall is terrible. The wall is fifteen feet tall and sheer with no sides. If it had a corner, at least, we might be able to bounce off the walls to get up, but there's nothing. No way to vault it except being thrown.

Of course, we try anyway. Nomi, the tallest, tries first and misses by several feet. Sidney has the strongest leap and she doesn't fare much better. Finally, we cave and Max excitedly runs up to the wall and plants her feet firm, facing us, hands down low and cupped, waiting for a foot to launch. One by one, we run to her and she launches us up to the top of the wall, then we leap down to the landing pad.

There is a twinkle in Max's eye as if something special is happening and I think I am the only one who notices it. It is as if she is finally doing something she loves. For such a big girl, I think she hates enforcing, as if maybe she is afraid to hurt someone. In past matches, watching her from the sidelines, I noticed her wince every time she eliminated another runner.

Having Max throw us over works but now we are down another runner and Max cannot be an enforcer until our final runner goes over the wall on her last loop. *First Cyndi, now this.*

Donavan claps her hands, saying, "Good job, girls! Good job! Now, what if an opposing team decides to try to push Max off the course?"

Max replies, "No one can push me off."

"I know, Max! I have faith in you! But let's be prepared for anything!"

I say, "We would have no way to go over the wall. Sidney might be strong enough to throw Cyndi up there, when she comes back, but without Max, we're sunk."

Qi sneers, "I strong. I do it," and everyone, even Donavan, turns to her in disbelief.

Impatience in her voice, Donavan says, "Okay Qi. Let's see."

I am the lightest next to Cee, so I run toward her and she tries to throw me up the wall, me placing my foot into her two cupped hands, she heaves me up with all her might as I spring up as hard as I can. Missing the top of the wall by about three feet, my hands scraping the side of the wall trying to gain traction on something, anything, I come crashing down on her head.

She rolls to the ground, yelling, "Gabriella, you stupid! You no good! Bad DNA! No jump good!" She stands and brushes the dirt off her forehead.

Apparently the NuGen 'modified is superior' mentality is seeping into her brain.

"Qi, shut it!" Donavan yells. "It's not her fault! You're not strong enough!"

Chapter Eighteen

We all surround Donavan and she says, "Okay, I am going to have to think about this. Develop a strategy." She turns and starts walking back to her office.

Leaning her head back she bellows, "Don't just stand there. Keep practicing!"

The Holy Grail

The match against DF comes quickly and the girls are nervous. It's our first match of the new season and we all miss Cee's bouncy optimism on the trip down. We are too quiet without her and everyone notices. It is a long plane ride to Mexico City and when we see the giant haze cloud hanging over the city, the smog from millions of vehicles and unregulated factories, we are wary but yet somehow glad that we are finally here, glad that the silence that reminds us that Cee is lying in a hospital is over. Even See's jokes don't seem as funny without Cee around to laugh with us.

We pull into the stadium lot and the huge sign that says *Districto Federal* stares down at us. DF, like the 'DC' of Washington DC, is a left over from the time that Mexico City was the capital of Mexico, back when it was a separate country, back before North America unification, before UNA. Even though conditions are much better now, people always seem to grow nostalgic for the old days, as if all they can remember is the good times. They still call it DF even though it is no longer the federal district, no longer the capital of Mexico; they still call it DF as if it is not just another city in Unified North America. DF is a rallying cry for Mexicans remembering a better time, even if it really wasn't better, they just remember it that way.

We have almost no fans here and the stands are a giant swath of Mexican green; shirts, hats and flags. Seeing that the DF team has a mariachi band, I wonder why we don't have something cool like that. Their Ultraball team, the field team, has always run a finesse game, but their Pre team is totally different; they have three enforcers and they are almost as big as Max. Seeing them, and their size, we know right away what they will do, take us out through eliminations, not speed.

Huddling at our bench, Donavan whispers to us, "Okay, we are running four first match and we are going to play a strong offense. I want Sidney and Qi to take out their two enforcers and that leaves Elektra and Max. You two are not to leave the starting line until those enforcers are out. Okay?"

"But Coach—" Elektra questions.

"No buts. Let's run this."

I see the flaw in her strategy right away. I guess Elektra does too. If we take out their two enforcers, we only have two people left. And since they cannot score either, their people will simply take out Elektra or Max and then no one scores. A stalemate.

The field game is going as expected. We don't train with them, so game time is the only time I have a chance to see our field team play. The field team has two balls in play at all times and teams can play up to three goalies but most teams only play two since goalies cannot score.

At the gun, as planned, Max and Elektra don't run, just stand there, and the Mexican runners look back at them, puzzled. Just before the big wall, See and Qi spin around and try to knock out the two enforcers. Sidney pushes her's out and Qi just barely makes her's step one foot out. All four must leave the course, disqualified. The two remaining Mexican runners stop at the wall and try to make it over while Max and Elektra start running toward them. Not being able to climb the wall they both turn and bolt toward Elektra and easily push her out. There is no way Max can climb the wall by herself so it is match over. No score.

Elektra is steamed. Slamming herself down on the bench, she looks over at me and says, "I tried to tell Coach!"

I am surprised she is talking to me, maybe some good will come from this after all. "I know you did. I saw it coming too."

At the second half, we can only run three and I am up, not knowing what I can do. Coach is besides herself, "I guess the best we can do is try to out-race them and if they try to take out our people we go for another stalemate. I can't see any other way."

"Coach?"

"What is it Gabriella?"

"I have an idea."

I give her my plan but she doesn't like it because it is not something we have trained for but she goes for it anyway, surprisingly. She must be desperate.

Qi, Nomi and Max sit; Elektra, Sidney and I run. Qi is a bit faster than me, but she is too short for my idea to work.

At the gun Elektra and Sidney blaze ahead and making it to the wall first, stand next to each other, locked into the wall so as not to be pushed off course. I beat out the huge DF enforcer, and the two girls launch me together. I barely grab the top of the wall with one hand when the DF enforcer arrives with her two girls. I pull myself over and turn around, balancing my belly on the middle of the top of the wall. The two DF runners launch over the wall next to me being thrown up by their enforcer. Hanging my arms down, first See jumps, we lock hands and I pull her over. Next Elektra does and we are all three over, but far behind.

On the second loop, the Mexican girls are over the wall when we reach it and the DF enforcer, feeling unthreatened, snickers at our struggle to pass the wall. My plan is working, but we are too far behind! *We have to do something!*

The three of us speed up to an all out sprint and See, our fastest, is dogging the heels of their last runner. Just as she is going for a swing rope, See screams, the Mexican girl turns, misses the rope, and falls in the mud pit. See flies past her then moments later Elektra and I are even with her.

When we reach the wall the first Mexican girl is already over and again we struggle. My stomach is rubbing raw on the wall edge. Finally See catches the first girl and the Mexican runner suddenly grabs See and yanks her off the course, taking them both out. Now it is two on two and we have no way over the wall. As we near the mud pit, I dive in, and Elektra screams,   "What are you doing?"

"You'll see. Hope this works."

As we round the bend, running toward the wall, I begin screaming in Spanish to the DF enforcer, "Get ready! Get ready!" and as I reach her, covered in mud, she heaves me over the wall, thinking I am the girl from her team. *I can't believe that worked!* Seeing me over the wall, Elektra pushes the mud covered Mexican runner off the course. I am the only scorer and we receive three points.

Coming in to our pit, Donavan is clapping for me and says, "Girls! You see what just happened? That's thinking on your feet! We need more of that around here!" As I start wiping mud off, she says, "Maybe you are going to earn your place here yet!" And it feels great. Everyone is celebrating my move, everyone except Max and I am the only one who knows why.

We finish the match, clean up in the locker room, go out to eat then head back to the airport. Just before the trip back, I receive a text from Michael that says:

> **Won't say much.**
> **Something about 'Holy Grail.'**
> **Nothing else.**
> **Sorry.**

'Holy Grail'? What's the 'Holy Grail'?

It is a long plane ride back so I have a lot of time to think about things. Well, one nice thing is that Michael actually replied to me. Even though it was only a text. Maybe we can be friends anyway. Well no, actually that would never work. At least I can feel good if he is not mad at me. I can't help it if I still love him, but at least if he is not mad at me—at least that would be something.

And what about this whole 'Holy Grail' thing? Dr. Duggan is a physicist, not a geneticist, so I am guessing that since they were all friends maybe he was in their labs for the experiments or maybe knew some of the ideas in general, but he probably doesn't know anything in detail. He might not even know what 'Holy Grail' means. Maybe it is something he overheard them say? Maybe 'Holy Grail' is a code word for the project like 'project Black Bird' or something like that? Hard to say, but I obviously need to do more snooping.

And Kyle. What about him? And his proposal? He is making arrangements for his parents to come down and do a formal engagement in a few days. No one knows about that yet. *Should be cool meeting them, I guess.* It is really getting too late to back out of that, so, I guess... I guess I am making the right decision. Well, what other choice do I have? Not marry him and hope that I fall in love with someone *like* him? Cee said her parents fell in love again after they were married. But that means they were in love before. Then maybe they were just mad at each other then got back together? Different situation in my case. Seeing as we don't love each other *at all* right now. *I hope this all works out!*

See, bubbling about our performance, bounces out of her seat and comes crashing down next to me, saying, "Got time for a few?"

"Not going anywhere," I say, smiling.

"Okay, okay, okay, I got a call from my old friend, Buffy, and she asked me if I could help her, saying, 'Well, I bought this jigsaw puzzle, but it's too hard. None of the pieces fit together and I can't find any edges.'

When I asked her what the picture was, she says, 'It's of a big rooster.'

So I agree to go take a look, drive across town to her house, go inside and enter the kitchen, Buffy leading the way to the jigsaw puzzle on the kitchen table.

After I take a quick look, I tell her, 'Buffy! Put the cornflakes back in the box.' "

I snort then she says, "Okay, you're gonna like this one."

"Go ahead."

"Err... What are those girls' names from Brazil?"

"Ahh... You mean Velocity and Carilla?"

"Yeah. Okay, okay, okay... So Velocity was in class cheating off Carilla next to her and the teacher knew that she was cheating, but he just couldn't catch her. So one day he was grading a test and noticed that Carilla had written 'I don't know the answer'. Looking at Velocity's paper, he smiled because he finally caught her. Velocity wrote, 'Me neither.' "

I chuckle and say, "Yeah, she is stupid. She thinks she's superior just because she's modified."

"I heard. Don't sweat that. That's just her thing. Hey, here's another. So Velocity was taking an important test and if she failed, then she would go on academic probation and not be allowed to play in the Ultraball game the following week. The exam was fill-in-the-blank and the teacher, knowing her predicament, wanting her to play in the game since he was a big fan, wrote a special test just for her. The last question read, "Old MacDonald had a _____.""

Velocity, stumped, had no idea of the answer and she knew she needed to get this one right to be sure she passed. Making sure the professor wasn't watching she tapped Carilla on the shoulder. 'Pssst. What's the answer to the last question?'

Carilla laughed, looked around to make sure the professor hadn't noticed then turned to Velocity and says, 'Velocity, everyone knows Old MacDonald had a *farm*.'

'Oh yeah,' said Velocity, 'I remember now,' and picks up her pencil and starts to write the answer in the blank, saying, 'That's so easy. Farm is spelled E-I-E-I-O.' "

We land and coach stands in the center aisle of the plane and announces, "I didn't want to distract you all during the game, but I have word from the doctors that Cyndi is conscious and they are releasing her for visitors. Now I don't want all of you—"

Everyone jumps up and quickly hustles off the plane and scrambles down the airport halls, each speeding up in front of the other, until we are all suddenly running, laughing.

"Hey where are you all going?" Coach howls, trying to keep up, "Hey come back here! Oh, all right. Let's all go to the hospital!"

Running through the airport, dodging people and bouncing off the airport planters and walls, it suddenly feels fun and innocent again, running obstacles, like the days back in Brazil. Elektra, See and I weave in and out of each other then finally reach the baggage claim, first girls from the team, and we are all laughing. I think the DF game bridged a gap between Elektra and me. I think now we might be able to become friends.

After we gather our bags we all pile into the team van and Donavan drives us to the hospital. Filling up Cyndi's room we can't stop smiling because it is so great to see her even though she is still asleep. Everyone can feel it. The long plane ride to Mexico showed us how important she is. She is the spirit of the team.

Sebastian is sitting in the corner of the room and apparently has been here all day. We greet him, making too much noise, then Cyndi wakes. As she opens her dreary eyes, everyone wants to know the same thing, 'What happened?'

Cyndi says, "I don't know you guys. I wish I did. I hit my head so hard. I think I lost some of my memory. I remember being in the room... alone. Sebastian and I had a disagreement and—"

Some of us glance back at Sebastian. "I needed to be alone, just for a minute. You know, just to clear my head. I want to say that, that, that I heard a noise—like someone else was in the room. But I can't be sure. I just can't remember."

Cyndi's response raises more questions than it answers, with me at least. The rest of the group probably not knowing what to think, stare at her, wanting more. I think most will be either blaming Sebastian, or thinking it was an accident. Hopefully Cee is not sick with some incurable disease and somehow just blacked out.

Donavan says, "It's okay, Cyndi, you need your rest. We are going to leave you now, okay?"

As we filter out Sebastian whispers to each of us, looking at each face, "It wasn't me. I would never... Cyndi. I love her." and a tear trickles down his cheek. He walks out with us and, suddenly angry, says, "If anyone knows anything! You have to tell me! I, I, I can't lose her."

See steps up to him, "Sebastian, don't worry. If we find out anything we will let you know. But Cyndi—she probably fell, slipped, who knows. It was an accident."

Now I am not so sure what to think. Why would Sebastian be hiding in the back of the room? *That doesn't make sense to me.*

If it was an accident, then okay, I can buy that but what did she hear? Why would someone be hiding there? And who? It would have to be someone from the team or staff.

And who would want to hurt little Cyndi? She is the bright shining light of the team, always happy, always optimistic. *Who would want to hurt her?*

The Proposal

"**G**abriella, what's going on here?"

"Mom, what are you talking about?" I say quizzically, trying not to smile.

"Wait. Something is going on here. You're up early, you're cleaning the whole house. I saw clothes lying out on your bed, your nice black dress. What's going on?"

"We are having company. It's a surprise," I reply, holding back a giggle.

"Surprise? I don't *think* so. I don't like surprises. Ohh no. You are going to tell me." She stands there in her house coat and footie socks, hair still a mess, and I smile broadly at her, not saying a word.

"Gabriella! Tell me! Come on! Who's coming over?" I can't stop smiling then she grabs my forearm softly and strokes it, "Tell me, Mija."

"Ohh alright. Micha—I mean, Kyle's parents are coming over to meet us." *Michael. I can't believe I almost said Michael.* Michael. Yes, he is still in there, somewhere.

"Are you serious? Why didn't you tell me? You know I have to get ready!" Throwing her hands in the air, she runs upstairs, still talking, "I have to fix my hair, I have to get my clothes ready. Gabriella! What are we going to serve them! Oh, how could you do this to me! You know I hate surprises!"

"Mom, don't worry. I have it under control." And I did. I ordered four pounds of sweets from the Turkish bakery, baklava and some others with pistachios. *I love pistachios.* The dishes were done, the house was clean. I bought a few gifts for his parents and I am ready for the traditional treatment. First we will sit in the formal living room and I will offer tea. After tea, I will bring sweets, then sliced fruit; mangos, watermelon, cherries and pineapples. After fruit, I will serve espresso and more tea.

And after that—Oh boy, after that, *it* happens.

It would be my job to not say too much, of course, just serve the food like a good, respectful, traditional girl who knows her place, smile a lot, make sure they have everything they need, sugar, spoons, forks, taking away the dishes with a twinkling smile, show that I will make a good wife, the traditional way.

It's a big day. I am nervous, but ready. I think.

Mom is rustling something fierce up there. *I'd better go fill her in on the rest or she will really be angry with me and I don't want her mad on this day. I can't let this be too much of a surprise.* She has been pushing Kyle and I together for some time, so I hope she doesn't become mad because I arranged all this, leaving her out of the loop until the last minute. I enter Mom's room and tell her who else is coming and what to expect and I wipe her happily crying eyes to stop her mascara from running.

A couple hours later, the door bell rings and I nervously run to the door, stop, smooth my dress, quickly look in the side mirror, check my hair and my teeth then open the door smiling. "Hello! Welcome! It's so good to see you! Come in! Come in! Hello!"

Mom comes behind me, immediately, insanely excited, insanely happy, just as I open the door, saying, "Hello! Come in! Come in!"

Smith leads the way, shakes my hand and kisses my cheek in the traditional way then does the same with Mom. Kyle steps in, greets us both with a brief cheek kiss then introduces his parents, Mr. and Mrs. Conrad. Both shorter and darker than Kyle, they look nothing like him. Mom and I shake their hands and kiss their cheeks. I take their light coats and put them in the hall closet and make my way for the kitchen.

Round one, coming up.

Mom takes them to the formal living room and the men sit on one side of the room and the women the other. Mom handles the conversation like an old pro. She deftly allows the details of our heritage and my pedigree to pop up in the flow of casual conversation, talking about our time in the old country and how we came to be in Venezuela and then in UNA. Of course, there is no mention of any hardship or bad luck. No one wants to marry someone who is cursed.

Kyle's parents smile and ask questions, but they seem much less interested in pedigree. *Kyle did say they were liberal.* Kyle's father tells the long, drawn out and terribly boring story of how their old country name, 'Awad,' became westernized into 'Conrad.' Mom, full of joy, grabbing hold of every moment of this experience, is eating up every word as if it is the retelling of some lost masterpiece of Shakespeare.

Standing at the kitchen entrance, just out of sight, I look out at the side of Kyle's face, suddenly wishing it were Michael's, wishing I wasn't trapped, wishing I had the freedom to choose who I wanted to be with. Kyle said he would give me 'freedom,' but it's freedom on a whole other level that I desire. A pain momentarily stabs my chest then quickly disappears. I exhale past my upper lip as if I could somehow blow away those dreams hovering over my head, trying to block out the desires of my heart, and exit the kitchen carrying the silver tray with cups, saucers, sugar bowl, teapot and teaspoons. I set the tray on the center table and expertly serve each person, in order of position of honor, just like I practiced, Kyle's father first, then his mother, then Smith, Kyle, Mom, and finally myself. Although I do not sit and drink with them, just take a few sips, out of respect, to join them symbolically, then head back to my place in the kitchen.

Kyle's father says, "We want whatever Kyle wants," just a few times too many and I hope he stops before it makes Mom nervous.

Both sides of the room, like enemy forces negotiating a truce, discuss questions that seem benign on the surface, but that can have far reaching implications in the way that the lives of their children will go, at least in their minds, questions that can only be answered with paragraphs of subtly nuanced phrases uttered in the style of politicians who want to somehow state that they support both sides of a position and thus really support none. Everyone in the room seems to be having a great time with this. Mom is lost in some mysterious marriage negotiation nirvana, the Conrads seem content, and Smith, well, Smith's morphing, exclamation-point, sinister smile is completely out of control, as if he has finally figured out some genetic mystery.

Their smiles stab my heart even the more, me standing there in the kitchen corner, just out of their reach, preparing their next round. All I feel, all I *can* feel, is loss. *Don't they see? I am losing everything here!* They are plotting and negotiating my future with Kyle, in their minds, and in such a way that they think they are guaranteeing me happiness when all my happiness is three-thousand five-hundred miles away.

Every few minutes I steel my mind, block out any thoughts of Michael, then enter from the kitchen with something else, smile broadly, walk slowly the long way around the room so Kyle's parents can get a good long look at me, and serve something. I engage in the conversation briefly if asked questions by Smith or Kyle's parents, trying to say something engaging, brilliant, and maybe even funny, feeling their joy stabbing my heart, then exit to the kitchen for something else.

Each trip out hammers the reality home, smashing pounding nails into my skull, that this *is* to be my life, the life that I don't want, the life that I have been born into and cannot change.

I return to the kitchen and I would love to let it all out and cry, that would certainly stop this runaway, slow-motion, train wreck happening right before my eyes, but I can't. I can't do that to Mom. No. I need to grow up and accept it. This will be my life. And that cold piece of driftwood named Kyle, sitting out there, will be my husband.

Mom excitedly tells them about me being a semi-pro athlete, so proud, so happy to share, but adds that I want children and a 'normal' life, pointing out that I am still in high school and there will be time for that 'soon enough.' Normally her saying something like that would make me yell, but right now, I smile and nod as I serve them. In my dead and dying heart I know that it is the perfect thing to say.

I serve the sweets and the fruit, walking slowly, smiling broadly, all the while holding back my terror, a terror that my fantasy life is all over. It is all I can do to make it back to the kitchen without bursting into tears or screaming out at the top of my lungs.

Leaning against the kitchen counter I feel my body trembling. It is happening. I am dying inside and I suddenly know why prisoners being executed struggle against the poison gas, strapped down tight, death at their door, refusing to breathe, struggling against the straps, holding on to even just one more second of life, even if it is the most miserable form of life. I *am* that inmate, right now, strapped down, in the gas chamber, being feed a noxious chemical named Kyle and I am struggling to breathe that fresh air called Michael, just for one second more, even though I surely know my death must come.

Death. Yes, you must die to what you want, Gabby, die to yourself. You were the one who arranged this; you created your own funeral. Yes, I know. I must die.

Kneading my cheeks, I force a smile on my face, and glance back into the living room and Mom catches my eyes for a moment. It is the happiest I have ever seen her. Laughing, smiling joking, she is the center of the universe in that room. Exultation and joy surrounds and radiates from her like dandelions seeds blowing in the wind.

I lean back out of sight and the truth stabs me down deep. I must die, today, right now, in this moment. My fantasy life must die, no matter how painful. I must let it die. *But it hurts so bad!*

Just after the coffee, we hear a knock at the door and I put my happy face back on and trot to answer it. Everyone stands. Opening the door, I introduce Archibald Duggan to the group, who greets everyone with cheek kisses in the traditional way and a shudder crosses my spine as I realize that we are close, very close, to the moment when my fantasy life dies, the moment when I must finally breathe in the poison gas and die to life and join the dead as the future Mrs. Kyle Conrad.

Dr. Duggan says, "Sorry I'm late," four times too many. I take his jacket and he bumbles into the room loudly and announces that he has been asked to be my male representative, since my father has passed. Everyone already knew this, but traditional people love things to be spoken out loud so there can be no disagreements later.

Dr. Duggan sits on the same couch as Smith, but near my mother, and I offer him all of the things he has missed. My hand is shaking as I serve his coffee and everyone notices. They probably think that it is due to my excitement at the quickly coming engagement to such a fine, successful and beautiful young man but it is really because I am dying inside and they can never know anything about that. Ever.

Mom says, "Well now. Down to business. Kyle, could you excuse us for just a few moments?"

"Sure," he says then steps out on our back deck. He seems too calm. This is our lives! He isn't the least bit nervous and I hate him for that.

The Proposal

I listen through the kitchen doorway, shaking, and I know that it is about to happen.

They call us in and everyone stands; Dr. Duggan, Mom and I on one side of the room; Kyle's parents and Kyle on the other; Smith in the middle, a room full of excited smiles. I put on a cheeky grin and wipe my eyes before a painful tear can fall, squeezing my emotions into submission.

Smith begins, "My name is Smith Dinklestein, son of Richard Dinklestein, and I am here as a common friend and a witness of Mr. and Mrs. Conrad and Mrs. Conceição. We are all here for the purpose of the family of Kyle Conrad to ask for the hand of Gabriella Conceição in marriage." His punctuation mark smile comes in full effect and the others are loving it.

Then Mr. Conrad speaks, "My name is Enrico Conrad, son of Benjamin Conrad, and this is my wife, Farideh Conrad, and my son, Kyle Conrad. We are from the village of Bethlehem and we respect Smith Dinklestein as our intermediary." His voice is suddenly deep and strong, and it sounds odd coming from such a small man. The Conrads are clearly proud to be a part of this moment.

Next, Dr. Duggan speaks, "Err... My name is Dr. Archibald Duggan. And—"

Mom, smiling broadly, whispers in his ear and Dr. Duggan says, "And this is Migdalia Conceição, wife of the late Jonathan Conceição, the parents of Gabriella—"

I wince when I hear Dad's first name with our new last name—it was never his and it reminds me of the lie we are living.

Mom smiles again, leans over and whispers in his ear once more and Dr. Duggan says, "She is from the village of Bayt Jala—and—I am from—well, I'm from Cleveland, actually."

Everyone bursts out laughing, savoring every morsel, everyone except me. I am doing everything I can to stop myself from running into the kitchen, out the back door and away, far, far away. All I want to do right now is escape. Escape and cry, long and hard.

Dr. Duggan, embarrassed, speaks the rest too fast, "Shenanigans. And I am here to represent Gabriella in these matters and we respect Smith Dinklestein as our intermediary."

Then Mr. Conrad suddenly grows very serious, yet somehow manages to still smile, saying, "It is my pleasure to ask for the hand of Gabriella Conceição for marriage to my son Kyle Conrad."

Terror grasps my heart and I cannot breathe. Every fiber of my being is in a sudden kaleidoscope of unbearably sharp pain. *It is happening! Now! Right now!*

Mom, smiling and giggling excitedly, whispers in Dr. Duggan's ear and he smiles, then nervously says, "We are honored and accept."

It is over. I am dead. My chance to run has past. My life with Michael, just a fantasy, is over. I am a shell, a dead shell, a carcass lying in the gutter, decaying, turning into earth, slowly. Misery and depression drapes me in shadows of death as I stare at the excitedly smiling faces.

Finally Smith says, "Let it be known that on this day Kyle Conrad and Gabriella Conceição are promised to each other and are to be considered engaged to be married."

A flood of emotions crashes in on me but they do not feel like they are mine; I am dead and do not have feelings anymore. I look across at Dr. Duggan, and wonder why did he have to give me away and suddenly it's as if I am still standing in our old living room in Venezuela and I am hearing about Dad dying for the first time and I miss him so much and I can't understand why he had to die. And looking over at Kyle, his smile painted on like some b-grade Hollywood actor, the loss of Michael catches me bare, once again, deep in my heart, piercing me sharply, then suddenly leaving me; it is not my emotion anymore. I am dead. I look at my sense of loss as a foreign object, not part of me, and analyze it, seeing it as weird in some odd way, because, in a way, I never had him. *How can I feel such a deep loss for him when he was never mine and even I knew, from the very beginning, that he could never be mine?*

I look down at my feet and forgetting where I am, begin to cry, completely out of control now, then Smith, with his stupid grin that I hate, comes up and gives me a hug, announcing to the rest, "Ohh isn't she cute! She's so happy that she cries!"

The knock at the door shakes me awake and See, Cee and Sebastian arrive to help us celebrate. Kyle introduces them to his parents and everyone kisses cheeks, smiling laughing and hugging.

Cee is still weak so Sebastian is babying her. The way he looks at her reminds me of Michael and I can't look at those two. *But what else can I do? Don't think about it. You can't help it. This is your life, Gabriella. Deal with it.*

Standing there, I contemplate the idea of Sebastian being the one that hurt Cee but the way he is looking at her I can't believe he would have done that; I push it out of my mind. She must have slipped, that's all.

We 'young ones' retire ourselves out on the back deck, me sitting next to Kyle, holding his hand, it feeling like a piece of wood, while the adults inside are planning the marriage details, the dowry amount, the approximate wedding cost, date, and location, a rough idea of all sorts of things that I can't believe they are even discussing, as if they are already planning out my life for me. It is all too surreal.

As the night wears on, me feeling dead, a ghost, a spirit watching the living, maybe, somehow, like the Void-man, I notice that Kyle and Sebastian are not so friendly, like they used to be. They both are laughing and having a great time with everyone but each other. *Something is going on there.* I try to keep my mind focused on See and Cee, forcing myself to interact, to not tip my hand that something is really, really, wrong here, to stay current with the conversations when my mind, bashed to a billion bits, is nowhere to be found.

See makes a dramatic stab at a few marriage jokes. She isn't married so she must have been searching for them, preparing for tonight, so we all give her some space. It would be awful to not let her tell them when she looks so excited.

The Proposal

"Okay, okay, okay, a husband reads an article to his wife describing that women use approximately 30,000 words each day, but in the case of a man it is 15,000. The wife replies, 'the reason has to be because we have to repeat everything to men.'

The husband turns to his wife and says, 'What?' "

Kyle shoots out, "Not me! Not me!"

See snickers then continues, "A husband says to his wife, 'No, I don't hate your relatives. In fact, I like *your* mother-in-law better than I like *mine*.' "

See sits there smiling, then Cee, eyes suddenly full of surprise, says, "Ohhh, I get it." and we all laugh at that. I am playing along, laughing on cue, but I'm not into it.

"Okay, okay, okay, a wife asks her husband, 'What do you like most in me, my pretty face, my sexy body or just me?'

He looks at her from head to toe and replies, 'I like your sense of humor.' "

Sebastian says, "Ahhh, poor girl. That's sad."

See says, "One more. a husband says to his wife one day, 'I don't know how you can be so stupid and so beautiful at the same time.'

The wife responded, 'Allow me to explain. God made me beautiful so you would be attracted to me. God made me stupid so I would be attracted to you!' "

We all snicker and the conversation flows here and there, and the evening draws to a close, finally, and this is a night that neither Mom nor I can sleep, both lying awake in bed, eyes wide open, both awake for completely different reasons, her alive with exultant joy, me lost in a miserable cave of depression, dark, fetid and full of the stench of death.

After I finally fall asleep the dream comes fast and hard and, as usual, I wake to the dark moonlight, streaming in through the window shade, in a puddle of sweat. His face is closer this time in the dream, the Void-man hovering over me, staring at me, as if he really wants me to hear the message this time. This night, more than any other, I feel so close to him, as if I am a spirit too. He repeats the phrase over and over and I wish I could figure it out. "Watch out... Don't trust..." I already knew that much. And, now, something new, it almost looks like, "Kyle." but that couldn't be it, right? This dream is all in my head, so maybe it is.

Of course, I am still completely miserable over what happened today so my dreams are filled with things that would make me want to run from him. Sure, that makes sense.

But, in reality, he is going to be my husband and I just have to find a way to trust him. I have to find a way to push past all of this.

Chapter 21

Michael, Sebastian and Kyle

Over the last three weeks we played two home games and one away game in the Philippines Islands and won all three so most of us feel like the high mileage and hard aggressive training during the pre-season was worth the pain as it is now paying off. Going to the Philippines was cool and unique for everyone except Qi, who grew up there. After we checked into the hotel there we had about five hours to kill so a few of us wandered about on the streets. There were children everywhere, some selling trinkets or candy, others begging for spare change, others calling customers into stores, banging metal cans together, yelling out, "Buy something! Buy something! Buy something!"

The effect on Qi was dramatic and it looked as if she was instantly transported back to her own childhood. I don't know her background but the way she reacted it was as if she was scampering along those same streets, begging and selling something, anything, for enough money to buy her next meal, to survive, for just one more day. Watching all that unfold and watching her cry as we listened to her childhood stories on the plane ride back made all of us understand her a little better and brought her deeper into the fold.

Coming up we have an away game in Germany and a home game against Montreal next Saturday. Cee's time off seems to keep getting extended day after day and some of the team are getting upset that she wasn't replaced right away when she got hurt. Donavan is not pushing us to train too hard, just light drills, due to the full match schedule, but I am throwing myself into training anyway, hard and fast, like an undead, emotionless zombie, keeping my brain focused on the nuances of each individual movement lest I remember that I am not dead, but alive, and lost. Killing myself with training, forcing my body to suffer is the only way I can feel alive and it helps me to block out the thoughts of my situation. During today's practice, See and Max put up a large sign in the training room. The sign lists our names and our best times minus a number of seconds. Mine is 30 seconds faster than my best ever.

"See, do you really think I can do that?"

"It's up to you to find that out." And I wonder where the funny, joking See went. She can be a completely different person on the track.

Donavan is trying out some new ideas on us and it is weird because what little speed work we do seems to be more about changing mind-sets than conditioning our bodies. Donavan makes us run a steady pace for the entire course except just before obstacles, where we have to speed up.

"Too many runners slow down before obstacles and that is hurting us. I am going to make you conscious of it by forcing you to run faster just before the obstacles."

She also has us work on not going too fast during recovery runs, standing on the side lines, looking at her stop watch, she screams at us to slow down if we are going too fast.

At the end of practice, Donavan makes a little announcement and everyone congratulates Kyle and I and I feel their love and just a glimmer of my former self lights up like a tiny candle in the depths of a cave.

The next day, Kyle and Sebastian approach me just as I finish tying my laces firm and tight, just as I like them and then they stand over me, waiting. Looking up at them, Sebastian says, "Gabriella, I understand that you are going to do the monitoring with us. Would you like to begin today?"

I look up at Kyle and I cannot read him. Then, on cue, he says, "Only if you are ready, my Dear," and it sounds completely foreign for him to call me that.

"Okay. Let's do this."

We go to the NuGen office and it is the first time I have been inside of it. I sit in the medical chair and take a deep breath.

Sebastian say, "First we need a full sample, to run your profile, then after that we will only need to do finger pricks. Okay?"

The full sample. It's what they have been after for so long. I think that they want it for a lot more than just to help me run a little faster and win a few races. They want to check for traces, find out if I am modified, and maybe something else, who knows. But right now I don't really care what they do with my blood anymore. I am tired of resisting them.

"Gabriella? Are you okay?" Kyle asks.

I must have been spacing out. "Sure, let's do it."

Finally, reluctantly, I pull up my shirtsleeve for Kyle, feel the needle pierce my arm and watch my blood drain into his sample vial as his mouth grins victoriously.

After he removes the needle and band-aids my arm, I stand up to leave as he stuffs my vial into his machine. As I head for the door, Sebastian says, "Hey! Don't you want to see your profile? Wait a few and it will be right up on the screen."

"Not right now. Show me later... maybe tomorrow."

I head back out to the track and push myself harder and faster. It is the only time I feel alive.

Mom picks me up after practice and I am silent for the entire ride home. As we enter the house, Mom says, "Gabriella, let's talk for a bit."

"I'm really tired Mom—and I have a long day tomorrow." True, but in reality I just don't want to talk about Kyle or marriage plans anymore.

"It's just—you don't seem happy lately. You're so—distant. What's bothering you? Is it the wedding? Is it too much stress?"

"No, Mom. I don't know, maybe... I guess... I just don't want to talk about it." I set my bag down and let my shoulders droop. How tired I am suddenly hits me.

"Well, darling, you know I am always here for you."

"I know that, Mom. I know."

I turn to head upstairs and just as I reach the staircase I pause when she says, "Don't worry, Mija. If you don't love him now... you will. You will. This has been the way for thousands of years. Don't worry, it will all work out." And I hope that she is right.

The next morning I wake just before my alarm and lie in bed, staring out the window. Out of nowhere I decide to text Michael.

Michael, need to tell you something.

He shoots me right back and then I remember it is lunchtime there.
What?

I type it all out then, holding my finger over the send button, pause, sigh, feeling the hand of death on me all over again like the day I became engaged, then mash the button.

I am getting married.

I wait for a while, listening to my own hard breathing, but there is no response. I turn off the alarm and go to the bathroom, shower and brush then get ready for school. Picking up my screen, there is a reply.

Call me.

After school Mom sits in the passenger seat and lets me drive to practice since I just picked up my learner's permit. I find myself driving like Kyle, hands at ten and two, sitting rigid, watching every car and truck that whizzes by and it strikes me odd because I think I am nothing like him. Mom tells me that she can't wait until I take my driver's test so she doesn't have to shuttle me around so much. I agree with her, but still we only have the one car.

I have been looking forward to calling Michael all day, even though I know I will only be giving him bad news, and today I am starting to feel alive again, excited that I can call him and talk to him but nervous about what I have to tell him.

After Mom drives off, I tuck myself in the corner of the parking garage and eagerly dial his number. Listening to the ring is torture.

"Hello? Hello? Gabriella? Are you there?"

It is pure joy to hear his voice. "Ahh... Yes. I am here."

"So what's up? Getting married? Is that true? Dr. Duggan didn't mention it."

"I asked him not to. I wanted to be the one to tell you."

"So... Do I know him?" He chuckles, but it sounds forced,   "Who's the lucky guy?"

"Do you remember the meet in Madrid? The boy there—"

He cuts me off, "Oh. Him," and in his voice it is as if it all makes sense. As if just by seeing Kyle once, and how good looking he is, it would all make perfect sense. Of course you would marry such a man as this. He is great looking!

"No, no, it's not like that at all. Michael? It's not—"

"Oh, Gabriella, you don't have to explain anything. I am happy for you—really, you are a great girl. You deserve to be happy."

"Michael, stop! Just stop! Okay! You don't know what this is like!" I stop yelling and breathe for a moment, then continue, "Don't tell me that. Okay? This is hard enough as it is without you telling me that marrying him is good and that I deserve him—" I nearly cry, grab a mouthful of air and then force myself to calm down.

"Gabriella? I, I, I... You are confusing me here. Why did you really call me?"

"I wanted to explain, to tell you that I don't have a choice. My mother—well, really it's all of them, my culture you see. I have to marry someone from the culture. It's our way." I pause, considering how much I want to say, how much of my heart I can expose, then continue, "Maybe if my father was still alive, maybe then... I like to think that I could have swayed him. That maybe he would have let me choose—who I wanted—but with him gone and mom—she has always been the traditional one. I just couldn't hurt her."

He is quiet for a time, then says, "And. So, you always knew this?"

"Yes, Michael. I know, I hurt you," I feel a tear running down my cheek but I refuse to wipe it. "But I need you to know this. Listen to me, okay?"

"I'm listening."

"If I could choose—" I know it is not wise to reveal my heart but I can't help it. Right now I just don't care. I have to tell him. "If somehow, somewhere, there was a way, I wouldn't be here right now. I would be with you, on a beach in Portugal." I dreamed of telling him this for so long but now that the words have been spoken I feel like they've fallen flat.

"I see." He is quiet and I am not sure what to say. Goodbye seems so final right now.

"Gabriella, let me say just one thing and I will let you go."

"Okay Michael, please tell me." I am sobbing inside.

"I don't have much experience with women. I mean, my life has always been the lab so when you showed up... and how we were together... you had me, I mean." His voice is suddenly cracking so he stops.

"Michael, it's okay. You don't have to—"

"No, no. If I don't say this now, I will never say it. The truth is... the truth is that I love you."

I wish I could say that this changes everything, but unfortunately it changes nothing. It only deepens my loss that much more and I still have to marry Kyle.

"Michael, I—"

"Maybe I shouldn't have said that. No, I am sure I shouldn't have. Gabby, I'm sorry." and suddenly he hangs up.

Just then a car whizzes by and parks not far from me. The doors fling open and Cee and See jump out.

"Hey, Girl!" Cee says, "The doctors released me to practice today!"

I trot over to her to help her with her bag, still shaking. "That's great! Welcome back! We missed you. Hey See." I try to sound enthusiastic but my voice is shallow and forced.

"Hey," See says, looking at me oddly.

As we walk in, both of them staring at me, Cee says, "You've been crying. What's going on?" And I realize that the tear I didn't wipe must have left a streak on my face. I wipe it.

"Oh, it's nothing. I just broke the news to an ex-boyfriend that I am getting married. That's all. Just a little teenager drama."

See chuckles, relieved.

We enter the break room and dropping our bags, start to ready ourselves for the practice. "So can you race?"

"No. Unfortunately just practice for now. But I will soon. Maybe the home game next weekend, I hope."

Sebastian jogs in, saying, "There you are," heads straight for Cee, his face illuminated, cups her head softly and plants a big kiss on her. Backing up he turns to me and says, "Gabriella, we can look at your results if you like and today we are going to press you during the workout. Don't take it personally."

I need something to shake me out of this funk and so far training like a maniac has been the only thing that has helped. That and talking to Michael, even though it was painful, at least it was an emotion, at least it made me feel something. "No problem, I'm ready for whatever you throw at me."

He backs out of the room.

After I change, I visit the NuGen room and Kyle and Sebastian show me my charts.

"See this," Sebastian says, pointing at a green squiggly line among many other squiggly lines on the screen, "That's your potential oxygen uptake." He pauses, looks up at me, then says, "I've never seen one this high, even from a fourth gen."

"Okay. So that's good, right?"

Kyle is silent and he looks upset.

Sebastian replies, "Good? Are you kidding me? It's great!"

"Well I guess that's why I made the team."

"No, no, no. Gabriella, you don't understand. These lines show us what you are capable of, not what you are doing now. You are performing far below your capability right now. This is what I was hoping for, that we could actually train you to be better. Once I get done with you, you will be the fastest on the team. And maybe... Well I am not for pointing at the fences, but I think you could be at the top of the sport. I mean of any team."

He can't hide his smile. Looking over at Kyle, the difference is striking. Sebastian is so excited and Kyle is so upset. What is going on here?

"That sounds good to me."

"And most of your other lines are solid also, almost as good as any of the other modified girls on the team. Now this one is also quite good, here," he says pointing at a red line, "this is your recovery rate, how fast your body can recover after exceeding your max oxygen. You recover very fast."

"That one I knew about."

"Yes. We have watched you and taken some notes. We think that you are under performing that line also."

I smile and say, "Okay I'm ready to be better, I guess."

"Okay then! Let's hit the field!" Sebastian jumps up and heads for the door.

I start to follow him, then seeing Kyle not moving, say, "Kyle, can I speak to you for a minute? Alone?"

"Sure," He says looking at Sebastian.

Sebastian says, "Hey, I will leave you two alone," then hustles out, leaving the door open.

I feel like I need to try to connect with him again. "Kyle-baby?" I say, grabbing his hand.

"What's going on?" He says softly, his eyes still dead to me, probably wanting to spend his brain power on some other puzzle than the one standing in front of him right now.

"*What's going on?* That's what I want to know. Sebastian here is so excited that you two can help me and you are sitting there like it's the end of the world. Are you going to get in trouble for this?"

"No. Oh no. That's not it. Just some internal NuGen stuff has me distracted. I am really happy about this, helping you run faster and all. That's great."

I stare down at him for a few moments then decide to let it all out, "Kyle, I know you can't tell me all your company secrets and I am okay with that, but I expect that you would never mislead me. Never lie to me. Right? I can actually trust you, right?"

That caught him off guard and he responds defensively, "Of course. We are getting married. I would never lie to you."

"Okay then. Because if you do. It's over." I stand to leave and he quickly grabs my hand.

"Stop. I need to... I want to tell you something."

I turn back around and face him, both of us now standing.

"I want to tell you more. more about myself. Clearly, from what you just said, you think I might be holding something back from you or maybe even that I have been dishonest with you, and that is not true. I have never lied to you and I never will. So then, in my mind right now, I think it must be my behavior or perhaps the way I said something that has made you suspicious of me and, yeah, I get that, so I just need to tell you something."

I brace myself, thinking he is going to talk about traces, but then he says, "I told you before that NuGen sent me to school and that I was test-tubed, right?"

"Okay?"

"Well, it goes a lot deeper than that. Now, no one, Gabby, no one can know this." He looks at me sternly.

"Okay."

"NuGen basically raised me. I was in a completely different program than the athletes. They tubed us, raised us from birth, sent us through special NuGen schools, everything. They trained us hard in all sorts of things, most I can't tell you about, but one of them is a deep level control of emotions, almost like being able to use your emotions as a weapon, using them to control any given situation, turning them on and off as necessary."

I have never seen him speak with such sincerity; there is absolutely no trace of dishonesty in his voice. At least this would explain his behavior.

"And I was one of the best. I can be as cold as ice, emotionless, whenever I want, or show deep emotions at the drop of a hat, but they aren't real. But now, with you, I want to turn them back on, just let my emotions flow, be normal, and it's hard Gabby. It's so hard. I am trying to be normal, to be a caring, loving fiancé to you but you know what? I don't even trust myself anymore."

His voice begins to crack and a tiny tear rolls down his right cheek. I was assuming that he was faking this because it is so over the top coming from him, but now I don't know.

He continues, "Every time I feel something I am second guessing myself. Is that a real emotion? Or is it something that I am fabricating because I think it would be a good response to the situation to provide tactical advantage? Don't you see? Do you see what they have done to me?"

It is possible, isn't it, that he is really opening up to me, trying to bridge a gap. Or maybe he is letting me see him weak and vulnerable, manipulating me, in order to play on my sympathy and win my love. Well he definitely is manipulating me, but that doesn't mean that he is not sincere.

I grab him, holding him and his wet cheek presses against mine and I don't want to let him go.

He continues, "Sebastian was there too, in the program, but back then—yeah, back when we were like eight, nine, ten years-old—I used to make fun of him. He was terrible at it but now, the way he can be with Cyndi, able to open up his emotions, I am jealous of him."

Seeing his weakness, I am not frightened or appalled; it is moving me in a way that I didn't think I could feel toward him.

"And that's what scares me the most, that I can't get my emotions back—that I am some kind of monster, that all I can do is use them to manipulate and control, that I can never have a normal human emotion, that I can never be human."

146

Michael, Sebastian and Kyle

I have never seen him like this, so weak, so vulnerable, and, if this is true, if he is not faking this, then it proves his point exactly, he is *not* a monster. Maybe somewhere in there he is calculating, unconsciously, gauging the effect of every tear and sob, but if there is another half of him that is really expressing these emotions, even though he is using them to some kind of dramatic effect, then maybe that would be okay, maybe that would be enough for me. I don't know why, but somehow I believe him.

Donavan, standing in the doorway suddenly, hollers, "Alright love-birds! Time to train!"

We walk toward the field and I don't know what to say so I just squeeze his hand.

The practice is intense and Sebastian wasn't kidding. He is laying into me something fierce, "Alright Gabriella! That wasn't good enough! You are way better than that! Look at your lines here, right as you run up to the last obstacle, you slow down and your glycogen level jumps by almost twelve percent. You need to push harder there!"

Each round we stick our fingers in the little machine, run, jump, swing, climb, bounce, squat and dive, then hustle back, stick our fingers in the machine, and Sebastian yells at us (well, mostly me) for not pushing hard enough at some point in the loop or for having poor, inefficient, energy wasting form.

At first it is great because he points out things that I hadn't noticed before and I actually can feel myself becoming better on every single lap. Later, it starts to become really irritating, like I would really like to tell Sebastian to just, 'Shut up.'

Even he treats Cee that way and I can't believe it. "Cyndi, why did you slow down right there! Look at your lines! Here! You know better than that!"

Cee, frowning, shuffles off.

Kyle doesn't say anything, only sits there behind the screen, running the tests, silently, pensively analyzing the data, occasionally pointing at a line and whispering to Sebastian.

The more Sebastian yells at Cee, the more I begin to wonder if I was wrong. Maybe he does have it in him to hurt her.

By the end of practice I am more sore than I have ever been and it feels like I have never trained so hard. I meet Mom out in the parking lot and she is sitting in the passenger seat already. It is the last thing I want to do right now, practice driving, but reluctantly I sit behind the wheel and drive home.

I do some Chemistry homework then get ready for bed. The instant my head hits the pillow I am out. The dream comes again and of course the thing I hate comes with it, the thing that wakes me up, the puddle of sweat. *It's so gross.* I go to the bathroom to wipe myself down, thinking about why this dream keeps returning. The Void-man hovering over me, repeating the phrase over and over, "Watch out for Kyle. Don't trust Kyle." But now that I know how Kyle really feels, and that he is trying so hard, the dream should go away soon enough. *It's all in my head anyway.*

Another day passes and today is our meet in Germany. Mom drops me off and I think about Dr. Duggan's machine and that I would love to use it for the trip right now instead of the five-hour plane ride. Cee and I sit next to each other on the plane and are several rows away from the NuGen boys, so, of course, we gossip about them once we are in the air. After a while of talking about nothing special, Cee whispers, "Oh! By the way, I found out more about the traces."

"Oh, me too. What did you find out?" I say, thinking she is going to tell me what I already know, that traces will show where a person's DNA was cooked and maybe who did it.

She starts with that, then adds, "Sebastian told me that Kyle wanted to know if you were modified because he couldn't understand how an unmodified like you could perform so well. Sebastian doesn't seem to care about that. But anyway, he said it is strange, like Kyle is obsessed with it."

"Did he say whether or not they found anything?"

"No. That's just it." She lowers her voice even more. "Kyle is freaking because your DNA looks perfectly unmodified. Like it is totally natural. There are no traces."

"Well, I kind of thought that much. My mom told me that I was born in a hospital. All natural. I wonder why he is so obsessed with it?" *But I am still not convinced myself that I am natural and not modded. Maybe Sebastian is lying?*

She stops, moves in her seat, looking up toward the front to make sure no one is listening, then says, "Okay, now this is where it gets real deep." She is whispering so low I have to concentrate really hard to hear her.

"Tell me."

"Somehow, and I don't know how he did this, Kyle compared your DNA to both of your parents, and they are not the same. So either you are modified and they can't find the traces or those are not your parents."

Cee leans back in her seat with a strange look on her face, staring at me, as the steward comes through with the beverage cart and I am left sitting there, in shock, the hairs on my neck on end, not believing what I just heard. *No. It can't be. They are my parents. That's it. I can't believe that.*

My head is spinning so I barely hear the steward ask me what I want.

Cee elbows me, then I say, "Sorry. Ginger ale, please."

After that bombshell, there is not much more I can say and I am lost in my thoughts for the rest of the ride. After we land, I walk to the baggage claim with Kyle saying, "Kyle, I really appreciate you telling me all that stuff yesterday."

"Whew, yeah, that was tough. I am not used to opening up like that. But we are going to be married, so I need to do that more."

"So is there anything else you want to tell me?" We are going down the escalator, toward baggage claim.

He looks troubled. "No, I don't think so. Why?"

"It's just, I don't want you sneaking around. If you need something from me, I want to be able to trust you. I want you to just ask me. Okay?"

"Oh, yeah, of course. Just ask. Sure."

We arrive at the baggage claim and stand a bit away from the group, so we can talk more privately.

"Alright then," he says, "There is one thing."

"Go on."

"I would like another full blood sample. There is something I can't figure out with the first and it would be nice if I could confirm it."

"Maybe. Tell me what it's for."

"Well. I'd rather not say. I mean, it's NuGen stuff."

"Then the answer is no." I begin to walk away as the bags start showing up on the ramp.

"Gabby, wait. Please, come back."

I turn back to him, disappointed, and say, "What?"

He exhales then says, "Okay. A few years back I interned in Smith's lab. That's why we are so close. I still do odd jobs for him sometimes, mainly because I find his research so fascinating and if I help him out he lets me check out what they are working on."

I stare at him and his face changes so he must realize that that is nowhere near enough of an explanation for me.

"Well, the truth is that I scanned your DNA, looking for modification traces for him. He thinks that you are modified and wants to know who did it. I haven't been able to find anything. I just wanted to run the test again before I told Smith that there are no traces."

I turn and grab my bag from the ramp, suddenly angry, saying softly, "You know what, Kyle, this is what upsets me. That you were running these tests behind my back. Why didn't you just ask? I would have given you my blood sample, no problem, if you would have just told me what you wanted it for up front."

I storm off and he doesn't follow me but what I don't say is what I am really mad about; that he is still not telling me everything. I suspect he wants my blood for much more than just looking for traces. There has to be more to it than that.

Chapter 22

Ultraball

Cee and Elektra are visiting Sidney and me in our hotel room and it feels like a slumber party when Donavan bangs on our door screaming, "Okay girls! Lights out!" and when we all laugh she barks through the door, "I heard that!"

After Cee and Elektra leave, I lay in bed and text Michael, wishing I could see him, knowing that he is so close. I have to stop doing this. I know. But just once more is all I keep telling myself.

The next morning no one eats breakfast before the match. The time change throws our bodies out bad enough without mixing in foreign food.

We pack up and head out to the stadium and it is already buzzing with fans when we get there. The stadium is sold out, every seat filled and standing room spots on the mezzanine are being sold. The Germans absolutely love Ultraball and their teams are very good. They run a split offense on the field team, five fast strikers that run the field, three in the backfield for defense, slow but great tacklers, and two goalies to protect the huge net. The game starts and we girls begin our warm up runs while the field team plays.

The announcer reports his play by play in both German and English. "Philadelphia Red running the blue ball down the field. But watch that green ball. Kirk has it, he goes for it. Deflected. Now if you look to the track you will see Donavan's Philadelphia girls warming up there. They are going to have a lot of work against our tough Deutsche Frauen." And he is right about that; the German girls are tough and brutal. The German Pre girls are four enforcers and three runners and their enforcers are known for being able to push out two or three runners each. Their enforcers are huge and I can imagine what being smashed by them will feel like. They look intimidating. Their three fast runners don't look like anything special but they have some of the fastest times in the league. It is a lethal combination and none of us are looking forward to this match.

Sebastian comes up behind me and says, "Gabby, you are the secret weapon today. They don't know how much you have improved in the short time we have been working with you. You are going to shock them. Make sure you use that. Don't waste the advantage."

"Let's hope so," Donavan says, overhearing what Sebastian said.

"Okay, so here is what you are going to do. You are going to run really slow during your warm up. Don't do anything special or anything we practiced during warm-up. Let them think you are still slower, like before. Okay?"

"Okay."

"Listen to me. You're okay. Trust the training, Gabby. Trust all your work."

In the first race, Donavan puts Elektra, Cee, Max and Qi out. The Germans run four also. Right at the gun, one huge German girl pushes Elektra and Cee off the course before they can even take two steps. We've never seen that before. A second enforcer takes out Qi and the final two German girls out-race Max and take first and second with Max taking third leaving the race score at five to one.

The Philadelphia Ultraball coach, John Bustoff, comes over to Donavan screaming at her, "What are you doing to me! You just gave up four points!"

Knowing better than to try to answer him, Donavan stands there nodding her head, smiling.

At half time, she says, "Well, now we have seen a new strategy and we have to prepare for it! We cannot expect that a team will wait until the first lap is finished before attacking! We have to be ready from the moment the trigger is pulled!"

Just after we enter the field, Michael texts me.

I am in the stands.
Section C106

I look for him, but can't see him. There are too many people. I don't know how to take that he is here. I mean, I am glad he came, but I don't know what to do about it. Kyle is over with the Ultraball men so I finally decide to call him, "Hey, Michael!"

"Hi. I can see you." His voice sounds soft and buttery.

"I can't see you. There are too many fans."

"Yeah, I know. It is really loud here."

"So now you are an Ultraball fan?"

"Yeah, something like that. Because of you I am starting to understand the game anyway. I like the two balls idea. Score the second one within twenty seconds of the first and it doubles the score from two to four. Gives it a lot more tension with the hurry up timer too."

"Yeah, that's one of my favorites. So how did you make it out here? Drive your convertible?"

"Yes, I did. Great weather for it too. You should come for a ride with me."

I remember our last ride, how terrible it was to have to tell him those things and how cold he was to me. Changing the subject, I say, "And how is the experiment coming? And Dr. Duggan, how is he?"

"We are making progress, sure. Maryann wrote us some new code. I can run the machine with only one person now. Open both gates from one side so I can jump through without having an operator on the other side. Cool, huh?"

"I guess."

"Yeah, I am thinking of coming through. It will be my first time as I have never done it yet, you know."

"Yeah, you said. Why not?"

"Well, kind of scared I guess and someone has to run the machine. Just didn't need to go to New Jersey back then."

"So what brought this change on?"

"I was kind of thinking. I asked her to do it for me, not tell   Dr. Duggan, so I could maybe come visit you? If you thought that might be okay?"

"Michael. I—"

"Gabriella, off the screen!" Donavan barks.

"I have to go. We'll talk later." I hang up and completely don't know what to do with him. I mean I know what I have to do. I have to stop it. It's over. But I don't know how.

See, Max and I head for the start line and they are running two enforcers and one fast girl and I know one of them wants to take me out immediately as she is way too close to me. I move right next to the edge of the course and she moves a few feet closer. I am down in my blocks like I am ready to sprint and at the gun then when it fires I flinch but don't cross the start line. The girl tries to push me out, but since I haven't crossed the line, I am not in play and she is disqualified; I am not. Now we have the advantage, three on two. Max takes out their other enforcer now it is two on one. I begin to move like Sebastian taught me, forcing myself to push where I would have slightly slowed, making my body twist and turn where I wouldn't have before. I pull out in front of the German girl. See and I take first and second, tying up the Pre score. At least we broke even, now it is up to the field team.

With a handful minutes to go and the game tied at twenty-four, the field team coach, John Bustoff, walks over to Donavan and tells her something. Cyndi, sitting next to me, elbows locked, hands on the bench, face pointed at the ground, starts crying. Donavan is yelling at Bustoff and he is yelling back, pointing toward us, waving his finger. Donavan throws both hands up in the air and screams, "Alright already!" then storms away, walking toward us.

Stopping in front of our bench, hands on her hips, she says, "Alright girls, the field team wants to put one of you on the field! There's only a few minutes left so just stay away from the ball and run up and down the field, I guess. Whatever you do, don't get hurt!" She beams down at all of us, angry but at the same time, sad. She doesn't look at me when she says, "Gabriella, you're up."

Our bench is shocked. Max and Sidney start to protest. Suddenly my peripheral vision disappears and all I can see is the green, green grass in front of my feet.

It's happening! It's happening! Just like Mom said it would! They are going to destroy me again!
Donavan bellows at the protesting girls on the bench, "I know! I know! I'm not happy about this either!" then turns to me and says, "Just do it! Okay! Get out there! And don't get hurt!"

Just then two large Ultraballers crash into each other in front of our bench, one of them flying off the field, barely avoid crashing into See and Max. I can't believe this is happening and as I stand, Bustoff screams, "Hurry up! Get over here!"

I hustle over to the men's bench and Bustoff says, "Okay girl, err, what's your name?"

"Gabriella," I say, my voice shaking.

"Okay then, I have been watching you and I like how you dodged the enforcers. You look real slippery. And you're small, not like our big men. We are going to use you as a distraction. Now don't worry, we won't give you the ball, so you won't be tackled. But I want you to stay close to the action. Run a lot, fast, and try to always be near the action, near one of the balls, got it?"

"I guess."

Looking in my eyes, he knows I don't understand anything.

"Look girl, err, what's your name again?"

"Gabriella."

"Look. Just stay close to the ball and when we have it, make a dash toward the goal. You're just a big distraction. Okay?"

Suddenly angry, I charge back, "No, it's not okay! But... but I will do it!" And inside I am already crying.

I wait on the field edge and looking back at the bench spy Cee still crying and the rest of the girls have terribly worried looks on their faces. I smile back, trying to give them some feeling that all will be well but it doesn't work, even for me.

The whistle blows loudly and I run on the field when one of the men runs off. I can't believe what is happening and I just stand there on the field as the men dodge to and fro. A ball whizzes by my head and at the last moment I dodge two giants crashing into each other near me and Bustoff screams, "Don't just stand there! Move girl!"

I look back at him and nod then look at the score board. *Just 45 seconds to go. You can do 45 seconds can't you Gabby?*

I sprint toward the blue ball, then back away, not knowing what to do, then toward the green ball. My complete confusion seems to be having an effect on both teams. Neither knowing what to make of me seeing as I am not following any of the prescribed patterns, just running around willy-nilly.

The blue ball is shooting toward the goal. *There it is. Okay, go, go!* I take off making a straight line toward the goal. A German defender deflects the ball and suddenly, shockingly, I look down and it is in my hands. *Ahhh! What do I do now!* Two Germans sprint toward me so I dive vault one and throw the ball away, quickly, anywhere, just to get rid of it. One of our men catches it, scores violently and the game ends.

Standing there in shock at what just happened, I spin in a slow circle, amazed. Many of the German fans are cheering. They have always been known to cheer for a well-executed play, even by the opposing team. Spinning, spinning, looking at the fans, I am still in shock, still not believing I am on the field much less that I just garnered an assist and will be listed in the Ultraball stats. The girls run out on the field and I can't help it; I start crying.

In the locker room everyone is running around celebrating, everyone but Cee. I go to her, grab her hand and pull her into a quiet corner near the showers.

"What's going on? I saw you crying."

"Ohh... It's just that—"

"Cee look at me." I stare deep into her eyes. "You can trust me."

She exhales then says, "I remember now. The night I was hurt, the night I fell. I remember."

"What? What do you remember?"

"Someone hit me from behind and I fell. I didn't see who it was, but as I was going down and just before I blacked out I saw a leg."

"And?"

"Oh Gabby! I can't say it!" She throws her hands around my neck and she feels so small and frail.

"Okay, you don't have to—"

She cries for a minute and I hold her, stroking her back.

"The leg. It was wearing a blue-black suit. I'm afraid it might have been Sebastian. Gabby? What do I do?"

"I, I don't know." And I really didn't. But I have to tell her something. "See and I, we will be with you. Okay? I will talk to her. We won't leave you alone. Okay?"

I lead her back to the girls and speak with See trying not to look nervous or worried.

The plane ride back is definitely uncomfortable for Cee, See and I. All three of us are putting on upbeat, happy faces while keeping our eyes on Sebastian, all of us suspicious of him.

I catch some much needed sleep for the remainder of the plane ride and as we arrive at the training center to drop off our gear I pop into the NuGen room.

"Hey Kyle, got a minute?"

"Sure, anything for you, beautiful."

The way he is smiling at me and the light, somehow, shining lightly on his broad chin warms my heart.

I step in and close the door behind me, "Do you think Sebastian could have been the one who hurt Cyndi?"

"No." He answers too fast and it surprises me.

"Why would you say that?"

He steps closer to me, wraps his arms around my waist, pulls me in close, then pushes his head next to mine, over my shoulder, then says, "Because it was me."

"What!" I wedge my arms between us and push hard on his chest, thrusting him away from me. *No! No! No! Not Kyle!* "What are you telling me?"

"Gabby, Wait. Give me a chance to explain."

My hand is on the doorknob ready to fling it open and run out when I see a tear streak down his cheek.

"Start talking. Now... Fast... before I walk out this door!"

He sits back in his chair and looks up at me, "It's our job, Gabby. Sebastian and me both. We have to get results. That's it. And when certain things happen, we are expected to handle them."

Now I am yelling at him and I can't stop myself, "Like what kind of things?! I mean, what could adorable, uplifting, little Cyndi have done to deserve this?! Huh?! Tell me! Why?!"

Suddenly Kyle stands, flinging his chair back against the wall, mad, the tear still glistening on his cheek, "Okay! You want to know why?! It was you! It's your fault! You ask way too many questions! You put her in danger! Using her like your own little spy! Who do you think you are?! Not her friend! A friend wouldn't have done that!"

I let go of the doorknob. Suddenly trying not to cry, I squeak out, "Kyle?"

"Gabby, this isn't a game!" He steps toward me and stands broadly in front of me. He tries to touch me and I recoil.

"You're terrible!" I say through tears, unable to look at him.

"Listen to me," he says softly, "I didn't mean to hurt her. I was talking to her and it got out of control. It wasn't supposed to happen that way. It was an accident."

I look at him and he looks so sincere, water pooling in his eyes. He whispers, "Do you think I wanted to do that? Do you think it made me happy? I hate myself for it. When I look at myself in the mirror, I don't know what I see anymore. I used to know, but now, I just wish you would stop. Let things be—"

"Stop, Kyle. Just please, don't tell me anymore!"

"Gabby, you told me you wanted the truth from me. And I was afraid to go there, but I think you are a strong girl, you can take it. This is our world, honey. This is the world you live in. It's not terrible; it's just life, just the way it is."

He puts his strong arms around me and something inside me wants to push away, really push away, really, really hard but something else really wants him right now, wants to just hold him, really, really tightly.

"Kyle, I don't—"

Touching my ear with his lips he softly whispers, "Listen, this won't happen again, okay? If you need any information, just come to me. Okay? I promise, I will tell you the truth. Okay?"

"Okay—"

He slides his arms off my body slowly and I step toward the door, confused, not knowing what to think.

Suddenly the window breaks, glass flying into the room, and someone slams the door open, pushing me hard to the floor, me sliding into shards of glass.

Sebastian storms in, a flurry of fists flinging at Kyle, screaming, "You! It was you!"

Kyle tries to defend himself as I scurry to the corner, avoiding flying furniture. The screen crashes down next to me, throwing sparks. Sebastian punches Kyle in the jaw then pushes the desk hard, pinning Kyle between it and the wall.

Kyle begs, "You know I had to! You wouldn't do anything! And it's your fault too! You kept opening your big mouth! You're lucky I didn't turn you in!"

"SHUT UP!!" Sebastian screams, swinging hard fists at Kyle's head, Kyle trying to cover and push out of the corner.

Seeing Sebastian this way, his anger, his rage, a realization strikes me. *How could I have missed this? Why didn't I see it before? Sebastian is one of the men who came to our store in Venezuela the day father died!*

Crawling through the shards of glass I sneak out of the room as they continue to fight, furniture being smashed and thrown around, them rolling in the glass and hammering at each others' heads and bodies.

I jump up and run toward the locker room, panting uncontrollably. Looking back down the hall I see a trail of my blood leading directly to me. *My blood is all over that room! My fingerprints are on the doorknob! I have got to get out of here!*

I clean myself in the sink, wash away the blood, wrap rags around the cuts on my legs and put on my running gloves to cover the cuts on my hands. Just then, my screen signals a message from Mom.

In parking lot.

Looking in the mirror, staring into my own eyes, I say, "Okay girl! Get a hold of yourself! Just walk! Walk out to the car. Tell Mom about how great beating Germany felt. All of that. Just move! Okay?"

I exhale, look away then back at the mirror saying, "Okay," as if I am answering myself.

I exit out the back door, avoiding the hall that leads to the NuGen room, go to the parking lot, get in the car with Mom and ask her to drive telling her that I am too jet-lagged to practice driving.

Chapter 23

Farewell to Falling Leaves

After I finally fall asleep, and I can't believe that I can actually fall asleep, the dream comes. I feel as if I am awake this time, in the dream. Lucid. No, I don't want to wake yet I tell myself in the dream. *Can I talk to him?* His face is close, oh so close, the Void-man hovering over me in my bed, staring at me. I am awake, but somehow I know I am still in the dream. "Don't trust Kyle. Watch out for Kyle." He repeats the phrase over and over, his voice distant and echoing.

"Wait—" I try to say but when I open my mouth I have no voice.

"Why?" I mouth the word without sound, staring up at him hovering there, above me.

The Void-man stops speaking, stops repeating and stares at me. A smile quickly flickers on the corner of his mouth then he disappears. Suddenly I am awake, but this time there is no puddle of sweat.

In the morning I hide my cuts from Mom with a few band-aids and explain it as a broken glass in Germany. She raves about my performance. She watched it on the Ultraball-E channel. "Oh Gabby, you were so great! I am so proud of you."

"You weren't nervous?"

"Are you kidding? Of course I was! In fact I was planning on going down there and busting off that Coach Bustoff's head."
We both laugh. "Until Smith talked me out of it."

"Smith, huh?"

"Yeah, I guess it's okay. I mean I don't like it one bit. But watching the game, I saw Kyle there and I thought, well, he will take care of her."

"Aww, mom! He can't take your place!" I jump up and hug her.

"That's nice, Mija. You two just make sure to give me my grandchildren. Okay?"

I don't know how to answer that so I say nothing.

Later Mom and I drive to practice and I marvel at the orange, red and yellow leaves falling from the trees. Autumn is something we never had in Venezuela and I can't stop looking at the colors. *Wow!* She drops me off at practice and being the last to enter I am surprised to see the entire team sitting on the benches, looking sullen. Donavan steps in and says, "Now that we are all here, let's begin! First off! Great job in Germany! We are 5-0 so far, leading the division and one more win will guarantee our spot in the playoffs!"

Everyone nods but no one looks happy.

"What happened on the field out there! I had a long talk with Bustoff and that won't be happening again! We reviewed the footage. Gabby, you were just too close to the action. I can't have that again! He wouldn't back down until I told him that his men obviously couldn't handle the game and he needed girls to come show them how it was done! Hurt his pride a little, I did! Heh heh." Donavan leans back and smiles broadly.

"Thanks, Coach," See says.

Everyone else chimes in, "Yeah, thanks, Coach."

"Finally, for those who haven't heard! The NuGen boys had a little tussle and busted up the place a bit late last night! It's all cleaned up now, but I threw them off site. The NuGen girls are going to have to get their monitoring offsite for a while. But with them being one of the primary sponsors, I won't be able to keep them away for too long, but at least this will send them a message! And by the way, I am requesting that when they come back, that they are replaced with two different people! Sorry, Cyndi and Gabriella, I know that you both had relationships with those two, but this is a business, and there was too much kissy-kissy going on here anyway!"

I say, "I understand."

Cyndi says nothing.

"Alright then! Lets get out there and get ready for Montreal! I want that playoff spot locked down!"

We all stand then Coach says, "And Cyndi?"

"Yeah Coach?"

"Show me your stuff today and tomorrow and maybe you can race on Saturday."

She smiles and we all start hooting, "Oohhh Yeeaahhh!"

We all push the training but everything feels odd and out of place with the NuGen table and the boys sitting behind it missing. And even with Cee back. She was out for just over two weeks and now that she is back the chemistry is all different. She's not the same bubbly Cyndi and See and I are the only ones who know why. She doesn't fit the same anymore and for the rest of the team it just feels awkward.

Saturday's game comes quick and I am so thankful that it is at home. Those long plane rides are a killer. We are the favorite by a long shot as the

Farewell to Falling Leaves

Montreal Pre runners have only scored three points all season. Their field team is quite good though so we will be expected to put up some good numbers to help the team win.

Walking through the long tunnel and out onto the field the crowds wearing Philadelphia red erupt and the echoing waves of their heartfelt love and appreciation grabs me down deep and tight. I love playing in front of them. Our people. My people.

We park at our bench and analyze the field before we warm up. Even though this is a home game, neither team knows what obstacles will be set up before the match. The Philly stadium is open, not domed, so the dirt path is real, actual dirt, not Astroturf or compressed rubber chunks. The field has real grass and I love that. It is so much softer to land on. The course has three oddly spaced hurdles in rapid succession, the typical stuff, a vault that is about five feet high immediately followed by an unavoidable mud pit about ten feet long, so we will all be covered, and something new, three huge spinning disks about ten feet in diameter each. *What is that?*

We all stand on the edge of the field trying to get a closer look at them. Apparently we must run across the three disks, kind of like large merry-go-rounds, each motorized, rotating in different directions. Weird, but okay, we will handle it.

After we warm up, Donavan calls us over, "Okay! Like us, Montreal is a speed team! They only have one real enforcer, like us, and they try to win on pure speed. Only problem for them is that we are much faster! So you all know what to do! Stay on the field! Don't be disqualified and run your race! After Germany, this should be an easy win!"

In our first half match up we run four, Max, See, Elektra and Qi and Montreal runs three, one of them is their big enforcer. At the gun See and Elektra are off and after one lap it is clear that no one will catch them. Our bench is cheering hard. The fans are losing their minds, shaking their red blow-up sticks and banging them together creating deafening shockwave of sounds. As See begins to lap the last Montreal girl, an enforcer, the girl spins and pushes See out, both being disqualified.

Donavan yells out, "No! She knows better than that! Argh! Why did she get so close?"

Elektra and Qi push ahead and on the fourth lap Qi twists her ankle on the second spinning disk. Falling off the disk and onto the grass, holding her ankle in pain, she is disqualified. She gets up and barely can limp back to the bench.

Donavan yells out, "What the? What's going on? We are falling apart out there!"

Elektra, now slowing for the disks on each lap, not wanting a twisted ankle, finishes second and Max takes fourth. We are down four-two in a match that should have been an easy six-point win.

As we wait on the bench for the half, Donavan sneaks over to the men's bench and talks to... *Wow! Is that? Yes it is.* It's Coach John Murray. I jump up and jog over to them. As I reach the men's bench, I overhear her saying, "I know, my love."

John Murray, seeing me approach, says, "Hey Gabriella! Good to see you!"

"I saw you there and I had to say hi!" I give him a big hug and a kiss on the cheek.

"Hey, you know you are in good hands here with Coach Donavan. Did you know that we worked together years ago?"

"No, I didn't." I look over at Donavan and her face is blank but it looks like she is holding something painful inside.

"Yeah! Those were the days. We were on the same coaching staff."

"Cool! Well, I better get back. Just wanted to say hi! Good to see you!"

As we head for the lockers at the half, I notice Kyle in the stands, wearing a red sweater and ball cap. Our eyes meet and I can tell he wants to talk to me.

In the locker room Donavan stands back and lets See speak, "Okay team. Listen to me," she takes a long dramatic pause, waiting for everyone to look up at her, then continues, "Don't worry about this. Okay? This is not real. What's real is all those miles we put in out on the road. What's real are all those twenty mile Saturdays. What's real are those twelve 200 meter sprints at AT pace."

She stops and we stare at her, unconvinced.

"Listen to me now. We are in so much better shape than those girls. Okay? They got lucky. And, I know, that happens sometimes. But us, there is not a team in the entire league that is doing the tough workouts that we do. I know. I have seen the scouting reports."

Cee, perpetually optimistic, yells out, "Yeah!" and somehow the rest of us start to come around. It's not exactly what See is saying, because any of us could punch holes in her logic, but the way she speaks, with such passionate intensity and conviction that we would almost believe anything that comes out of her mouth right now.

"So what we are going to do right now—"

Max and Elektra stand up.

"is show them—"

The rest of us stand up.

"Who—

We—

Are!"

We all howl, "Yeaaahhh!" and slap each other's hands.

Just then, the team doctor steps in and whispers to Donavan then steps back out.

Donavan announces that Qi has a stress fracture and the blood drains from my face. We are still all pretty excited about running though and ready to go when Max holds up her big hands and we are all surprised that big, shy Maxine wants to speak.

"You all know me by now. That I am quiet, shy even, and I was as surprised as the rest of you when Coach picked me to be a team captain. But I really feel like I need to say something."

We all sit down and look up at her as she flushes red.

"You all know there is a sign over the entrance door at our training center that says, 'Enter this door and join the greatest athletes in the world' and that is true. We know that it is true. But why is it true?"

She looks around at us then continues, nervous and voice quivering, "There are so many people who run in races, hoping to make this team but don't, and to be honest it is not for lack of talent. The real reason is they didn't have the heart for all the hard training, the heart for the fight."

She pauses for a moment, her confidence growing. "There are so many people that want to be you right now. Do you know that? So many want to be you, in your shoes, right now. Some fast, some slow, some posers and fakes, others want the fame or glamor, and others, schemers. We have seen them all in off-season races, fast girls, good genetics, good blood-lines, that just don't make it. They didn't have it. They didn't have—what did coach call it? Mental fortitude? I call it heart. They didn't have the heart for the fight. I want you to look at each other. Take a good hard look. These faces you see are the ones who had the heart for the fight."

Max pauses and all of a sudden Cyndi hops to her feet takes two giant steps, leaps onto the bench then catapults herself at Max and gives her a giant hi-five. Max catches the little waif's swat as Cee howls, "Alright Maxie!"

As we head up to the field, I hear my screen ringing in my locker and duck back to check it as everyone else leaves for the field.

It's Michael.

I really don't want to speak with him, now of all times, but glancing back and seeing that everyone else is gone, I mash the answer key.

"Hello?"

"Gabriella. It's Michael—"

"Yes, I know. What's up?" I say quickly.

"Do you have time to talk?"

"Not really. Half-time is just ending and I only have a few minutes until I have to be on the field."

"Ohh, okay. Can I call you back later?"

"Michael. I, I don't know about that."

"It's just what you said before, and what I said, and now with the machine. We could see each other and—"

"Michael, no—"

"Gabby, no one would—"

It hurts me but I have to do this. I know. I have to do this.

"Michael. No. That's it, see? I am getting married and I can't see you anymore. I can't talk to you anymore. See? It hurts enough as it is without dragging this out. It's over. I can't talk to you anymore. I can't see you anymore. This is it. Okay?"

The line is quiet. It is a heart breaking moment, waves of deep emotion, a combination of bewilderment and sadness, somehow coming through the silent screen. I feel like words are no use at all. This is our final farewell and the silence feels so awkward and painful.

"Michael, are you still there?" My voice cracks.

"Yeah," he says and I know that he is crying.

"Michael, it wouldn't be fair to you. I can't be with you, that's all. This is the world I live in now." *I can't believe I just said that.* It's what Kyle said. *Who am I? Who am I becoming? Like him?*

"Okay. That's it then—"

"Michael?"

"Yes—"

"Don't be angry. And I know it's hard but try not to be hurt. It's not your fault. This is just how it is."

We hang up and I look at my watch. *Shoot! I'm late!* I throw the screen in the locker, wipe my cold face, dart out of the room, sprint up the hall and out onto the field.

Donavan screams, "There you are! Get out there!" and I sprint straight to the start line. Taking Elektra's place, I say, "Sorry I'm late."

She steps back and says, "No problem, drama queen," then gives me a cheeky smile.

Nomi, Cee and I are lined up against the four Montreal girls and I am pumped about the run but still have a feeling that this could go badly.

The Philadelphia fans are excited to see the return of Cyndi and there are giant signs everywhere that say "C B 4 ME" and "CYNDI 'BATTLES' TO WIN." A row of six men in the front row section are screaming, arm in arm, topless, their naked torsos painted red with one large white letter on each chest spelling B-A-T-T-L-E, Cyndi's last name.

On the line, I hear Nomi muttering under her breath, "This is fake. This isn't real. What's real is those 1200 meter sprints," and suddenly I realize she is right. We can run the disks slower, as a recovery, and sprint the remainder of the course. It would be just like our AT runs, the runs I hated so much. We quickly huddle and I tell the other two.

At the gun, the three of us are out fast and hard, running a blisteringly fast sprint. We put fifty meters between us and the other team and with Cyndi in front the stadium is shaking from the fans stomping and screaming. Hurdle, hurdle, hurdle, dive, jump, vault and on to the spinning disks. We slow for the disks and take them cautiously, one at a time, Cee in front and Nomi in the back. The Canadians are catching us then. Leaping off the disks, barely recovered, we burst in full power, blinding speed and I can't wait for the disks so I can rest, even for a few moments. By the fourth lap we have 100 meters on the other team and by the halfway point we have 200 meters on the four Canadians. Realizing we will take all the points, two of their runners slow down, allowing us to catch them. They are going to try to push all of us out, or at least two of us. If they can take out two of us then the best we could do would be 3-3. *We can't allow that!*

I yell to Cee and Nomi, "Stay in the middle of the course and don't pass on an obstacle!"

Farewell to Falling Leaves

Cee is the first to reach them so she slows down and stays about 5 meters behind them. Good strategy, I think. We don't have to pass them and there's only two laps left.

Another lap gone and we are on our last. C'mon, just hold on! Suddenly the last Canadian girl stops, turns around and dives toward little Cee, arms spread wide like she is going to tackle her.

The Philadelphia crowd erupts, "Booo! Boooo! Boooo!" echoing in the stadium. Cee, treating her like an obstacle, dives to the ground and rolls past her, leaps up and continues running. The Canadian turns back around and speeds up behind her. Now Cee is trapped between them, one in front slowing, one in back speeding up and the disks are coming! I slam down the gas and give up what little energy I have to catch them. The second girl is so focused on catching Cee that she doesn't see me sprint past her until it is too late.

Catching Cee, I yell, "Let me pass you!"

She says, "What are you doing?" but there is no time to answer.

I sprint past her and slow slightly just before the disks. The Canadian girl is waiting for me, standing on the second rotating disk. I hop across the first disk and try to run past her on the opposite side of the second, running against the rotation. Running on the other side, the motion of the disk aiding her, she catches me quickly and grabs my waist, trying to throw me off. Refusing to fall, I stagger to the third disk then fall to my knees, both of us rotating on the disk around and around. The whistle blows and she must release me and exit the field. She failed to push me out of bounds.

After she lets me go, I stand and continue running. Cee reaches me and we sprint together for the finish line. Nomi is pushed out and the second half score for the Pre is five-one and together with the first half score we are up seven-five. Basically, we gave the field team two points when they were expecting at least six so Bustoff is not happy with us. After the game ends and we clean up, we head out to the bus for the short ride back to the training center. Cee sits next to me and whispers, "I heard what happened with the boys."

"You did?"

"Yeah, why didn't you tell me?"

"I don't know. Nervous, I guess."

She looks out the window for a while then says, "Yeah, makes sense. Heard your blood was all over the hall. Got cut up, huh?"

"Sebastian broke the window."

"I don't know what to do with him, Gabby. I mean, I love him—at least I thought I did, but with him hitting me... No, I can't take that. As hard as it is to say, it's over."

"What? What do you mean?"

"He hit me and I mean, I forgive you and all—for telling Kyle—and I understand he would get upset and fight with Sebastian for that. Gabby, you're the lucky one."

In shock, I don't know what to say. *Should I tell her the truth and let her hate Kyle? And when I marry him, she will hate me too. Probably everyone on the team will also. But if I don't tell her then she is going to leave Sebastian. Either way I lose.*

I hug her and don't say anything. I have to think this over. If I decide to tell her, I need to know how to do it. I don't want to mess up one of the only friendships I have.

The bus pulls in and after we unload we all head to the lockers to prepare to leave. Coach Donavan is in her office but the door is half open so I stand in it and knock lightly. John Murray is on her wall screen. She says, "I have to go. Talk to you later?" then the screen goes gray.

"Come in!"

"Sorry to interrupt, but the door was open." She is wiping her face and I think she may have been crying.

"Good game today, huh?"

"Sure Gabby, sure. You are coming along nicely. I am glad you decided to go with the 'bot monitoring. It has made a world of difference in your technique. And protecting Cyndi today shows real character. The Liberty will surely take notice of that. But that is not what you are here for. What can I do for you?"

I close the door, walk in and stop just in front of her desk, "I need some advice. Can we be private?"

"Do you mean, can I keep a secret?"

"Something like that."

"Well, depends. If you tell me something that affects the team, then I will act on it."

"It's about Kyle—"

"Ohh." She leans back in her chair and looks at the ceiling. "Before you go on, let me just say that was very hard for me. You don't know how hard it was for me—to move those two out. You wouldn't know this but I was something like you once."

"What do you mean?"

"Well, not just like you, but I was in love with someone and we worked together, like you and Kyle, and I let the work and my career come between us and I always meant to get back with him, but before I knew it, years had passed and somehow—I don't know—I lost him."

She sits up quickly and stares right at me. "Gabriella, you are young now so you really have no concept of time. Let me tell you, time is relentless. It's merciless. You can't stop it. You can't rewind it. And time is completely unforgiving."

"Okay."

"Let me tell you something about life and I want you to listen to me, okay?"

"Yes, Coach."

"You love this boy Kyle, I assume because you are supposed to marry him, right? So don't let anything, and I mean anything, including me, stand in your way. Understand?"

Her voice grows more distant and it is now as if she is talking to herself as she says, "To live life, to make the journey, going through the trials and tribulations, ups and downs, fighting the battles, running the races, winning and losing, and never allowing yourself to embrace what you truly, truly love? What is that? You haven't lived life at all."

Her eyes glisten with personal experience and I realize that John Murray was the one she lost. Her eyes grow increasingly distant as she continues, "I am not talking about this bubble-gum love that the commercial-fed networks sell, that garbage can full of fake drama. I am talking about real love, real passion, someone you can't live without. Someone who you *have* to be with. Without that person you have no life and it feels like you're all dead inside. When that person hurts, you hurt. When that person succeeds, your heart flutters, full of electricity, full of joy, full of life."

She stands, comes around her desk, grabs my hand and says, "I say this, Gabriella. Don't make the same mistake I did. Don't let him get away. Marry this boy, Kyle. Embrace him, hold him, fall head over heels in love with him and never let him get away. If your head is telling you something different then stop listening to it. Listen to your heart. Do you hear me? Listen to your heart. Marry Kyle."

She keeps saying 'Kyle' and I wonder if she would say the same thing about Michael. *Yes, I think she would.* But she is not in my situation.

"Sorry to get so dramatic with you. When I start talking, sometimes I forget and slip back into coach mode."

"No problem. You gave me a lot to think about."

"Good. Now is that all you needed?"

Unable to bring up the real reason I came in, I say, "Yeah, I guess that's it. Thanks again, Coach."

I turn to walk out and just as I reach the door I say, "Coach—"

"Yes?"

"I really hope you get him back."

"Me too."

Closing the door, walking into the locker room, I can't stop thinking about what she said and I am more confused than ever. I just ended it with Michael, who I really love. At least I think I do. And he said he loved me. But how much can two seventeen-year-olds know about love? And I am engaged to be married to Kyle who, well, he has a lot going for him, successful and gorgeous, but I don't love him. *Will I ever?* And him "accidentally" pushing Cyndi down. *What about that? Is there some secret temper there that I need to know about?* He said he had all his emotions so under control that he was like an ice-man. *Well, then how did that happen?*

"Hey Mija! Good game!" Mom is in the locker room waiting for me, talking with See. I give her a kiss on the cheek.

"Thanks, Mom."

"You almost ready to go?" she says, handing me the car keys.

I take them and reply, "Yeah, let me just put a few things away then we can head out. You can hang out here for a few if you want, okay?"

"Okay."

I walk out the door and down one hall then another when I find some-one huddled in the corner talking on their screen, his back toward me. *It's Kyle!*

I walk up to him and softly whisper, "Hey! What are you doing here! You know Coach banned you. You're not supposed to be here!"

He hangs up and says, "I know, I know. I just had to see you."

"And what's that you were talking about I heard?"

"You heard? How long were you standing there."

"Long enough," I say, baiting him as I heard nothing.

"Okay," he breathes in deep, saying, "I can explain."

I whisper, "Lower your voice!"

"I was going to tell you eventually anyway. You know it would be so much easier for me to not tell you all these things. But I am trying here, like you said, to be honest."

"Kyle?"

"My parents. The people that came to your house for the engagement. They are not my real parents. NuGen paid them."

"What?"

"Ssshhhh! The problem is I don't have parents. And when you asked me. I didn't know what to do. I'm sorry I tricked you."

"So, you're an orphan?"

"Not exactly. NuGen cooked me in their lab, from DNA of, who knows, a thousand different people. I am a product of complete and total genet-ic engineering, raised in a sterile environment and trained all my life."

I feel the blood draining from my face and I don't know if I can believe him. He must be telling me the truth or why would he tell me something so hor-rible? Now I don't know if I really want the truth.

"Kyle? Am I one of your assignments?"

"Listen to me. Gabriella, listen." He puts his hand on my neck and pulls me in close. "Maybe I don't know what love is, but the way I feel about you. It must be love."

I push him away, needing some space to breathe. "Please. Just answer the question."

He looks down at his feet. "I could get in real trouble for telling you this. But my assignment is to find out if you are the 'holy grail'."

Holy grail, holy grail; there's that phrase again. The same thing that Dr. Duggan said Smith and my father were working on in the old country so many years ago. It can't be a person; it was an experiment.

"And you would stop at nothing to get this information?"

"Within reason."

"Tell me what that means. What is the 'holy grail'?"

His eyes, wrinkling at the corners, lose some of their wariness. "The 'holy grail' of genetic modification is to be able to perform an untraceable DNA modifica-tion, to be able to alter DNA and have it look like it had not been tampered with, as if it was naturally occurring." Suddenly he gets excited. "Gabby, do you know what that means? If there were no traces then there would be no lines of division. Who could say what was original and what was different? Who could say what was human and what was added? We could change our genome and no law could stop us!"

"That sounds terrible! What are you trying to create? More freaks!"

"Your father didn't think so. He made you."

"I'm all natural. Mom said so."

"But how do you know? How do you really know? You have no traces. If you are the first untraceable modification then no one would know. Not even your mother."

"I just can't believe that he would—"

"It was what he was working on."

"And NuGen killed him for it," I sneer.

"Listen. Don't keep blaming NuGen for all society's ills. I read the files. He was under contract and he stole his research and disappeared. That was NuGen property. They owned that research and paid tons of money to have him perform it. He had no right to disappear with it. He stole it."

"So when he didn't give it back. What? They sent two goons to kill him?"

"Well, I wasn't there. I don't know but from what I heard it was an accident. He was protecting you."

"So now it's my fault?" I say angrily, trying not to raise my voice.

"Why does it always have to be about blame with you? Can't you understand that accidents happen?"

"Some things look like more than accidents." And suddenly I decide that I do not want to marry him. "I have to go. Maybe we can talk more another time."

He grabs me and yanks me close and his voice is suddenly harsh. "Listen, Gabby! I've had a lot of patience here. You wanted the truth so I gave you that. I have kept up my side, now it is time to keep up yours."

"What do you mean?" I say, fear in my throat.

"We are going into Smith's lab to find out if you are this 'holy grail.' I need to take you in."

"And if I refuse? What are you going to do? Force me?"

"It's not going to get to that, is it?"

Not whispering anymore, I yell, "I am not going back to that freak show! I am not a lab rat! Got that!"

A spacey, dazed look steals over his face and he squeezes my arm tight, too tight, and it hurts.

"Hey! You're hurting me!"

Suddenly surprised at what he is doing, as if he is not in control of himself, he releases my arm and mumbles, "Sorry, I don't know what just happened."

I push his chest hard, he slams back against the wall and I dash for the rear exit to the parking lot.

Chapter 24

Getaway

Get away. Get away! I just have to get away! Running down the hall and toward the parking garage, I realize that I still have Mom's car keys in my pocket and I think about using the car to get away. *But I only have my permit! I'm not supposed to drive without an adult in the car! What am I going to do?!*

Just as I reach the car, fumbling for the keys in my pocket, wondering what I am going to do, maybe hide in the back seat, Kyle enters the parking garage screaming, "Gabby! Wait! Just stay right there!"

"Oh no," I mutter, open the car door, jump in, slam it shut, start the engine and pull out of the parking space. Kyle slams into my door, trying to open it and I slam the door-lock button down hard. He is screaming at me through the window and pounding on the roof, running alongside the car, "Gabby! Wait! Don't go! Gabby! Wait!"

I can't look at him, can't look at his face. *I just have to stay calm. Drive. Gabby, drive. Stay calm! Don't look at him.*

He pounds on the roof harder, screaming, "Gabby! Wait!"

"Ohh noo..." I mash the gas pedal and speed out of there, leaving Kyle behind, standing there with a distressed look on his face, tires squealing, car bouncing airborne over speed bumps, my head hitting the ceiling, sparks flying out behind Mom's poor car as the undercarriage makes a terrible scraping noise.

I turn the corner and turn another, moving down to the lower level, slow through the parking exit and quickly wave to the attendant all the while looking for Kyle in the rear view mirror, trying to smile and appear unrushed and normal when inside nothing is normal, nothing is sane, in fact, everything is insane. I pull out onto the roadway and Kyle steps out of the building exit door, hand still on the doorknob, screaming, "Gabby! Wait!"

He sees me not stopping then runs back into the building. I drive the car through the streets, heading toward the highway.

I am going to lose my permit! I am going to lose my license! Mom is going to kill me for this!

Just calm down. You can do this. Drive normal. Don't do anything to get yourself pulled over. Drive normal.

I pull up to the stop light, highway entrance just in front of me, when I notice my hands trembling. I squeeze down harder on the steering wheel, trying to make them stop. I bite my lower lip.

It's okay, girl. Just make it out of here. Everything is going to be okay.

A car pulls up in the lane next to me and unconsciously I turn to look and—*Oh my God! It's a police car!* Why did you turn and look, dummy?! Now you did it! Why did you turn away so quick?! Now they are going to think you did something wrong! *Whatdoldo? Whatdoldo? Whatdoldo?*

Okay! Calm down! The light's green. Ease your foot off the brake, nice and slow. Okay that's it. Put it on the gas... slow... easy... that's it. Just drive away, just drive away.

Whew! That was close!

Pulling onto the highway, I merge into the traffic and pick up speed. *Drive like everyone else. Speed limit, Gabby. What's the speed limit? Okay, there it is. Sixty-five. Okay, do sixty-three. Just drive straight. Don't even change lanes.*

I wish I could call someone. Mom. Michael. See or Cee. Anyone. But I can't risk using the screen on the road. And what would I tell them? It would all be hearsay. My word against his. And then what? You know it would be all over once the word got out. I can't take that chance right now. I just need to get away—to think for a minute. I just need time to figure all this out.

Beeeeeep! Beeeeeep! Beeeeeep! Beeeeeep!

I swat the button on the car screen.

"Gabby, I need you to turn around and come back. C'mon. This is silly. Let's just talk this over."

The screen is black, thank God, (only the voice comes through when the car is in motion). I quickly slam the button to cut off the call. No way am I talking to Kyle right now. Not after what just happened.

I must have fat-fingered the button because a call list comes up and I realize that the car synced with my own personal screen and Michael's name is at the top. Keeping my eyes on the road, I think about calling him then reconsider. I don't want to drag him into this. I mean, no way is he going to want to talk to me right now anyway, after I just hurt him. And the way I did it, so cold.

Just drive. Just drive. Keep it in the center of the lane. Sixty-three. No sudden motion. Just drive.

Wheeew! Wheeew! Wheeew! Wheeew!
Wheeew! Wheeew! Wheeew!

The police siren is suddenly in my ears and the red and blue flashing lights blast full on, into my car, in my eyes, as if they are pointing directly at me. I look in the rearview mirror and see the police car directly behind me. I take my foot off the gas and begin to slow down. *What am I going to do now!* Maybe I could tell the police officer that I am in danger. Tell him who I am, my situation, what's going on. Kyle will be questioned at least. It would open this up. Give me some space anyway. NuGen won't like the negative publicity. Of course, they would deny everything but at least it would get them off my back. Hopefully keep Mom safe.

I pull over and stop on the side of the road, the police car behind me, siren off but lights still blazing when I realize—*Oh no! It's Kyle driving the police car! What is going on here!*

The car's screen rings again. *Beeeeeep! Beeeeeep! Beeeeeep!*

I swat the speaker button once more.

"Gabby—"

"Kyle! What are you doing! You stole a police car!"

"Gabby! Listen to me! You have to stop this before it goes any further! You don't know what I am willing to do for you!"

"*For me! For me!* This is not for me and you know it!"

"Listen to me Gabby! Just calm down! Okay? Calm down. Okay listen, I am going to turn off my lights and come and get in the car with you, okay? Then you are going to drive away, okay?"

He turns off the lights, exits the car and begins walking toward the passenger side of Mom's car.

"I don't think so." I bash the accelerator and speed out onto the highway. Looking in the rearview mirror, the police car is still sitting there, lights out.

What is he going to do now? Kyle, how far are you willing to take this? Is this how Dad died? This craziness?

I have got to get out of here. Get away. I need time to think.

As I drive I hit the screen button, highlight Michael's number and press dial. Through the car's speaker system, it rings and rings and rings.

C'mon Michael! Answer the screen! Pick up!

The call times out so I hit the dial button again. It rings and rings and rings.

Pick up! Michael! Pick up!

"Hello?"

"Michael! Oh my God! Michael!"

"Gabby? Why are you calling?" His voice sounds irritated.

"Michael. Oh, I'm so sorry to call you like this—"

"Listen, you can't keep calling me like this. I can't take the drama."

"No, no, no. You don't understand! I need your help! It's an emergency!"

"What's wrong?" His voice softens.

"I can explain everything—when I get there. I need you to start the machine for me. Can you do that for me?"

I notice that I have sped up without realizing it. *Slow down. Slow down. Sixty-three. No faster.*

"Ahh... I don't know, Gabby. I mean, I don't want to abuse Dr. Duggan's trust."

"Listen Michael! Someone is chasing me and I need to get away! Okay? I just—need to—get—away. Can't you help me? Please?"

I hear silence on the line as I enter Princeton, then one word, "Okay," and he hangs up.

Just then, behind me, the sirens are on again.

Wheeew! Wheeew! Wheeew!

Wheeew! Wheeew! Wheeew!

The red and blue, full blast, is in my eyes. Looking behind, there are three of them. *Three police cars! And is that?* Yes, it is. Kyle is driving the lead car. *I know I am going to lose my permit now!*

Ignoring them, I take the exit and stop at the bottom of the ramp. Kyle gets out of the car and starts walking toward me. *He should know better.* The stop light turns green and I speed off. *That should buy me a little time.* The other two police cars can't go around him so they have to wait until he gets back in his car. Just a few more minutes and I will be there.

Beeeeeep! Beeeeeep! Beeeeeep! Beeeeeep!

"Kyle! No! I am not talking to you again!" I scream at the dumb blank screen, refusing to press the answer button.

The campus is a block away and the police cars have caught up to me.

Wheeew! Wheeew! Wheeew! Wheeew!

Beeeeeep! Beeeeeep! Beeeeeep!

Wheeew! Wheeew! Wheeew!

Beeeeeep! Beeeeeep!

"Aarrgh!" I abuse the answer button, yelling, "Okay! What is it!"

"Gabby? I, I am at the controls? Are you there?"

"Michael! Sorry—"

"What's all those sirens I hear?"

"Don't worry about that right now! Please? Just start the machine and soon as I come through, shut it down! Okay?"

I hang up before he can answer and smash the gas pedal all the way down, running the red light, trying to avoid the cross traffic, barely missing two cars, a little red Honda and a green truck, speeding down the lane and skidding across the Forrestal Campus entrance of Princeton University. The car's wheels dig deep into the dirt just off the road as it fishtails down the curving road. Pulling up to the front of the building, slamming on the brakes, skidding through the fresh construction dirt, I throw the door open, jump out without closing it and roll across the hood of the car. Just as I hit the building steps I hear, "Freeze! Stop right there!" and I don't have to turn around to know that the police have their guns drawn.

What did Kyle tell them? How am I going to get out of this mess? How am I going to get away?

Chapter 25

Running in the Void

No stopping now, I snatch the door handle and *(Thank God, it's not locked!)* open it. Entering the building, I run up the steps two at a time, then three, leaping up to the second floor, rounding the staircase and as I reach the top I hear the door below open and the police entering, yelling, "Stop! Stop! Don't move! Stop right there!" Ignoring their cries, I run down to the third door on the left, swipe the passkey that Dr. Duggan gave me, throw the door open and am immediately sucked into the room, tumbling head over heels.

Floating, flying, bouncing off file cabinets and large screens, my body shoots toward the void entrance, suddenly flipping, out of control, arms and legs flailing, sucked toward it as if I am an insignificant particle being drawn toward an immense black hole, papers everywhere swirling in the air. My body somersaulting over and over, uncontrollably, I hear the door bang open and I realize it didn't close behind me. From a weird angle, head upside down and crooked, I see Kyle sucked in and the door slam behind him. He flips over a few times then is somehow able to right himself and flies toward me like a bullet, him sailing straight at me, pointing his fists, soaring, smiling, me still flipping end over end. I smash my head, hard, on the ring edge as my body feels like it is being ripped in two, a spike of mind-numbing pain in the center of my brain as I cross the threshold and then skid across the brilliant white, hazy, cloudy, Void floor.

I squeeze my eyes down hard, instantly remembering that I do not have the welding goggles that See let me borrow. Head throbbing in intense pain, I touch my wet forehead, running my blind fingers back and forth, trying to determine the length of the gash. My fingers are really wet.

Sitting down, my body shaking, I holler, "Kyle? Are you in here?"

My words are swept from the air and ripped out of my throat. Silence. There is no echo to my voice as if the Void eats sound; my words consumed before they can exit my mouth.

Maybe he didn't make it through?

I take off my light jacket and then my shirt, tear my shirt into strips, tying one strip across my cut forehead and another across my eyes so that I can squint through them a little. How else can I find the exit? I put my jacket back on, zip it up and peek one eye open. "Aaaaahhh!" Still too bright! I tear my shirt again and wrap a second strip around my eyes and then I am barely able to squint through and look around.

I stand up and call out, "Kyle?" looking around, squinting, spinning in every direction, frantically, "Are you in here?"

A deaf person can feel the vibrations of sound. Here there are none. Just silence. My ears begin to ring for the silence. *I forgot how quiet this place is.* It's unnaturally quiet; any noise is consumed.

Turning, squinting, I make out the dark exit circle and quickly forgetting about Kyle, start walking toward it.

I'm alone. No Kyle. No Void man. No one. *I could just stay in here, couldn't I? I would be safe here wouldn't I? I could just sit here and think for a minute. Figure it all out.*

I reach the Portugal gate and look out at the frozen picture of Michael hovering over the control panel, hand still on the giant blue button, eyes looking at the gate as if he is staring at me staring at him, frozen, a tiny slice of time, a frozen moment of time. I feel like I could stand here forever, staring through this gate at this three-dimensional picture. It's so hypnotic and motionless, like there is no air. The longer I look, the more the strange details jump out at me. There, right there, a fly, stuck in the air, tiny wings in mid-flap. And the flash of the fluorescent bulbs spooks me, there, right there, one on, another off, and another, and another. Then I remember that a teacher told me once, long ago, that they did that. They turn on and off many, many times a second, maybe like one-hundred times a second, or maybe sixty times a second, I think, something about alternating current, the AC of the power outlets. It happens so fast that our eyes just can't see it. But I can now. The world is frozen to me.

Suddenly, swirling around me, the smell of lilac. And jasmine. I turn, squinting, looking around for the clouds and the Void-man. *He was right, you know. Warning me about Kyle. He was right, in the dream. Could that have been him? Or was it in my mind?* Then cold. Oh so cold. *Why do I feel cold?* It's as if something suddenly jumped between me and a campfire, blocking the heat, sucking the cold from the air around me.

Pfeeeetzz!

"*Aaaarrrrr!*" Something grabs me from behind, hands on my neck, strangling me, choking me and I can't breathe! It feels like death. And cold. Like death is easing into me through his touch.

"Get off me!" I shake my shoulders back and forth, trying to shake him off, twisting, pushing, trying to see who it is. *It must be Kyle.* But I can't see anything. I run in one direction then swing my body around, throwing my hips to the side and he falls off. I turn to see him and—nothing. No one is there.

"Kyle?"

Silence. Just sound eating silence.

"Kyle? Is that you?"

I just need to get out of here. That's it. I will jump through the gate. Michael will push the button, closing it. Then Kyle will have to exit out the other side, or who knows, be stuck in here. It will give me time to think about what to do at least. Maybe we can get the police, have them waiting at the Void exit when Kyle steps out.

I walk toward the gate, determined to exit when just in front of me the white deepens to a dull yellow, then blue, then a deep indigo, a completely un-natural shade of indigo, a saturated deep indigo, like some kind of weird ancient dye made from some kind of weird ancient shellfish. Everything feels all wrong. Everything is all strange and I feel nauseous and, more than that, like something is pulling on my mind, like thoughts are really difficult to make right now. I struggle to think. *What is happening to me!*

Pfeeeetzz!

Out of the indigo leaps a metallic face, black and bronze and brown and silver and platinum, dull but shimmering, coming right at me, then, too close. I try to step back then cold, metallic and black hands grab my shoulders, holding me still, as the face comes right at me, inches from my face and flickering, fad-ing in and out, the mouth opens and hisses, "Gabby! You should have came with me!"

Like falling down off a mountain, tumbling, watching the earth rushing up toward me, it feels like I am dying, like I am watching myself die. The touch, his touch, it brings a choking, stifling dread. And fear. And everything terrible and awful.

"Kyle? What's happening to you?!"

Kyle's face, all bronze and shimmery, reminds me of the solar eclipse that Dad and I saw many years ago. It was the middle of a hot summer day in Venezuela when the moon came and blotted out the sun. The very edges of the sun still provided some light but the spectrum was all wrong; everything went cold and bronze and indigo.

"Ohhh, Gabby! You should—told me! I feel so—in here! I can—feel—" His voice fades in and out just as his form shimmers as if there is an external battle between the light and dark, as if the Void light is rejecting the darkness. The moon blotting out the sun; the moon blotting out the sun.

Looking down at his hands, my skin fades silver where he holds me and—

I—

Feel—

So—

Cold—

"Kyle? Let me go, Kyle. Please? Just let me go. Okay?"

Bronze light shines off his shady black face, the black of night, the black of decay and death. I can barely talk and I feel like he is draining me, as if life is being pulled out of me—

I think—

I feel—

Weak—

Suddenly—

He grates his forehead back and forth against mine and the fresh gash burns cold as his voice hisses, "Never!"

I pull back my head and slam it into his, head butting him as hard as I can. Him letting go, I turn and run away. *Get away! Get away! Get away!*

Oohhh, that hurt! My head is throbbing and the blood is dripping down onto my face.

I am almost at the New Jersey gate when the cold wraps me again and he appears halfway between the gate and me. Standing there, I can now see his entire body, fading in and out, metallic and black, shimmering like one of those old picture imprints from the middle ages, pressed into a sheet of copper, finely detailed yet old and dull, coming in and out of focus, as if the Void light is struggling to push the black away, as if it is something unnatural here in this place of light and clouds.

Extending his hand toward me, he hisses, "Come with me! We will jump through together!"

I feel so weak, suddenly, and I cannot resist him.

"Kyle. No," I say, even as I find myself slowly walking toward him, a tear falling from my eye.

His form is black and dead and as his metal eyes move I suddenly recognize him, recognize his former self and what he used to look like when he was alive, before he became night and darkness and death. I recognize the face I held, the face I kissed, the face I was to marry. Somehow I am drawn to him like a fly to blue light, knowing that he will kill me yet unable to pull away.

"Look! Look! You are becoming like me!" he yelps, voice full of glee and looking down I see the silver spreading, like some splotchy, sick disease, spreading from where he held me. I touch my forehead and it feels so cold and I know it is spreading from there too. I am becoming night, becoming darkness and death. I feel sick and diseased but there is nothing I can do to stop it.

"Kyle! What are you doing to me!" I howl as I shuffle step toward him slowly, resisting with all my might.

A surprised look comes over his face and he begins to fade away to nothing, the space where he stood fading back to white, right in front of my eyes.

Gone.

Run, Girl!

I run as fast as I can, but I feel so weak, so drained. I struggle to move my legs and feel crippled, as if my mind-body link has somehow been severed, as if controlling my appendages is oh so difficult all of a sudden. Reaching the gate, I throw myself through, awkwardly, and as the Void gate sucks me through and I am flung out into the space of the New Jersey control room, Kyle's arms, appearing out of the clouds, wrap themselves around my legs. We both fly out, a mass of tumbling flesh, flinging, flicking, flying through the air, papers floating about everywhere, bodies three feet off the ground when, oddly, we pause, floating in the air for a moment, then are both sucked back into the gate.

That's right; it makes perfect sense. Why didn't I think of that? Michael has it set up to exit in Portugal. We can't go *out* through the *in* door. I skid across the bright white floor.

Looking all around, I don't see Kyle. He has disappeared again. *I have to move, to make it to the other gate.*

I scamper as fast as I can toward the Portugal gate then trip over my own uncontrollable feet, falling head over heels, sprawling out onto the cloudy white.

Pfeeeetzz!

Kyle's upper body appears, bronze and platinum and shady black, fading into white at the hips, face sneering yet powerful. Life is being sucked from my body as he stands over me and I feel my eyes rolling into the back of my head. The gate, and my survival, seems galaxies away, light-years away, at the edge of space, an impossible distance. And that voice in my head. What's that?

Why don't you just give up? He has won, don't you see? How can you beat him Gabby? It's over. Just lie down and die. Give up. You can't win. It's over.

I slump to the ground, drained, no energy. I can't fight. I lay my head on my arm. "Noooo! Please!"

And it will be so easy. You don't have to do anything. Just don't move. Stay right there. He will take care of the rest. Don't struggle. Don't fight. That would take too much effort anyway. Just give up. It's over.

Tears roll from my eyes and it is all I can do to barely whisper, "*Noooo.*"

A bellowing, screaming, yelling of a sound echoes, and wind, a fierce powerful wind, shakes through the Void, "*Haaaaaaaa-Taaaaaaaaaaaaaahhhh!!!*" then suddenly Kyle is gone. It is so difficult, but I struggle and lift my head. Turning it, I see the Void-man, fading but struggling not to, as if to fade or not to fade is dependent on will, him hoarsely crying out, "Gabby... Run... Go." Then nothing, gone. He's gone.

Get up, Gabby.

Gabby, get up.

But it would be so much easier to just lie here.

I hear myself breathing.

Gabby. You have to get up.

But it is so comfortable here.

Gabby.

You.

Have.

To.

Running in The Void

Get.

UUUUUUP!!!

"Whoaa... What's that?"

I fight to stand up and limp to the gate, struggling over every step as every fiber of my being fights me over every motion and every movement. Arriving at the gate, I momentarily turn, seeing the Void-man, clutching his ribs, fading in and out, a wispy, clear shadow.

He calls out to me, desperately, his voice hoarse and shallow, barely whispering, "Go!"

It is all I can do to leap through the Void exit, flying out into the Portugal control room and skidding my knee, shoulder and the side of my face on the floor, turning to see Kyle's metallic face breaking the plane of the circle and the grid pattern suddenly turning a brownish bronze color.

"Shut it down! Shut it down! Shut it down!" I force myself to scream.

Michael squashes the button, the Void closes and Kyle's metallic head is sucked back into the Void.

I can't move. I can't move. Staring at the ceiling, the beautiful ceiling, old, yellow cracked plaster and oh, is it so wonderful to lie here on this floor.

Then darkness.

Chapter 26

Epilogue

Light. Bright, white. Light.

My eyes slowly easing open, I squint down hard as they are flooded with bright white light. *Am I still there? In the Void?*

No, it is only the ceiling light, so bright.

"Uuuuuhhh..."

"Look! She's waking!"

As my eyes come back into focus, I see Mom and Cee and See and Sebastian and Michael and Dr. Duggan. I try to smile.   "Hey,   you guys—"

Mom says, "Don't try too hard. Don't get up. Just lie there, you have to rest. We are all here. We're not going anywhere."

"Where am I?"

"You are in a hospital, in Portugal. We all flew out," Cee says.

"Portugal?" I look at Mom, wondering what she thinks.

"It's okay Gabriella, I explained everything to your Mom," Dr. Duggan says.

I know he couldn't have explained everything. He doesn't know everything.

"And Kyle?"

Mom's face grows puzzled as See and Cee look pained, then both say, "We haven't seen him."

Sebastian adds scornfully, "But the police in New Jersey are looking for him."

"Oh," I say, somewhat surprised.

Dr. Borges enters the room and exclaims, "Gabriella! You are awake! Good. Good."

Sebastian and Michael step back to give him some space and he continues, "A mild concussion and some cuts and bruises. After your forehead heals, we'll laser it so you don't have a scar. A few weeks and you will be as good as new. "

"Thank you, Doctor. Sounds good." But the ringing in my head and the weakness in my bones tells another story.

I look at Dr. Borges then at Mom and exclaim softly, "Ayi, que bagunça."

Cee whispers to See, "What'd she say?" and See replies, "I have no idea."

Dr. Borges whispers to them, "What a mess," then steps back out and I look at Mom saying, "Mom? Michael here, he works in Dr. Duggan's lab."

"We met." she says, briefly eying him suspiciously.

"He saved my life." My eyes quickly dart over to him and back to Mom.

"Oh, I didn't know that," then edging closer to him, looking him in the eye, she says, "I guess I have you to thank for my girl being alive then?"

Looking down at his feet, sheepishly, then back up at her, he replies, "I guess, yeah. But it was nothing."

Suddenly, she hugs him fiercely and I think everything might be okay in the end.

A nurse comes in with a needle on a tray, saying, "Okay everyone. Gabriella here needs her rest. I am going to administer her meds. You all can visit in the morning." And as she injects the solution into my drip IV, me fading to a forced sleep, I wonder where Kyle is and if he made it out. I wonder what would happen if he stayed in there for twenty years. *Would he exit the Void like only a microsecond had passed for him?*

And Michael. *Will he ever forgive me for all I have put him through? And will Mom ever accept someone like him?*

And what about Kyle being all dark and black, like that? Both Michael and Dr. Duggan described the Void as all black and darkness, yet what I saw was pure white light. There must be some explanation. *There is always an explanation.* But I am beginning to realize that we might not always be able to understand the explanations. I guess there are some things that we might never understand.

And with Kyle gone, how will I ever really find out about my father? And me? How will I find out who I really am and where I really come from? How will I find out whether or not I am modified? How will I find out if my parents are really my parents?

As the last glimmer of consciousness fades away, forcing myself to barely hold my eyes open, I look at them, Mom and Sebastian, Cyndi and Sidney, Michael and Dr. Duggan, edging toward the exit. *Well at least I have them.* I look at them and I realize right then that I already know who I am. *My group, my people, my tribe, the ones I belong to. And for now that is enough.*

Chapter Twenty-Three

Acknowledgments

I am happy, pleased and overjoyed to recognize the following individuals who have aided me in my quest to bring the characters of this book alive and tell an engaging, informative and challenging tale; some who have provided valuable insights into South American and Mideastern thinking, cultures, and customs; others who have stepped into the minds of the characters, breathing life and authenticity into them, sharing their own personal life experiences, many of which have found their way into the pages of this book, proving the point that truth *really is* stranger than fiction; and finally, others who have offered encouragement and support when the words stubbornly hid themselves in the folds of darkness.

Alexandra Sarigianidis-Wright

Majdalin Cardona

Sam Cardona

Yaser Abdelkader

Questions

1) The coaches offer lessons that they say apply to life in general. Do you think sports provide a good analogy for life? Do you think any of the lessons the coaches provide are accurate for life? If so, which ones?

2) Throughout the book Gabriella grapples with who she is and who she wants to be. She appears to think that she is defined somewhat by her relationships with others, such as her parents, her friends, her team mates or even her fans. Is that an accurate way to define one's self?

3) NuGen is a company that treats the people that it has test-tubed as a commodity, maintaining some amount of ownership over their behavior throughout life. Some of the characters think this is a good thing as they feel it has benefited them, others see the negative side of it. How do you think you would feel?

4) Some of the genetically modified people in the story think they are superior to *mere* humans because their DNA is supposedly better. Do you think they are better or do you think they may have lost something?

5) The writing tries to balance typical, real-world events in Gabriella's life with the extraordinary, science fictional or supernatural. Does providing the details of her mundane daily tasks make these extraordinary events seem more or less real?

6) The "Silence in the Halls" chapter contains some of the strongest repetition and rhythm of the book, such as this passage:

> Slowly moving up and down the halls, up and down the halls, the creaking of the wind in the trees outside echoes through the silence of the halls as it is beginning to hit me. Up and down the halls, up and down the halls, as the quiet descends on me, calm and content, giving me pause, I listen, far away, far away, I listen; silence.

What underlying message does the repetition and rhythm of the writing in this section provide? How does it make you feel?

7) Chapter three ends with this sentence:

> Those words, like heavy sledgehammers banging steel anvils, sharp, tight and abrupt, echo painfully in my ears, then I leave for the blue bus.

What message do you think the anticlimactic ending of the sentence (and the chapter) provides? Why or why not is this effective?

8) Gabriella and Michael speak briefly about their observations of different young-adult mindsets toward sports and intelligence in the "Out of The Corner of My Eye" chapter. Do you agree or disagree with their observations?

9) Do you see any similarities or differences between Gabriella's family's matchmaking process of searching for a "good boy" with emphasis on bloodlines and the "modified genetics" mindset of altering genes to improve bloodlines?

10) Literary style is a difficult term to define in a few words without becoming annoyingly abstract, yet it is something that almost every reader can immediately recognize. The author has placed a handful of style "easter eggs" in the book. The "Silence in the Halls" chapter has a few sentences written in imitation of the style of Virginia Woolf and the "Fantasy Land" chapter has a few in the style of F. Scott Fitzgerald. Can you find them? What makes their styles so recognizable?

11) Gabriella, Kyle and Smith have a brief discussion about what it means to be human in the "NuGen Biotechnics" chapter. How would you define "human"?

Gabriella and The Curse
Of The Black Spot
(Book 2 of the NuGen series)

Coming soon : February 2014
ISBN: 978-0-9850284-7-3

How can unmodified Gabriella compete with genetically designed super athletes? Could it have something to do with her father's disappearance? And why are people with odd black spots following her? A mind-boggling teleportation machine lies at the center of this riveting adventure.

Santa Claus vs. The Aliens

ISBN: 978-0-9850284-6-6

When Edwin cuts his finger, dripping a few drops of blood onto a bone-colored tracking device he becomes a target of a group of aliens that think he holds the secret to the human race's defeat. The only person who seems to know what to do is a fat man wearing a Santa Claus suit and he somehow seems to know just a little too much. Who is he and why does he know so much? Where did the aliens come from and what are they after? Can a Fourteen year old wandering the cold, empty streets of Manhattan late on Christmas Eve and an odd character dressed as Santa Claus stop the aliens, save the planet and discover the true meaning of Christmas?

About the Author

James Cardona has written four books as yet, two non-fiction works and two young adult science fiction novels, and is planning on writing many, many more. For his fiction, James tries to make his words come alive by pouring his real-life experiences into his characters such that many of the details described in his books actually happened and are told from the perspective of someone who was there. He also enjoys integrating a hard science approach to his science fiction, feeling that all aspects of his story telling, although perhaps not currently possible, could actually happen once our technology evolves.

James enjoys all things that can unleash the creative process including drawing, painting and creative writing and the not-so-typical such as robot design and writing computer code. He loves tinkering with computers, electronics and building robots and is the Lead Engineer for FIRST Robotics Team 316, a High School Robotics team operating out of Salem Community College.

Additionally James helps organize and run the PSEG Nuclear Salem County Math Showcase which he created back in the year 2000, a math competition for students from grades four through eight, typically attended each year by approximately 500-600 students.

James received his Bachelor's degree in Computer Science from the University of Delaware with a minor in Religious Studies. He lives in Southern New Jersey and works as a Senior Test Engineer for the Laboratory and Testing Services group of the Public Service Electric and Gas Company.

www.ingramcontent.com/pod-product-compliance
Lightning Source LLC
Chambersburg PA
CBHW020634180626
46816CB00003B/954